EVER WORLD

BOOKS I & II

K. A. APPLEGATE

SCHOLASTIC INC.

New York Toronto London Auckland Sydney
Mexico City New Delhi Hong Kong Buenos Aires

Search for Senna, ISBN 0-590-87743-7, Copyright © 1999
by Katherine Applegate. *Land of Loss*,
ISBN 0-590-87751-8, Copyright © 1999 by Katherine
Applegate. All rights reserved. Published by Scholastic
Inc. SCHOLASTIC and associated logos are trademarks
and/or registered trademarks of Scholastic Inc.
EVERWORLD and associated logos are trademarks
and/or registered trademarks of Katherine Applegate.

12 11 10 9 8 7 6 5 4 3 2 1   4 5 6 7 8 9/0

Printed in the U.S.A.   01

This edition created exclusively for Barnes & Noble, Inc.
2004 Barnes & Noble Books

ISBN 0-7607-5608-2

First compilation printing, May 2004

Contents

THE SEARCH BEGINS . . .

It happened the next day. The terrible thing. It was early. Gray dawn. More gray than dawn, really, because the clouds were hanging low over the lake. It was chilly, which is how I like it when I go for a run. . . .

I crept down the stairs past my mom's room. . . .

The street was quiet. . . .

I headed toward the lake. . . .

Senna sat gazing out at a mist-shrouded lake, hands pressed down on the rock, legs drawn up to her chin, a little girl. She was wearing a jean jacket a couple of sizes too big. She looked so small. . . .

And then I saw the others. And they saw me, and I swear the chill breeze became a frozen wind that went right through my skin and iced my insides. . . .

"What is this?" Christopher demanded in a loud voice. Deliberately loud. Maybe loud enough for Senna to hear if she was listening.

"Ask *her*," April said.

Slowly Senna climbed to her feet. She turned and looked at us. She was maybe a hundred feet away.

I could see confusion on her face.

Her mouth formed the word "no."

And then the entire universe ripped apart. . . .

EVER WORLD

SEARCH FOR SENNA

FOR MICHAEL
AND JAKE

CHAPTER I

The fight started at the Taco Bell where a lot of seniors and some juniors went for lunch. I'm a junior. I fit in there as well as anywhere. Which is not very well.

I'm new, in a school where almost no one is new. Not just "a" new kid. I was "the" new kid. Worse yet, I was the new kid who'd been seen with Senna Wales in his car on Sunday. Down by the lake. Lake Michigan.

It was stupid of me. I shouldn't have rubbed Christopher's nose in it. I didn't know for a fact that he'd be down at the lake. I didn't know for a fact that he'd see us. But when you have an unusually warm, sunny Sunday right in the middle of a rainy late September, well, it doesn't take a genius to figure out that kids will be hanging out down at the water.

I drove Senna down there. Top down on my big old Buick. Senna on the cracked, white leather seat beside me. Long blond hair whipping in the wind. Pale face with Julia Roberts lips. Eyes the color of the rain clouds that had stayed for weeks and would return the next day.

I drove down there knowing that people would see. I don't know what the point was. Probably just some lame "look at me!" thing. I was with Senna. I wanted people to know it. I wanted them to say, "Whoa, that new guy David Levin is going with Senna."

Like that really meant something.

Maybe I just wanted Christopher to see. Christopher, who'd been with Senna ever since the last week of sophomore year. Christopher, the wit, the comedian. He'd left half my English Lit class peeing themselves from laughing so hard. At me, as I read aloud a poem I'd written as a class assignment.

Christopher is a funny guy. I mean, he has a real talent that way. You know a guy is funny when a week later you can still feel the little knives he stuck in you.

Senna wasn't the most popular girl in school. Not even the most beautiful. A lot of guys were scared of her. Truth. There was always something about her that seemed remote, cool. Like she lived behind a veil. Like she could see you but you couldn't quite see her, not really her, just a shadow.

So she scared some guys. But me? First time I saw her I knew that everything that had ever mattered to me just didn't anymore. I could feel the course of my future suddenly swerve. I was like a planet drawn into the gravity well of a black hole. No escape. No desire to escape.

Surrender, David.

I didn't walk the three blocks to the Taco Bell that Monday lunch, I drove. So did lots of kids, so they could roll down their windows and crank their stereos. Or sneak a smoke. Or sneak whatever.

My old Buick's stereo was just an AM radio. The FM was broken, and I only got three stations on the AM: some political talk station, some religious talk station, and a classic rock station.

Hard to tell which I wanted to listen to least.

The car's a beast, but I wanted a convertible, had to have one. I hate the feeling of being all cramped in. And this was all the convertible I could afford.

I drove the few blocks with the top down and elbow stuck out, driving with one hand, praying I wouldn't stall out at the stoplight and have to get out and push the old beast over to the curb.

By some miracle, there was a parking space. I slid in and jumped out. It didn't take long for Christopher to spot me.

People figure a guy who's class clown is probably a wimp. Maybe Christopher is. But he had a lot of friends. So when the door of the Taco Bell blew open and Christopher came out, bristling and scowling, he had three other guys helping him hold up that bad-ass act.

I didn't pretend not to see him. I stopped walking and waited. He came right up to me. I gave him credit for that. I have a rep as a fairly tough guy. Maybe I deserve it, I don't know.

Would he have confronted me without his crew along? Don't know. He looked mad enough to.

"We have a problem," he snapped.

"Do we?" I asked.

Then, *wham*!

I never saw the blow coming. It wasn't Christopher. It was one of his boys. Just loaded up on me and nailed me with a left hook that connected with my right cheek. I staggered. I went down on one knee. My knee crunched a soda cup someone had dropped. Pepsi or whatever soaked into my jeans.

Then, *wham*!

The punk's knee came up and caught me in the nose. It was like someone exploded a hand grenade in my face. It was stars and Tweety birds, just like some old Looney Tunes cartoon.

I heard a lot of shouting. A lot of it was Christopher. He was dragging the guy off me and yelling, "I didn't say hit him, you moron! Get out of here or I'll kick *your* butt."

Someone, or several someones, dragged and frog-walked me away around to the back of the Taco Bell. Back to the greasy Dumpster.

"Leave me alone!" I yelled, trying to stand up. I stood up for about three seconds before I tottered back into the wood fence that surrounded the Dumpster.

The rain decided this would be a good time to start pouring. So down it came. It was a blessing. It helped me straighten out my whirling, loopy head.

It was Christopher himself holding me upright. And beside him, this girl named April. She's Senna's half sister. Three months and a universe of differences separate them. Senna is cool, blond, and remote. April is all green eyes and auburn hair and big, mocking smiles. Be with Senna for a million years and you won't know her. Be with April ten minutes and it's like you grew up together.

Jalil was there. I knew Jalil from school. The poem I'd had to read that Christopher ridiculed?

Jalil came up afterward and told me exactly, precisely *why* it sucked. But with no rancor and no ridicule, just because he knew.

Jalil doesn't believe the truth should piss anyone off. Or maybe he doesn't care if it does. He just cares that it's true. That's giving him the benefit of the doubt. Take away that grace and maybe he's just a condescending know-it-all.

He was one of the first kids I got to sort of know at school. Not friends, exactly. More like two off-center loners who recognized a bit of themselves in the other person. We were guys who nodded at each other. Once he stepped over and just sort of made his presence known when I was getting hassled by some black kids. Once I did the same for him when he was getting some grief from some white guys.

Jalil has this habit of not turning his head much, just moving his eyes, skeptical, appraising, not impressed by much. It takes him a while to talk and you might think he's slow. But you get to know him you realize he's slow to talk because his brain's already jumped ahead three spaces and he has to back up to deal with you.

Me, I'm not that smart. Not schoolbook smart, anyway. I don't have the focus for that. When I was a kid I had that attention deficit disorder thing. I was always jumping around, looking at all the wrong things, missing what I was supposed to get, and getting the things no one else thought were important.

Here's my entire childhood: "David, settle down!"

By the time I was thirteen I was a confirmed skateboard freak. Pants so big I could have had another couple people in there with me. My board was, like, surgically attached to me. Could not be without it.

Here's my entire junior high existence: "Hey, kid, get offa there!"

Now I was older. A year away from college or a job or the military. Now I didn't know what I was.

Oh, wait. Yes, I did. I was a chump with a piece of raw burger where my nose used to be.

"What are you all staring at?" I raged.

"I can't speak for any of the others," Christopher said, "but personally, I'm looking at a guy who got sucker-punched and looks like he needs a new nose. I mean, damn, what are you going to breathe with?"

I felt my nose. Gingerly. It didn't hurt. Not yet, but it would.

"You let that punk do your fighting for you?" I demanded.

Christopher shook his head. "Uh-uh, don't lay that on me. What you and me have going on, you and me can deal with. That wasn't my idea, what happened back there."

"What the hell is the matter with you two?" April demanded, but in a tone that was at least half amusement. "Let me guess. This had to involve Senna."

I glared at Christopher. He glared back at me. Some of my blood was on his shirt. He'd helped me stand up.

"We should move on," Jalil said. "Someone may have called the cops."

"I didn't do anything wrong," I said, intensifying my glare at Christopher.

"Who cares about you?" Jalil asked blandly. "I'm a young black male. The cops show up, they'll bust me on general principle. So come on, let's take this show down the road before I end up playing Rodney King over your problems."

That was how we all came together the first time. Me wobbling along holding my face, Christopher propping me up and showing no sign of guilt as he made jokes at my expense, April thinking the whole thing was amusing and touching and idiotic, and Jalil looking out for himself even while he helped me out.

That's where it all began: around a girl named Senna who wasn't even there.

Chapter II

"You look terrible," Senna said.

"Thanks. So do you." A lie.

It was later that night, after the Taco Bell Incident. We were in my car. The top was down. We were driving. Driving nowhere. Just driving.

We stopped at a light. She slid across the seat. Her bare knee pressed against my jeans. She reached with long, sensitive fingers to touch my swollen, smashed-plum nose.

Her eyes were glittery in the neon of city night. She looked at my messed-up face. She looked a little too long, maybe. Her expression was . . . I don't know what it was. It made me look away.

I guess she spaced, because suddenly her fingers were pressing too hard. Pain shot through my nose.

"Hey!"

"Sorry," she said. She pulled her fingers away. There was blood on her fingertips. She looked at it and did not wipe it away.

"It's okay," I said.

"You were fighting over me," she said.

Green light. I pulled away slowly. Too slowly for the cab behind me. He gave me three seconds of horn.

"I would have been. Fighting for you, I mean. If I'd given Christopher half a chance. But instead I decided to grab that punk's knee and use it to beat the hell out of my face."

She smiled, teeth blue and gold from a Blockbuster sign we were passing.

She slid closer still. "Christopher wouldn't have fought you. He's not that way."

"You don't have a very high opinion of him. Why'd you go out with him?"

"I liked him. I still like him. He's smart and funny."

That stung. "Yeah? So why aren't you still seeing him? Why are you with me?"

"Don't tell me where I am or who I'm with, David," she said.

I shot a look at her. Red light. She considered me, her eyes roaming over my face. Not at the injured nose anymore, but at my own face. My chin, like she was judging it. My eyes, but without making contact.

Then she kissed me.

Green light. This time I took off a little faster.

We drove to a place where we could watch the moon come up over the lake. I parked the car.

I looked at her. I knew nothing about her. I knew her face, her eyes, her hair. Nothing.

What I knew about Senna Wales was really about me, not her. I knew that if only I could have her, if only she could somehow be with me, be a part of me, if only I could get up each day knowing she'd look at me, see me, smile at me, then she would be a wall to block out everything, a chasm between past and future.

But that was about me. That was all about the twists in my head. About her, I knew nothing.

"Sorry the radio sucks," I apologized.

"I like it quiet."

So we sat there, side by side in silence, and listened to the breeze and the not-so-distant sound of traffic and the mellow lapping of water at the shore.

I was trying to work up my nerve to kiss her again. But there was a wall around her. Untouchable.

"Something is going to happen," she said, gazing out at the water.

For a moment I didn't know if she was done talking or not. And then I didn't know if I should say anything.

"What do you mean? What's going to happen?"

Slowly, very slowly, she shook her head. "I don't know. I only know something will happen. Soon. Something . . . terrible."

I shivered. I don't shiver. I don't scare that easily. I shivered.

She turned and smiled at me. "Sometimes I know things before they happen. Sometimes I can see a scene in my head. Like watching a movie. And then it will happen. I think, did I make it happen? Or did I just see it somehow?"

I shrugged, helplessly confused. Not wanting to make her turn away, wanting to keep her eyes looking at me. "I don't know. Maybe a little of both."

I had no idea what she was talking about. But she acted like I did.

"Yes. Maybe," she said. Then, almost shyly, she asked the question that would enslave me. "David, when it happens . . . when it happens, David, will you save me?"

I don't know what I thought. That she was crazy. That I didn't care if she was crazy.

"Yes, Senna. I'll save you."

She kissed me then, and then again. And each time she opened her lips to me I felt another part of myself drained away. And I didn't care.

CHAPTER
III

I dreamed about Senna that night. I almost always remember my dreams, although I always pretend not to. There are some things that pop up in my dreams I don't want to remember. Stuff from a long-gone, faraway time, rising up to torture me.

But I dreamed of her that night. And that dream I wanted to keep forever.

She came to me. Right there in my room. She just appeared. Even before I'd opened my eyes. She wasn't smiling. She looked distant and distracted and wary.

But she came to stand beside my bed and took my hand in hers. I felt something like electricity, only, no, no, not electricity. Electricity would travel from her into me, and that's not what I felt.

I felt her hand and it was cold. Not death cold, steel cold. Emptiness cold. My own hand, hot, could not affect her. My heat could not raise her temperature by one degree, and that fact, that physical fact made it seem that my own hand was burning.

She looked at me but there were other eyes looking out through hers.

She scared me. I felt she could reach down and take my throat and squeeze and I would be helpless, helpless, batting at her with weak arms, unable to so much as bruise the liquid steel of her delicate body.

She waved her other hand, and all at once the walls of my room were gone, and we were outside in sunlight, in a field of wildflowers. All fake, I knew that right away. I knew it and it made my insides churn. An illusion she had created, that was it, a movie backdrop for the big scene.

She bent low then, low to me sprawled on the grass, and pressed her lips to mine. Her hair whipped my face, stinging. I flinched but she smiled and I smiled, too, a different smile as she kissed me, and now I was screaming in silent pain as the burning in my hand spread through my body.

I reached for her to pull her down, but I might have been tugging at a marble statue.

No control, David. You have no control. She said that. Or was it me? Or was it some voice from someone watching, unseen?

She laughed. David the Dragonslayer, she said. General David. David the Fool. Lord David. And more names, more titles, all mocking, but as she went on, more bitter, more angry. Like she was seeing a list reeled off, a list she liked less and less.

Then her eyes saw something that made her mouth form into a snarl.

Plans within plans, she said thoughtfully, wary again. Secrets within secrets.

But you will never betray me, will you, David?

No, no, no! I cried, as if someone were ripping the words from my throat.

You will always be mine, she said.

She kissed me again and pressed her body against mine, and now at last she was warm and real. And then she disappeared.

It happened the next day. The terrible thing.

It was early. Gray dawn. More gray than dawn, really, because the clouds were hanging low over the lake. It was chilly, which is how I like it when I go for a run.

I run maybe three times a week. I'm no athlete; it's just that sometimes I'll wake up way too early and be full of this dangerous energy. The kind of feeling that makes you go looking for trouble. Maybe it was some hangover from my dream. Maybe I just hadn't slept well.

All I know is I woke up tingling, teeth grinding, eyes way too clear and alert. So I got up and ran.

I rolled out of bed and pulled on a pair of gray shorts, a faded Radiohead T-shirt, and a sweatshirt with the arms cut short. I dug in my drawer for clean socks and laced up my shoes.

I crept down the stairs past my mom's room. Her door was partly open. A man's leg was sticking out from beneath crumpled sheets. I looked away.

We have a house in a kind of old neighborhood. It's a nice house, with a standard lawn and a fence around the backyard. The street is quiet. It's eight, nine blocks to the lake and downhill all the way.

I headed toward the lake. No warm-up. I wasn't planning a long run. Through the still-sleeping downtown, past the Breugger's and the Barnes and Noble and the health food store.

I listened to the sound of my shoes hitting sidewalk. I listened to the sound of my own breathing, calm and steady for the first few blocks, getting a little harsher after that. I had to breathe through my mouth. My nose hurt less that way.

Down to Sheridan, still mostly devoid of traffic. I caught a red light, shot a look each way, and ran across. There's park all along the lake. Grass and big trees and winding paths for runners and bikers. People take their dogs there. Kids play there. At this hour of the morning, though, there were just a few runners spaced far apart on the crushed shell path.

There's an L-shaped pier of concrete blocks. It shelters the powerboat launching ramp. I saw someone sitting out there on the end. Past the railing, perched on a rough, white concrete boulder. I knew right away it was her.

Senna sat gazing out at the mist-shrouded lake, hands pressed down on the rock, legs drawn up to her chin, a little girl. She was wearing a jean jacket a couple of sizes too big. She looked so small. Weak. Not the creature from my dream.

My steady steps faltered. I heard the different rhythm as my feet slowed, then sped up, then slowed again.

I should have wanted to go to her. But I didn't. I should have felt lucky. Lucky to see her alone on a morning when I expected to be alone with myself.

But that's not what I felt.

Dread.

That's what I felt. Dread.

There was a voice in my head, a lunatic voice screaming, *Run away! Run away!* A panicky voice.

"What's the matter with you?" I asked myself, wanting to hear my own, true voice. "Getting jumpy? That knee in the face must have rattled your brain, David."

I headed toward Senna, toward the start of the pier. But my feet were listening to that other voice, that faint but insistent madman in my brain. My feet were out of rhythm, they missed steps, they dragged, they didn't want to go any closer.

And then I saw the others. And they saw me, and I swear the chill breeze became a frozen wind that went right through my skin and iced my insides.

Jalil was just pulling up in his car. I saw him clearly. He saw me. I guess we were both trying to look normal, but we both knew there was nothing normal here.

Christopher was walking from the other direction. He looked worried and harassed. Like a guy who's late for an appointment he doesn't want to make.

April was sitting on a bench, looking out at Senna. I would be next to her in a dozen steps. I stopped.

"Hi, April," I said, trying to sound normal.

She turned her startling green eyes on me. "What does it mean, David?"

I shook my head. "I don't know."

I heard a car door close. Jalil joined us. He said nothing. He looked at me. He looked at April. Only his eyes moved. Then, as if he didn't want to look, as if he didn't want to have to turn his head, he looked at Senna. At Senna's profile, because she did not turn to look at us.

"Excuse me, but does anyone else have a case of the unholy creeps?" Christopher asked. Christopher's a big guy, bigger than me. Blond. Looks like a surfer dude. His tan was looking a little green.

He had walked up and stopped, like me, a few feet away from April.

"I was blaming it on brain damage," I said, pointing at my bandaged nose.

"My brain's fine," Jalil said. "It's my stomach telling me to get the hell out of here."

"Too weird," Christopher said. "We're all here? *She's* out there? What is this?"

"I heard her leave really early this morning," April said. "We share a wall between our rooms. She . . . and then, I felt like I had to follow her." She shrugged.

"What is this?" Christopher demanded in a loud voice. Deliberately loud. Maybe loud enough for Senna to hear if she was listening.

"Ask *her*," April said.

Slowly Senna climbed to her feet. She turned and looked at us. She was maybe a hundred feet away.

I could see confusion on her face.

Her mouth formed the word "no."

And then the entire universe ripped apart.

CHAPTER V

It was like a fade. Like on a TV show when they fade from one picture to another. One minute you're seeing one picture, then slowly another picture emerges beneath the first.

Only this was not TV. And this was happening in three dimensions.

The picture had sight, sound, smell. It had the breeze that smelled of damp. It had the soft sounds of water sighing against the shore. It had the feel of chill, and of soft grass under my soles, and of sweat cooling on my body. It had low, heavy clouds that seemed to squeeze the air out of my lungs.

It had Senna, alone, at the end of the pier, and the memory of her lips on mine.

In one sickening moment all that began to shimmer, as if it had all been a reflection in a bowl of water and someone had tapped the bowl. It shimmered and sent a wave of fear-sickness through me.

The clouds twisted as if a tornado were forming. The pier seemed almost to curl, like a pig's tail. I looked at Jalil. His face was turning inside out. Inside out! I could see the back of his eyes, the gray wrinkled brain, the heaving, gasping trachea in his throat.

I held my hands up instinctively, blocking that vision, but my own hands were twisted and deformed. The skin was flayed and spread out, as if I'd been skinned. I could see the blood-soaked muscles beneath, the white bones. I saw the arteries pumping blood up through my wrists.

I cried out. But my moaning voice came from somewhere outside of myself and rang distant and false in my ears.

The ground opened, opened until I could see buried rocks pushing up beneath me. But I didn't fall. The sky split apart, a blue-gray curtain drawn back to reveal black space and a sun burning too close. The clouds boiled madly.

I've gone insane, I cried, but the thought itself was nothing but dancing electrical charges, sparks between neurons that I could see behind my eyes.

And in all this twisted chaos, all this hallucinatory madness, I still saw Senna, whole, complete, herself.

The gray, choppy surface of the lake swelled up, rising higher and higher, as if it would crash down on us in a tidal wave. It rose, and as it did, the chop roughened, lengthened, formed itself into a mountain of shaggy gray fur.

The mountain pulled up and back, bringing more into view. Two ears, a brow, eyes! Brown and yellow eyes the size of backyard kiddie pools. Intelligent, cold, gleeful, malicious.

Up rose the snout of the wolf's head. Up behind Senna, who still looked at me, right at me.

Up it came and opened wide, with glittering teeth that may have been six feet long.

The wolf's mouth opened wide and lunged.

Only then did Senna turn away from me and face the wolf. She held her thin arms up in a pathetic gesture of resistance, but the wolf snatched her up in one swift bite.

It closed its jaws around her, but gently, holding her helpless, limp, unresisting now.

"Senna!" I shouted. "Senna!" And now the voice was coming from inside me, and it sounded real and raw and impotent.

The ground became the ground again. My hand was skin over muscle over bone. Jalil's face was a face twisted by shock, but a human face.

It was ending.

It was ending with the wolf, the monstrous wolf, sinking slowly back into the water. In a few seconds it would be gone.

I had been frozen in place, but now my legs moved. Shaking, wobbling, my stomach twisted, I ran after her. Down to the pier.

"David! Don't do it!" Jalil yelled.

It was Christopher who answered him. "Like hell," he said. "That thing's got her!"

Then Christopher was running, too. And April behind him, and Jalil behind her. We were all four running, our footsteps pounding.

The closer we came to the wolf, the more the universe around us became twisted and distorted again. The pier itself suddenly swooped uphill, soft and twisted as a piece of taffy. But we ran.

Courage? Panic? Rage? Some stupid, animal instinct?

I don't know. I don't know why we ran after that monster from another world.

We ran as it turned away. We ran, the twisted universe receding with us, racing the wave of distortion.

Suddenly, the sound of feet on damp concrete stopped. There was nothing beneath my feet. I leaped!

CHAPTER VI

I leaped and was frozen.

Still, utterly still, unable to move, unable to do more than slowly, slowly aim my eyes. I shifted my slow-motion gaze from nothing to nothing to nothing more.

I was buried in cotton, cloud, whiteness all around me. It didn't touch me. Nothing touched me.

I floated, naked. Exposed.

Watched?

Yes, maybe. I felt something. Yes, watched.

"Play your story for me, David. Show me your secrets."

I was in summer camp. I didn't want to go to summer camp. My parents made me. Good for me, you see. But I knew things were wrong at home, I knew there was trouble between my parents; I had felt the hard, sure edges of my life beginning to crumble.

I said, *"But I don't want to go."*

"Once you get there, you'll like it."

Awake, pretending to be asleep in my bunk. Listening to the snores and farts and crying and sleep-mumbling of a dozen kids around me.

Pretending not to hear Donny's footsteps. White nylon camp windbreaker bright in reflected moonlight, moving confidently, arrogantly. He had the power. The counselor. We were just kids.

Why was he doing it? Why didn't he just go away?

He stopped beside the same cot as before. It was wrong, what he was doing. It was bad. Why didn't the kid cry out? Why didn't he yell?

Save him, David. Don't pretend to sleep, don't inch the blanket higher around your head. Don't press your hands over your ears. Don't . . .

"Will you save me, David?"

Later, older, last year. Last year?

Walking out of the gym, sweaty from some after-school one-on-one. Walking past the coach's office. It was none of my business.

A loud, berating voice.

"What's the matter with you!"

I slow my walk and look through the glass

door. Some kid from the junior varsity football team, in jersey and shoulder pads, sitting there, head hung.

"You disgust me, you make me sick, your attitude out there on the field. You make me want to throw up. You might as well be a little girl. Are you a man, or are you some kind of faggot?"

I open the door. Some part of me, some part of my brain has taken over my body in a flash, no thought, no hesitation. The switch has been thrown. The rage adrenaline is flooding my arms and legs, stiff with repressed energy.

The kid is crying. Crying in his cot.

"Leave him alone."

"What are you doing in here, Levin? Get the hell out of my office!"

"I can take care of myself," the kid yells, nearly hysterical, face streaked with mud and tears, turning his anger on me.

I'm two feet away from the coach. He's my size. Older, though, fat in the middle, slow.

"Leave the kid alone."

"I ought to kick your ass!" the coach roars.

"Screw you! Screw you!" the kid yells. At me. *"You think you're so tough."*

I walk away.

"Ah," a voice says. *"I see."*

CHAPTER VII

I woke in agony.

Pain in every muscle fiber, every joint. I tried to move but something was wrong. My arms were pinned, my legs seemed to be dangling, my chest was stretched, my spine . . .

My eyes snapped open.

I couldn't make sense of what I saw. It was like that moment when you wake from a dream and look around your room, unable to figure out where you are or what things mean.

I was hanging by my arms. My back was against a stone wall. Stones as big as cars. Chains were attached to my wrists with shackles. The chains and shackles could have held King Kong.

A dream! Had to be. Wake up!

Come on, David, wake up!

I slammed my head back against wet, mildewed stone. The pain was real. I closed my eyes tight and opened them again.

I was still hanging by my wrists. My clothes were shredded. I could feel my partly bare butt scraping against the stone. My heels kicked back and hit rock.

I was hanging like a piece of meat, dangling, stretched, helpless.

"Hey! Is anyone there?" I yelled. Not a brilliant thing to say. But what do you say when you wake up to find yourself hanging against a wall?

"We're all here," a harsh, strained voice said.

"April?" I pushed my head out and twisted it to look around my own armpits.

She was hanging about ten feet away on the same wall. I could see her wrists. They were scraped raw. Blood had run down her arm and dried. We'd been hanging for a while. I was cold. Very cold.

"Yes, it's me," she said. Her voice came out in ragged gasps. I guess mine did, too.

"Where are we?" I asked.

"I don't really know, David," she said with surprising gentleness, despite her strained breathing. She even managed just a hint of mockery. "I don't think I'm familiar with this place. But I can tell you one thing: Don't look down."

I looked down. Down was a long, long way. My

running shoes were hundreds of feet above jumbled, jagged rocks that formed a shoreline. If I fell, I'd have plenty of time to scream before I was sliced and smashed.

I looked up. This was harder to do, but more reassuring. There was an end to the wall. A parapet, I guess you'd have to call it. The wall rose only six or eight feet above my head, topped by tall, stone teeth. My chains went up between two of the teeth.

"Are you okay?" I asked April.

"I'm alive," she said. "I think Jalil's breathing, but he's still unconscious. I can't see Christopher very well. He's on the other side of you."

I twisted my head to the left and saw Christopher. He must have just awakened. He was looking around, wild-eyed, till he spotted me.

"Well, this isn't good," Christopher said. "Where are we?"

I sighed. Then, a thought. "Senna? Is she here?"

"No," April said. "At least not that I can see. Maybe on the far side of Jalil. I can't tell."

"Jalil!" I yelled. "Jalil, wake up!"

"What? What?" he said. "Oh, man!"

"Got that right," Christopher muttered.

"Jalil, is anyone hanging to your right?" I asked.

"No. No one else."

"This is one bitch of a dream," Christopher said.

"Not a dream," Jalil said. "Doesn't feel right for a dream."

"Of course it's a dream," Christopher said scornfully. "What, we're actually hanging by our wrists on some castle wall? I don't think so."

"Maybe he's right," I said to April. "Maybe I'm dreaming."

"Then dream me up a parka. It's cold," April said.

I looked away from her and out across the landscape. It was a gray day, just like it had been. But nothing else was the same.

The castle, if that's what it was, seemed to be at the end of an unbelievably steep chasm. Rugged, bare, black stone walls rose sheer on both sides. In the bottom of this canyon was a lake, or maybe an inlet. One way or the other, there was dark, glass-smooth water. It reflected the harsh cliffs so that they seemed to go down forever.

It was a picture in shades of gray, from near black to near white, but with never a splash of color.

Until a dot of red appeared. I squinted and focused. Down along the left-side cliff wall, maybe a half mile away, there was a boat. It was bow-on to us, so I couldn't see how big it was. But it was flashing out a sail as it rounded a point of land. A square sail with some sort of logo or symbol in red.

Were there people on that boat? I couldn't see that far.

"There's a boat," I said.

"Maybe they'll help us," Christopher said. "I can't take this, man. My arms . . . my wrists are all bloody. I think maybe one of my shoulders is dislocated."

"I have Advil in my backpack," April said. "I think I still have it on. But it's going to be hard to get anything out."

I glanced over. She was wearing a backpack. It pushed her out from the wall. It must have been painful.

This was ridiculous. We were hanging by our wrists! Where was the lake? Where was the city? There's no castle in the Chicago area. Where were we?

I took a couple of deep breaths, fighting down the urge to start yelling. If I started acting scared I'd start being even more scared. I was scared plenty. I was good and scared.

But being scared was one thing. That was normal. *How* you acted once you were scared — that's what mattered.

My dad told me that. He has two Purple Hearts and a Silver Star that prove he has a right to talk about fear.

"Has to be a nightmare," Christopher grunted, trying to reassure himself. "Has to be. The whole thing. Senna, the wolf, this, all of it."

"I don't think so," Jalil said. "It's going on too long. It doesn't have the *feel* of a dream. It's bizarre, but I think it's real. I push my legs back, my body goes away from the wall: cause and effect. In dreams you lose normal cause and effect. You jump around in time. This is reality."

"Dammit, someone help us! Help! Help!" Christopher yelled. "Help us! Help!" I guess he was tired of hearing Jalil analyze things.

I kept my attention on the boat. It was something to focus on. Something better than focusing on pain and fear.

I like to sail. My dad had a forty-two-footer, back in Annapolis, where we used to live. A wooden boat, practically an antique. When I was younger we'd take it out on the bay on Saturdays. Him and my mom and me.

Then my dad retired from the navy and we ended up in Chicago. We brought the boat with us, but since then my folks got divorced. My dad remarried a woman with her own kids. So I don't see my dad as much. Anyway, you can't compare sailing on Lake Michigan with sailing on the Chesapeake Bay.

The boat with the red-emblazoned sail was turning slowly as the wind caught the canvas. I could see that it was bigger than I'd expected. Longer. Riding low in the water.

Oars? Were those oars I saw? And . . . yes, there were figures moving about on deck. I caught faint suggestions of blond hair, flashes of polished metal.

Then I saw the figurehead. The graceful prow that rose high till it ended in an ornate carving of a dragon's head.

I barked out a laugh. "No way."

But it was true. There was no mistaking the unique lines, the very sight of which had once sent brave men running.

"It's a longboat," I said.

"Yeah, really long, who gives a rat's ass how long it is?" Christopher demanded. "Help! Help!"

"No. It's a *longboat*," I said, not believing my own words. "A Viking longboat."

CHAPTER
VIII

The fitful breeze was in our faces, and the longboat swiftly closed the distance to the castle.

It was easy to see the rows of shields arrayed along the sides, each painted with the identical red emblem: a snake, mouth open, fangs out, dripping venom onto an agonized, upturned face. It was the same emblem on the big, rectangular sail.

"Nice logo," Christopher said darkly. "That's right up there with the Pillsbury Doughboy and Betty Crocker. Those boys need a new sponsor."

On deck, some sitting at oars, others standing around in conversation, were forty, maybe fifty men. They were big men, most of them. Big in size and in body language. Most were bearded. Not trimmed, Lincoln Park yuppie beards, but big, bristling, red or gold or brown beards, glistening with grease. Their hair was long and wild.

They wore a motley array of garments: baggy trousers, long chain-mail shirts, and what might have been bearskins and goatskins draped down from their massive shoulders and cinched at the waist with wide leather belts. Some had crude high-top sandals laced over rag socks. Others had knee-high, buff leather boots.

At their sides most wore long, heavy swords. Others carried crude axes, some like tomahawks, others with handles maybe four feet long.

From time to time a few would look up at us, hanging a hundred feet or so above them. They pointed and guffawed loudly. But the laughter died quickly, followed by a cautious hush.

They were burly, rough-looking men. Fighters. Killers. But they were nervous. Afraid.

As they came within a few dozen yards of the rocks below, they struck the sail. They worked their oars till someone yelled a signal, at which point all the oars rose clear of the water. The helmsman leaned into the one long steering oar and guided the craft into a slow turn that brought the longboat kissing up against what I could now see was a dock.

Fore and aft, men holding ropes jumped ashore

and tied the ship off. But though they looked as if they'd done this many times before, there were frequent nervous glances up at the castle.

Baaa! Baaaa!

I heard the bleating of sheep. Three of the animals were being dragged up from the hold of the longboat. They were manhandled over the side onto the rock slab shore.

Half a dozen of the Norsemen jumped out after the sheep and wrestled the first one up onto a flat obsidian stone.

An altar, I realized.

I glanced at April. She was staring down, transfixed. Her hair kept blowing in her face. Even Christopher was silent.

"You may not want to see this," Jalil warned in a quiet voice. Talking to April? To me?

An old Norseman, big but stooped with age, climbed painfully out of the ship. No one offered him help. He looked like the kind of man who'd chop off a hand offered in help. His beard was mostly gray, but you could still tell that it had once been blond. He was mostly bald, and even from high above I could see a scar from an old wound that must have opened his skull.

The old man walked, with the cautious gait of arthritis, over to the sheep. The first sheep was bleating and squirming, stretched out on its back on the stone.

The knife flashed, coming up with surprising swiftness from the old man's belt. Down it arced, slicing the sheep's throat, silencing its stuttering cries.

"No!" April cried, but softly.

One after the other, the two remaining sheep met the same fate. Blood ran from the edges of the altar.

There was no ceremony. Simple slaughter, carried out hurriedly, nervously.

The old Norseman glanced up at the castle, as if he were looking at us. But I knew, as a chill of premonition tingled from my tailbone up to my neck, that it was not us he saw.

I craned my head back, looking upward. I could see nothing there. But I heard the deep, rasping breathing of some huge creature. A slow, long inhalation, followed by a blast of reeking, carnivore breath.

The wolf.

The Norsemen turned and boarded their ship. The oars were extended and the longboat backed swiftly away.

From above us, a hard, unnatural, animal growling said, "Pull them up. Take them to my father."

Suddenly I felt a sharp, excruciating jerk that

made my chest and shoulders scream. My back and butt were scraping up along the stone wall. Jerk and agony, jerk and agony.

I was afraid, but mad, too. I tried to prepare myself for whatever might be happening, but pain overwhelmed me. Tears came to my eyes.

Rough hands grabbed me, hauling me over the parapet. They threw me down onto stone. I cried out. My kneecaps hit hard. I was on all fours. The second time in as many days.

April landed before me, flung down just as roughly.

I tried to climb to my feet, but pushing myself up, my arms gave way. They were weak, limp. My hands were numb.

A foot, iron-booted, was before me. A hand reached and grabbed my arm. A hand so big it closed all the way around my biceps.

A hand with only three fingers, each as thick as a salami.

I jerked my face upward, still fighting the pain, trying to shut off the flow of tears. I looked up into a face that had never been human.

"Who are you? What's happening?" I heard Christopher ask.

Instantly came the thud of a short, hard punch. Out of the corner of my eye I saw Christopher crumple.

"Silence!" a brutish voice yelled. Then, more quietly, but with seething malice, "Be silent while you can. You will speak soon. You will say all your words and pray for more words to offer when you come before Great Loki."

They unlocked our manacles and tossed the heavy chains aside. They stood us up, supporting us as they trotted us along the stone walkway. And now I could see them clearly. They were maybe eight feet tall and almost as broad. They looked as if they'd been chiseled out of living rock, with limbs so thick they could have been live oak trees.

They had three fingers on each hand and clanking iron boots. They wore simple tunics, a rectangle of fabric with a hole for the head, a thick belt, a sword, and a knife.

Their heads were low, forward-thrust. Like rhinos without the horn. From the back they looked headless.

Someone shoved me in line behind Jalil.

"Jalil," I whispered. "Lopi. What's Lopi?"

He spared a quick, wondering glance for me. I swear he would almost have smiled if he wasn't grimacing from the pain.

"Loki," he corrected. "The Norse god of destruction."

CHAPTER
IX

There was only one thing keeping all four of us from falling apart: I don't think any of us thought it was real. How could we? It was completely impossible!

Life makes sense, mostly. Maybe not people's behavior, but for the most part, one thing follows from another. Cause and effect. But what was the cause here? What was this effect?

It had to be a nightmare. A hallucination. Something. Anything but reality.

But it did feel real. They marched us along a wide battlement. The walls of the castle must have been twenty feet thick. On our left, the tall, daggerlike teeth of the crenellated walls. In the gaps between the sharp merlons we could see the water, the valley. On our right we looked down on sharply pitched tile roofs. As we marched, the roofs gave way to reveal a large courtyard. Our guards slowed us down a little at that point so we could get a good look.

The courtyard was only vaguely rectangular. It was maybe two-thirds of a football field in size.

In the courtyard were half a dozen more like our lumpish guards. Tall, wide, thick, slow-moving creatures who seemed to be drunk and working on getting drunker. They sat against a wall on the ground and on low stone benches. Most held crude wooden bowls, like something your mom would make salad in.

They dipped the bowls into a cut-down keg and drew out something with a head on it. Then they threw back their rhino heads and quaffed it down.

Christopher gave me a look. His lip was split from the guard's punch. He looked as bad as me now. "It's a freak show kegger," he whispered, winking to show he hadn't been totally intimidated.

There were humans in the courtyard, too. Over wool trousers they wore tunics with the snake and face emblem. They had helmets the color of old bathroom faucets. The helmets came down to below the ear and had a nose guard. Nothing elaborate.

These men were practicing sword fighting. The

clang, clang of steel carried up to us. A hard, one-armed man swaggered around among them, slapping whoever annoyed him with the flat of his own sword, yelling, berating.

But that's not what our guards wanted us to see. What they wanted us to see was a man, black-haired, smooth-faced, with deep-set eyes. Not a Viking. He was dressed in rags, but rags that had once been an elaborate costume. He was being dragged across the courtyard toward a hole. The hole was six feet across. A pair of the big rhino heads dragged the prisoner to the edge of this pit and bent him forward so he could look down into it.

I guess this was supposed to scare the prisoner. And maybe it did. But he wasn't giving anything to the guards. Even as they were yanking him back and forth, teasing him, hoping for a few good screams, the man delivered a speech in high, fluty tones.

"I came in peace from my lord Amon-Ra as an emissary to Wise Odin. Hear me all, and witness! I came in peace carrying the words of Ra!"

The guards didn't much like this show of spirit. They dragged the man back from the pit and took turns slamming pile-driver fists into his face. Only then did they throw the dark-haired man into the pit.

The guards laughed and slapped one another on the back. Then they stood around the lip of the hole looking down, laughing and pointing. Bloodthirsty fans at a prizefight.

I don't know what was in the pit. But the man who had been brave was now screaming. And each scream brought fresh hilarity from the brutes.

Our own guards shoved us to get us moving again. They'd shown us what they wanted us to see. Message delivered.

Through a dark arched doorway. Then down a winding stone staircase. Down and down forever. Finally we reached a series of dank, torchlit tunnels. It took a while for me to notice the torches. They were tarred sticks jammed into holders mounted in the walls. The holders were skulls.

We marched past a series of archways that opened into a vast kitchen. Dozens of filthy, grease-spattered men and women turned spits above roaring fires. The spits were long enough to impale four or five sheep and pigs. The smell of roasting meat reminded me of how hungry I was.

I should have had breakfast. Maybe lunch by now. Yes, I was hungry enough that I should have been getting lunch. Maybe back at the same Taco Bell. Maybe just a Coke and a premade sandwich from the machines outside the school cafeteria.

I guess your mind looks for something normal to grab on to when you're scared enough. Familiar hunger. Familiar memories.

What was I doing here? I raged silently. *What was happening?*

We left the kitchen behind, with its charred meat and boiling black pots. Gradually we left the smell behind, too. Then it was up, up, up a long stairway. Three times as high as the one we'd taken down. We were going up into some sort of tower that was higher than the walls.

What was it they called them? I strained my memory. Hadn't I read *Ivanhoe*? Sure. Oh, no, just the Cliff Notes. Yeah, and a B minus on the paper, too.

A "keep." Yeah, that was the word. The big tower, the castle within the castle, the holdout. That must be where we were headed. I'd seen it rising impossibly high above the courtyard. But I'd been paying attention to the courtyard.

At the top of the stairs, just as my thigh muscles were screaming, we found ourselves in a hallway. We emerged suddenly up through one of several doors.

Here the decor improved. The ceiling arched high overhead, maybe ten stories. Huge, intricately carved timbers supported the roof. Dim tapestries hung on the walls. Along the left wall it looked as if something had disarranged the tapestries. A dozen pinched, dirty, anxious-looking women were using long-handled hooks to straighten them again.

The floor was paved in lustrous black flagstones. They echoed flatly with every footstep of our monstrous guards. Our own footsteps were slight, light, insignificant.

I saw an immense doorway ahead. It stood open, with flickering yellow light coming from beyond. And then a smell reached my nostrils. One of the guards muttered something under his breath. He jerked me rudely aside to walk around what looked like a pile of dog crap. But a pile that came up to my knees.

More of the anxious, starved-looking women in pinafores and cloth caps came rushing with shovels and mops in hand.

Suddenly we were in a room so big you could have lost a cathedral in it. It could have been a hangar for 747's. It was more enclosed space than I had ever experienced. I felt like a bug.

Across the room, a football field away, was a massive throne. Someone had started with a slab of stone the size of my house and then chiseled it down into a throne. In one wall, high up, were narrow arched windows that glowed dully with gray light.

A man sat on the throne, with a wolf pacing the floor before him.

Only there was something wrong. Either I was confused about size and distance, or the man and the wolf were each impossibly large.

The guards lowered their already low-slung heads and formed into two more or less straight lines with us between them.

We marched at a fast trot. My legs were cramped from all the climbing. My hands had gone from numb to painful. But I could keep up.

Christopher tripped on a flagstone. He was probably still woozy from the monster's punch. He stumbled. A guard violently yanked him to his feet.

Closer and closer we came, and still the man and the wolf refused to retreat to normal size. The man sat in his throne, gripping the arms, slumped down with his chin on his chest. He was dressed much as the Norsemen had been, but in a version more like a Ralph Lauren designer-label Viking outfit. His boots were knee-high, shining supple leather trimmed in black fur. His trousers were deep green. The long, belted shirt was golden chain mail. Gathered across his collarbones with a golden chain was a fur from some huge white beast.

His hair was blond, long, and combed. His

face was thin, cruel but not stupid. He was handsome in a way. Handsome like a poisonous snake can be beautiful. But he was nervous, too. Drumming his fingers on stone. Rocking just slightly back and forth. Yeah, nervous. Afraid despite his power.

Or maybe I was putting my own feelings off on him. Maybe I was seeing what I wanted to see.

I could feel fear bubbling up inside me. But I had it under control. I was not going to show anything. I arranged my face into a rigid mask. Indifference. That's all I would show.

Give him nothing, I told myself. *Show no fear and he'll at least have respect for you. Show fear and you'll feel the fear even worse. And then it might get away, might boil up out of control.*

I gritted my teeth hard. I clenched my fists. *You don't scare me,* I said silently. *You don't scare me. Not me.*

The wolf paced back and forth. It was a huge gray beast the size of an elephant, but it moved with the easy grace that comes from tremendous strength. It watched us with yellow eyes that burned with more than canine intelligence. The same eyes that had gloated as it snatched Senna from the end of the pier.

The wolf was so big he made the ten-foot-tall man on the throne seem small. And yet despite

the teeth the wolf showed us, it was the man who
held my attention.

He had not looked at us yet. Had not spoken.
He didn't need to. I could feel his power.

When I was little, my dad took me aboard his
ship when it came in. It was an assault carrier.
Mostly helicopters, but with a few Harriers, too.
You know, jump jets. He showed me around the
big belowdecks hangar where they keep the
planes. I remember standing beneath a big, muscular Harrier, already loaded up with its comple-
ment of weaponry.

It's funny about warplanes. You could live your
whole life in a cave and never even see a Piper
Cub, but when you see a warplane for the first
time, you know it's deadly. You can feel the
power and the danger.

That was my first impression of Loki.

I had never seen a god before. Never known of
such a creature, never suspected one existed, but
I felt the power and the danger. I understood
what I was seeing.

Then he looked at us. And I knew I was wrong.
I understood nothing.

This creature was not simply dangerous. He
was evil.

I felt my stomach lurch. I felt my knees buckle.
To my amazement, I sank slowly to my knees.

The four of us knelt in slow motion, knees hitting flagstones.

Loki looked at us with amused contempt. He looked as if he might burst out laughing. He looked as if he might have us dragged away to the pit in the courtyard. He looked as if he might step down off his throne and rip us apart with his bare hands like four rag dolls.

"Welcome," Loki said in a voice that echoed around the vast hall. "Welcome to Everworld."

I was shaking. I'd always hoped, assumed, believed I was brave, but I was shaking. I glanced left and saw April. She was crying. I couldn't see Christopher, but I did see Jalil. His eyes were narrowed, his lips pressed tight. Scared but not panicky.

I shook myself, trying to get a grip on the wild images of terror my own imagination had called up to torture me.

"This is my humble home," Loki said, waving a ham-sized hand around casually. "You've already met Fenrir, my son."

He nodded in the direction of the wolf, who stood poised, ready, bristling with barely contained energy.

I should have wondered how in hell he had a

son who was a wolf, but there was a long list of things to wonder about.

"Eat? Drink?" Loki asked, mocking.

I shook my head. No. I had a horrible moment of thinking Christopher might make some smart remark. But no one said anything.

Loki leaned forward, bringing his face closer to us. His lips actually drew back in a snarl that would have been appropriate for his son. "Good. Then, if we have the necessary pleasantries out of the way, let me ask you: WHAT HAVE YOU DONE WITH THE WITCH?!"

The blast of sound knocked me back. It was a hammer! I hit my head hard on the floor. My ears rang. The wind of his voice, the heat of his rage was like opening a furnace door.

Then I felt more than that. Suddenly Loki was no ten-foot man, but a towering monster that dwarfed the wolf Fenrir, reducing his foul-breathed son to Chihuahua size.

He reached down and grabbed me. Fay Wray in King Kong's grip. He held me, helpless, up to his gnashing mouth.

But this time his voice was gentle and sinister. "What have you done with my witch?"

He could have swallowed me. He could have bitten my head off and chewed my skull. He was huge; I was helpless. I shook. Uncontrollably. Just shook as if I were coming apart.

"Speak up, mortal," Loki said, suddenly all sympathy and reasonableness. "I realize you've had a difficult day. It can't be very pleasant hanging from my wall. But I had to know whether you were mortal or some more significant foe in disguise. Only a mortal could have allowed himself to be hung in chains like a criminal, so now I know *what* you are. Do you hear me? Are you paying attention?"

I nodded, but even that familiar gesture was jerky with trembling.

"Good, good," Loki said. He reached over and set me back down alongside my shocked companions. I noticed Jalil's eyes glance down at my shorts. They were wet.

Loki shrank back to his normal ten-foot dimension. "Now that I have your attention, tell me: Where is my witch? What have you done with her? Speak up."

"I . . . I . . . I don't know any witch . . ." I stammered. I cringed. I couldn't help it. I cringed on my knees before him.

"Oh, but you must," Loki said, still reasonable, suave. "You came through the barrier with her. I went to incredible trouble to allow Fenrir to cross over, all so I could have the witch. I have exhausted myself! I have borrowed power from others that I must now repay. Do you have any idea what that witch cost me? And now, NOW, NOW I don't have her. And you tell me you don't know any witch."

Loki blazed. Literally. His hair was on fire, his face twisted, his eyes seemed to burn into me. Burn right into my brain, burn through my pathetic teeth-clenching tough-guy pretensions.

"Leave me alone," I whispered, begging.

His expression changed to one of bemusement. He laughed. "You really *don't* know. Blind little mortal." And then he did something that rocked me to the core.

The room filled with a blinding glow. An instant later, where Loki had stood now stood Senna.

She was beautiful. Dressed in the clothes she'd worn on the pier. "Fenrir penetrated the barrier and brought me back to serve Great Loki," she said. The voice was not hers. It was a feminine voice but not hers. A parody of a girl's voice.

"I came through the void, but the four of you came through, too. And somehow in the confusion, the imbalance of that moment, I slipped from Fenrir's jaw and disappeared."

Senna, who was not Senna, walked over to me. She stood very close. Her face. It was her face. Her eyes, her mouth. She touched me gently on my wounded nose. "What have you done with me?" she asked.

And then she dug her nails into my nose and twisted.

"Ahhh!" I yelled. I batted at her hand, turned my face away to break her grip.

"Leave him alone!" April yelled. "No one knows what happened to Senna. We didn't do anything to her."

Loki became Loki again. He was breathing heavily, as though he'd just climbed the stairs to his own tower. He was weary. The rage was burning out.

Fenrir decided to take a leak. He pissed a firehose stream against the far wall. The wolf urine steamed.

From the shadows behind Loki's throne a figure emerged, gliding across the floor.

He was not large, no bigger than me, maybe a little smaller. But the wings he kept folded back made his shoulders seem very broad. He moved on thin, bowed legs that ended in soft pads rather than feet. They made a faint squishing sound, a little like someone with new sneaks. Just above the feet there were knees, and from the knees sharp, forward-aimed spikes protruded.

The head was round, dominated by two large,

flat insect eyes. But the single thing that caught my attention was the mouth. It was almost human at its center, but three jointed, grasping claws ringed the mouth. The claws worked constantly, reaching, grabbing at nothing, then pulling in toward the mouth.

Loki, for all his evil power, was clearly a creature of Earth. Fenrir, the huge wolf, too. But this monster, this . . . thing . . . was just as clearly not.

Loki didn't look at the figure, but I could see that he felt his presence. Loki's lip twitched into a sneer.

"They know nothing," the winged insect said in a fluttery, whispery voice.

"They have stolen my witch!"

"You have failed," the creature said without a trace of emotion. "You have not opened a door into your Old World as you promised Ka Anor you would."

Loki turned to look at the creature. "I could have Fenrir chew you up and crap you out, you Hetwan filth."

"You are a treacherous creature, Loki. Ka Anor knows this. Ka Anor will not be surprised if you kill me. But Ka Anor will not be happy, either. I will leave now and report to Ka Anor. I think Ka Anor will eat you."

All this without any sense of fear or worry. The

delicate alien creature seemed unconcerned by Loki. And he had no interest in us.

Loki looked at the huge wolf and jerked his head ever so slightly. Fenrir lunged and snapped up the Hetwan. The Hetwan offered no resistance. He lay passively in the panting jaws. One of Fenrir's huge teeth was drawing yellow blood.

Fenrir carried him to Loki. Loki twisted his head sideways to look right in the Hetwan's blank eyes. "You tell your Ka Anor that I don't die easily." Loki threw out a hand, pointing at a tapestry embroidered with the red serpent picture we'd seen earlier.

"Do you see that? Do you know what it means, Hetwan? Odin, the All-Father, imprisoned me, bound by enchanted chains between massive rocks. And he created a snake to writhe above my upturned face, a snake that dribbled its venom into my eyes. The pain . . ." Loki flinched at the memory and swept a hand over his face as if wiping something away.

"It was agony. Day after day, year after year. Odin meant me to lie there in agony forever, for the crime of killing Baldur! But when the Great Change came, when Everworld was born, in that cataclysm I escaped. I lay in wait and I found the time." Loki's voice was a whisper now. "And I found the way. And the weapon. And I seized the indestructible Odin. And now it is Odin who lies writhing in torment."

Loki's face was suffused with remembered pleasure. He savored the memory. "Odin One-Eye, all-powerful Odin, is in my power now. I entertain myself devising new tortures for him."

Loki took a few deep breaths, shaking off the happy visions. He smiled at the Hetwan. "So, you see, there's a moral to the story. One you should pass along to that alien interloper, Ka Anor: Loki is not easy to kill. The bastard of Asgard now entertains Asgard's former master in his dungeon."

He nodded at Fenrir. The wolf let the Hetwan fall.

The Hetwan picked himself up. His three-clawed mouth still sought for food that did not exist.

He walked calmly to one of the tall, arched windows, spread his wings, and flew up and through it without another word.

Loki glared after him.

"Double the guard," he said to Fenrir. "Have our vassals kept alert. I will kill the fool who lets any Hetwan enter my domain. Likewise any creature of Huitzilopoctli. They're of a piece, these aliens and those bloodthirsty madmen. Death-worshipers all."

Fenrir nodded his shaggy wolf head. "And

what of these mortals?" he asked in his strange, animal voice.

Loki shrugged. "Have the trolls take them to the pit. Kill them." He looked right at me and curled his lip in contempt. "Have them kill the cowardly one slowly."

CHAPTER
XI

We marched from the great hall away from Loki and Fenrir.

I had to get up off my knees to move. I had to get up and walk with my own piss drenching my shorts. Christopher was behind me. He had to see. He had to know what I'd done.

My God, I was a coward! Loki was right. I was a coward.

I was still shaking. I was glad, relieved to be away from Loki and his foul-smelling son. But terrified of what lay ahead.

All my life I'd wondered. Like every boy. Like every man. Maybe girls, too, I don't know. But there has never been a male born who did not wonder whether he was brave.

You hear stories, you read books about men who were brave when they had to be. Men who had stood up against unbelievable odds. I'd failed. And not for the first time.

Was it Loki who had opened my mind and looked in at my secrets when we crossed over? Had it been Loki whose voice I'd heard as I hung, suspended, in the blank white void between worlds?

Ah, I see.

No. Someone else. Not Loki. But Loki hadn't needed to open my mind to understand me.

Kill the cowardly one slowly.

I wasn't ready. I hadn't known it was going to happen, I told myself. This wasn't what I'd ever pictured. A war, maybe. Yes, I could be brave in a war. I'd thought about it many times. But this! My test had come and I wasn't ready.

No excuses! Coward! Coward! I'd wet myself like a little baby. I had cried. I would have begged if I'd had the chance.

Oh, my God, how could I be a coward?

Now they'd kill me and it would almost be a relief. How could I ever tell my father what I'd done?

I was in a haze. Disconnected from what was happening. Like it was all happening to someone else. Some far-distant person was being marched down that long stairway. Someone else, someone I didn't even know, was blinking in the sudden light of the courtyard. Someone else was walking meekly toward the pit.

Not me. Not David Levin. Not me. That wasn't me shuffling along, head bowed, tears welling in my eyes behind a swaggering troll. No. No, that wasn't me.

"NO!" I yelled.

It happened in a flash. I lunged. My hand grabbed the sword hilt. My fingers closed around it, unfamiliar yet expected. I pulled.

It was long. It seemed to take forever to draw out of the troll's scabbard. Then, there it was: a blade. Not glittering but dull. There was a fine coating of powdery rust below the pommel. It was heavier than I'd thought it would be.

The troll turned his brute face to me. Seeing the sword in my hand, he registered slow surprise.

I held it awkwardly, pointing straight out but with my wrist all wrong. I saw the sword point. I saw the troll's chest and neck and head.

And in that awful moment of suspended time, some clockwork part of my brain, some cold, distant, untouched part of my brain told me, *The neck will be most vulnerable.*

I thrust, blindly, wildly. No art. No style. Just a convulsive jerk forward.

The iron blade entered the troll's neck and

stopped. In sheer panic, I leaned into the sword, thrusting with all my weight, all my adrenaline-powered strength.

The troll gaped at me, amazed. He reached up and touched the sword that now protruded through his neck, skewering him.

A second troll began to draw his own sword.

I yanked the sword from the troll's neck and swung it hard. My panicked, sweeping blow nearly decapitated April, but she was just short enough. The blade caught the sword arm of the second troll.

The arm dropped, bloodless, to the ground, still holding a sword. It stiffened. It became rock, like something hacked off a statue.

"Run!" Christopher yelled.

I hesitated, but only for a moment. The troll I'd stabbed was not bleeding from the gaping wound in his neck. The area of the wound was already stone. Hard. Lifeless. It was spreading out from the wound, turning what must have been living flesh to granite.

The troll still looked puzzled. Then the stone-stiffening reached his face and the look became permanent.

I turned and ran.

Jalil, April, and Christopher were already racing back down the tunnel we'd come through. There were too many men and trolls in the court-yard to stand and fight there. Trolls and men were coming after us, but the two nearest, our re-maining troll guards, were too slow for teenagers in running shoes.

We pelted down the stairs but leaped off after only a few dozen feet of descent. We were in a tunnel, colder, darker than before. Dustier, as if it hadn't been used much lately.

I still held the sword, which made it awkward to run. Several times the blade scraped on the stone wall and set off sprays of sparks. But I'd give up my life before I'd let go of that sword.

The tunnel came to a three-way divide.

"That's the direction we came from," Jalil said breathlessly, pointing at the left branch. "Back toward Loki."

"Yeah? Then how about another choice?" Christopher suggested.

"Right," I said, and led the way into darkness.

I was fifty feet or so down the right-hand tun-nel when I realized April wasn't with us.

I stopped and grabbed Christopher, who was running past. I yanked him to a stop and Jalil plowed into us. We froze, backs pressed against dripping walls, scared of making a sound.

I looked back and saw April silhouetted in torchlight. Trolls and men, all with swords drawn, were descending on her.

If we went back for her, we'd all be killed. If we didn't . . .

"They've gone to murder Loki!" April screamed. "Stop them! Stop them! They've gone to murder Great Loki!"

She kept yelling and pointing down the left-hand tunnel.

It was idiotic. No way anyone would fall for such a lame trick.

And yet the motley assortment of men and trolls roared away down the left tunnel.

One man, a large, brutal-looking Norseman, hesitated. He looked at April and squinted, as if trying to form a thought. I tensed, wondering if I could take him on.

"Yeah, right," I muttered under my breath. "He's been swinging a sword since he was four!"

April didn't give the Norseman a chance to form his suspicion fully. "What will happen if they reach Loki? His anger will be terrible! Do you want to be the *last* to defend him?"

That penetrated the thick blond head. Loki's anger was something he could understand. Showing up late was probably not a good idea when your boss was a lunatic god.

With a battle roar, he went off in pursuit of the others.

April ran to us, panting.

"Not bad," Christopher said. "You should be an actor."

"I *am* an actor," April said shakily. "Obviously, you missed *Cuckoo's Nest* last year. I killed as Nurse Ratched."

"Which way?" I asked, like someone might have an answer.

"How about away from the last troll we saw?" Jalil suggested.

"Fair enough," I agreed. We took off at a trot. We were all exhausted, hungry, and thirsty, but adrenaline is an amazing substance. If you're scared enough, you find more energy than you thought possible.

And we were definitely scared.

XII

It was a long tunnel. And a long way between flickering skull-sconce torches.

Worst of all, the tunnel was not straight. It was curving, and the more it curved the more we feared it might lead back to Loki and the men and trolls who must be looking for us. Our footsteps seemed awfully loud. And we were leaving prints in the dust.

We talked in low, muttering whispers. Scared. But relieved, too. We should be dead. We weren't.

"So are we definite that this is not a dream?" Christopher asked at one point.

I had been off in dark thoughts, remembering my shameful terror before Loki. "Not a dream," I muttered. I smelled of urine. I smelled like a men's room.

"Then what the hell is it?" he demanded. "I

mean, what is going on? Is this someone's idea of a joke? Loki? A Norse god? A wolf the size of a bus? Some creepy alien? Trolls? Vikings killing sheep? I mean, what's the deal?"

"Loki called it 'Everworld,'" Jalil said. "Not that that tells us much."

"Maybe we've all gone nuts," April said, laughing a little at the idea. "Maybe we're psychotics walking around a padded room wearing paper slippers and straitjackets."

"Sounds like you took *Cuckoo's Nest* a little too seriously," Christopher said.

"Did you see it?"

"Yeah. I needed some extra credit in English so I wrote a report on it."

"And?"

"And you were very good, April," Christopher said. "But nothing compared to your performance with that dumb Viking back there."

April laughed again. It annoyed me. What right did she have to laugh? She would laugh at me, no doubt. Probably already had. Big deal David, tough guy David, David with the attitude, crying and squirming and . . .

I couldn't think about it. It made me want to crawl out of my own skin.

"This is all connected to Senna," Jalil said. "This didn't start with us hanging off a wall. This started with all four of us being there at the lake this morning. And her being there."

What was he talking about? I tried to tear my mind off my own self-loathing.

Jalil was right. Only it may have started even earlier. I said nothing, but I wondered if it had started with the fight at a Taco Bell. Why had we all been there? Was that part of some plan?

I flashed on my car, Senna beside me.

"Something is going to happen." That's what she'd said.

"What's going to happen?"

"I don't know. I only know something will happen. Soon. Something . . . terrible."

Yesterday. A million years ago, and yet I could still see the way her eyes glittered. *"Sometimes I know things before they happen. Sometimes I can see a scene in my head. Like watching a movie. And then it will happen. I think, did I make it happen? Or did I just see it somehow?"*

Good question, I thought grimly. *Very good question, Senna.*

Senna, the "witch" Loki wanted so badly.

"David, when it happens . . . when it happens, David, will you save me?"

I grabbed my head with my two hands and pressed hard on my temples. *No, I won't save you*

Senna, I'll shake and quiver like a scared rabbit. That's what I'll do, Senna.

"Hey, watch where you're waving that thing," April said, looking at the sword. "You have a headache or something?" She swung her backpack around and began digging inside.

The question was so mundane I had to laugh. A headache? Did I have a headache? I was living a nightmare inside a nightmare.

April dug out a small blue-and-white bottle. She twisted the cap off and handed me a round, dark rust-colored pill — an Advil.

"Here. You'll have to swallow it dry. I better ration them, so see if this one works before you take another."

"Oh, April," I sighed, shaking my head.

"What?"

"Nothing. Save it. You're right, we may need it."

Jalil quickened his pace to catch up to us. "What else do you have in that backpack?"

"Good question," Christopher muttered. "And if you say, 'I have my nine-millimeter Glock and an extra clip,' I'll kiss your feet."

We kept moving as April searched by dim torchlight. "The Advil. Bottle of a hundred, maybe half gone. Um . . . my CD player."

"What CDs?" Christopher asked.

"Alanis Morissette . . . Um, that Lilith Fair CD . . ."

Christopher and I both groaned.

"The Bach B-minor mass. And the sound track from *Rent*."

Jalil groaned. "Oh, man. Show tunes? We're stuck a long way from the nearest Sam Goody and all we have is whiny women and show tunes?"

"Hey, she brought some Johann Sebastian, too," Christopher said, changing sides. "Lighten up on the girl. Broaden your tastes."

"Sorry, if I'd known I was going off to bizarro world to hang out with trolls and Norse gods, I'd have brought a wider selection," April said. "Not to mention extra batteries. And don't dis *Rent*, drama club is putting that on this year."

"Not just Norse gods," Jalil said, thoughtful once more. "There's that alien and that Ka Anor thing. And Loki said something about Huitzilopoctli. And the prisoner was talking Ra."

"Didn't he play third base for the Cubs back in the eighties?" Christopher said.

Humor. The just-nearly-died brand of giddy humor.

"I have this vague memory that Huitzilopoctli

is some kind of Aztec god. And, of course, Ra. Egyptian."

"Aztecs? Why would there be Aztecs?" Christopher demanded.

"Why would there be Loki? Why would there be a big freaking wolf?" I demanded, suddenly angry. "Why would we all go trotting down to the lake and end up hanging in chains? You want to start with the 'why this?' and 'why that?'"

"Touchy, isn't he?" Christopher mocked. "Must be the wet pants."

I was on him before he finished the last word. I grabbed him by his collar and shoved him against the wall. His hair was inches from the flame of a skull torch.

"Don't push me!" I yelled at the top of my lungs. "Don't push me or I'll shove this sword up your ass and see how brave you are!"

I was panting. Christopher looked amazed.

Jalil grabbed my sword hand, whipped his other arm around my neck, and yanked me back. He spun me away.

I stumbled but kept to my feet. I clenched the sword and tensed my arm, ready to do murder.

April stepped between me and Jalil.

"What are you, crazy?!" Christopher yelled.

"Shut up, all of you!" April hissed. "We're in a

tunnel, you idiots. Voices carry. You want to have those . . . those trolls all over us? I don't. So shut up and calm down and stop acting like little boys."

She was right. Obviously. But I almost didn't care. Christopher had as much as called me a coward. I couldn't let that stand.

April sighed and smoothed her hair back. In a calm voice she said, "Listen to me. We don't need this. We stick together or we don't have a chance. Even if we do stick together, we don't have much of a chance. We have to figure out what's going on and get home, and stay alive in the meantime. We'll need food and water and warm clothing."

"And weapons," Jalil interjected.

"That, too. What we don't need is a bunch of macho crap."

For a while no one spoke. Christopher and I both sort of came down at the same time. Like a pair of balloons someone had poked holes in.

"We're dead meat, anyway," Christopher said.

"Oh, really?" April said. She pointed back down the tunnel. "Then head back that way, go find the nearest troll or whatever, and die. Okay? Otherwise, if you want to stay with us, work on helping and stop being a baby. And, by the way?

We're not dead meat. We have one big advantage: We're smarter than those guys."

"We are?" Christopher asked skeptically.

"Would you have fallen for that 'They went thataway' routine back there?" April asked him.

I avoided looking at Christopher. But I saw Jalil nodding agreement. "The Trojan Horse," he said to himself. Then for the benefit of the rest of us, "Trojan Horse. You know, war of Troy, Greeks against Trojans."

"The Greeks fought against condoms?" Christopher asked.

Jalil ignored him. "The Trojans are inside the city, Greeks can't get them out, so the Greeks build this big horse, hide a bunch of guys inside it, the rest sail off and leave the horse for the Trojans, telling them it's a surrender gift. The Trojans haul it into the city, the guys climb out at night, open the gates, bye-bye Trojans."

"Who would be that dumb?" Christopher asked.

"I think that's his point," April said. "Not dumb, maybe. Just naive. I mean, we come from a cynical age. Suspicious of everything. Maybe that's an advantage we have."

"Yeah, our bad attitudes versus their swords and axes and giant wolves," Christopher said darkly. "Let's just find the trapdoor to get out of here and back home."

"I'm for that," April said.

We started walking. April searched through her backpack again. I had to say something. I couldn't let it all just lie there.

So I said, "Okay, we look for a way home. But we all go. All or none. The four of us *and* Senna."

No one said no.

No one said yes, either.

CHAPTER
XIII

Fifty-seven Advil.

A Sony personal CD player with headphones.

Four double-A batteries, mostly charged.

An Alanis CD, the Lilith Fair CD, Bach, and *Rent* CDs.

Two books: *Great Poetry of the English Language*, and *Chemistry: Principles and Application*.

One spiral notebook.

A pencil, a felt-tip pen, and two ballpoint pens.

Tampons.

Clinique blusher.

Keys.

That was what we found in April's backpack.

Jalil had keys, a Swiss Army knife, eleven dollars and forty cents, a watch that had been crushed by the chains around his wrists, and his dad's Shell credit card. Christopher had keys, twenty-one dollars and nine cents, a receipt from Marshall Fields for a three-pack of underwear, and a phone card.

I had keys and a quarter.

"Well, if keys turn out to be money around here, we're pretty well set," Christopher said. "Lots of keys. No Uzi, which is what we need in this nuthouse. No grenades, which would come in very handy. Nope, a little pocketknife and a lot of keys."

"How do they keep these torches lit?" Jalil wondered. Then, "Forget the pocketknife and the keys. The most important thing is the chemistry textbook."

"Why? You thinking we'll whip up some —" The joke died on his lips. He grabbed April and pulled her to the side of the tunnel. We all froze. "Shhh!"

We listened, straining. Nothing. Then . . .

Voices!

"Behind or ahead?"

"Behind," April said. "They're after us." She didn't mention that they'd probably heard Christopher and me going at it.

"Let's run," Jalil said.

"But quietly."

We ran. One big advantage we had over the

Norsemen and trolls: They wore boots, we wore sneakers. Hard for men in boots to outrun teenagers in sneakers. Harder still to hear sneakers if you're busy stomping around in boots.

We ran and now, ahead of us, gray light.

"That's not torchlight," April said, panting.

We soon reached the source of the light. A tunnel that went off to the left. It was not meant for people to walk through. It was no more than four feet square. But at the end I saw a perfect square of blue.

"Ventilation shaft," Jalil said. "I don't know how high up we are, but we're definitely up. We go that way, we're probably looking at a long drop."

I snagged a piece of the frayed sleeve of my sweatshirt and ripped it off. I wedged the fabric in a crack in the rocks. "Maybe this'll make them think we went that way."

We continued along the tunnel, running at a pace we could all handle. The noise behind us was fading. We were gaining. Then, a sudden turn in the tunnel, around the corner with Jalil in the lead, and —

"Stop! Back! Back! Back!" Jalil stopped fast, jumped back, and spread his arms to stop the rest of us.

I glimpsed a sheer drop. The tunnel simply

came to an end, opening into a vast natural cave. Stalagmites shot up from the floor, natural skyscrapers. Stalactites hung down from above. An eerie glow filled the cavern. It was a glow that came from a living creature.

There, curled and coiled, its loops wrapped casually around pillars of stone, lay a snake. It was radioactive green, with a pattern of hollow squares, like yellow leopard spots, all along its length. The yellow spots were each the size of a basketball court.

It was a snake the size of a fifty-car freight train. And that was only the part we could see. There was no way of knowing how far back down the caves this hideous, impossible creature stretched.

"You know that film they showed in, like, fourth grade?" Christopher said. "That nature film where they showed a python eating a small pig and you could see the bulge of the pig going through the snake?"

I didn't remember ever seeing that film. But I knew what Christopher was talking about.

"Well," he said, "this snake could swallow a cement truck. With no bulge."

We stood rooted in place at the edge of the precipice, the four of us pressed against Jalil's arms, staring down at the snake.

Just then, I guess someone finally told Loki we'd escaped.

"FIND THEM!"

The voice blasted down the tunnel. It was thunder! It was bombs going off! It shook the rock beneath our feet.

April fell against Jalil.

Jalil windmilled his arms madly, trying to fly. I stuck out a hand and grabbed his right arm. He spun to face me. His foot slipped. He fell.

Chapter
XIV

I gripped Jalil's hand but his fingers escaped.

His face hit hard on the edge of the floor. His hands scrabbled on stone. April screamed.

Jalil was slipping. I dropped to my belly. Jalil's left hand waved, helpless, unable to grab anything but air.

I clamped both my hands on his right arm, but it was a weak grip. His fingernails clawed at stone. Sweat slicked his forearm.

And now I was slipping. I snatched his sleeve to improve my grip. But I was being dragged, dragged toward the edge.

He looked at me, eyes huge, mouth open like he was screaming, but no sound came out.

Slipping . . . slipping . . . I had to let go or I'd —

April landed on my back, too hard, almost

knocking the wind out of me, but stopping my slide.

I caught a flash of Christopher down on his belly, too. He was extended out over the edge, trying to grab Jalil's flailing hand. My fingers slipped. Damp, smooth flesh. I couldn't hold on. I dug my fingernails, ready to tear Jalil's skin to save him.

Slip!

"Ahhh!"

I caught him again at the wrist. Now his other hand was too far for Christopher to reach. But I could hold onto the wrist better. Both hands tight around Jalil's wrist till they cramped.

Then, behind Jalil's head, I saw it.

The snake's head rose up, up, slit eyes amused and eager. A bluish tongue, forked, thick as bridge cable, thirty, forty feet long, whipped out, whipped back, whipped out and quivered, tasting the air.

I flashed on Loki's tapestry, the uniforms of his men: Was this the snake who'd been used to drip venom on the god's face?

"FIND THEM!" Loki cried again. The sound hammered at my head, confusing my thoughts.

"I HAVE THEM, FATHER!"

This voice had come from the snake. No lips had moved. It had no lips. But the sound had come from the snake with the intelligent, mocking eyes.

"Father? Father?" Christopher demanded shrilly. "I thought *my* family was messed up!"

The snake's mouth opened like an automatic garage door. It opened and then there were the fangs, glittering in the puffy pink-flesh mouth.

Jalil flailed. Christopher nearly toppled over the edge, reaching for his hand. In seconds the snake would strike.

"April! Backpack," I gasped. "Give it to Christopher."

I could feel her on me, squirming, getting it off her. "Here!" she yelled.

Christopher wrapped one hand through a strap and swung the pack out, trying to lasso Jalil's other hand.

A grab, a miss! A grab . . .

Yes!

Jalil's hand snagged the strap, Christopher clamped his own hands around Jalil's wrist, and we pulled. Jalil's feet scrabbled at the sheer wall below him and found some tiny edge to push against.

Up he came.

The snake's eyes darkened.

Like a bullwhip, it struck!

Jalil clambered up as the snake's head slammed

against the tunnel opening, fangs out. Fangs so big I could have stuck my fist up inside the hypodermic hole.

But the snake's head was too big for the tunnel. We wobbled to our feet and ran. Then we stopped very suddenly.

Christopher yelled a curse. We were face-to-face with a tunnel crammed with trolls and men, all with swords drawn and axes held ready.

Behind us, the enraged snake reared back and slammed itself against the tunnel opening again.

"Down!" Jalil yelled. He shoved me face-forward. I plowed into April. Christopher must have figured it out on his own because he hit the dirt like he'd been tackled from behind.

The snake's forked tongue shot just inches above us. It darted forward down the tunnel, knocking down a handful of the trolls and men like bowling pins.

The forked tongue curved and wrapped and snapped back.

Snapped back over us with several hundred pounds of bellowing trolls and wild Norsemen.

I was kicked, pummeled, and nearly slashed by a sword blade. I raised my head just enough to see them sucked, screaming, into that pulpy pink mouth.

The two men and single troll who were left

backpedaled fast. I charged, sword held straight out in front of me.

Taken by surprise, the two men slammed back against the tunnel wall. The troll stood blinking stupidly. I rammed the sword into his chest and kept on running.

April was right behind me, Jalil, Christopher.

Suddenly, the sound of a bag of cement hitting the ground.

One of the men had tripped Christopher. The Norseman was drawing a long knife from his belt. He pulled Christopher's head back by the hair, exposing his throat.

Jalil fumbled in his pocket.

"Damn it!" I yelled in utter frustration. I had no weapon. Nothing! The remaining Norseman was grinning. Grinning at April. He grabbed at her. She evaded him.

Just then I saw the tiny Swiss Army knife open in Jalil's hand. He slashed at the knife hand of the guy who had Christopher. The big man gaped at the small red wound on his hand. Christopher twisted around on his back, pulled both his legs up into fetal position, and unloaded with every muscle in his body.

His feet hit the big Viking in the very location that no man — not even a big Viking — wants to be kicked.

"Argh!" the Norseman said. He stumbled back and grabbed himself.

His companion guffawed like an idiot and said, "Now I'll have the woman to myself! Haw, haw, haw."

April swung. The heel of her hand came up and nailed the end of the man's nose. I grabbed his sword arm, slammed his elbow against the rock, and yanked his sword from his numbed hand.

We didn't stay around to see any more. We hauled.

"The air shaft," Jalil panted. "Only way."

It was just fifty feet down the tunnel. A hundred feet down the tunnel was a new rush of armed men.

A race.

I hit the air shaft first, about three seconds before the wave of Norsemen. I jumped to block them from reaching the opening.

"Go! Go! Go!" I yelled to the others.

I held the sword out, ready. A huge man, blond hair greased into Heidi pigtails that hung down from his dingy helmet, stood facing me. He was holding a long-handled battle-ax.

He looked like I was the best thing he'd seen in years. He laughed. He grinned the happy grin of a mad warrior getting ready to do battle.

He roared a threat at me, like some World

Wrestling Federation character putting on a ferocious act. Only this was no act.

The others were all in the air shaft, crawling like infants. An undignified parade of butts.

I could stay and fight. I'd lose. I barely knew which end of a sword to hold on to. Or I could run for it.

I backed up into the air shaft, keeping my sword out. The Viking looked disappointed. But he wasn't going to let me get away. In he came after me.

I was crab-walking, scuffling, backward-crawling, losing more skin off my knees, banging my head on the low ceiling. I swung the sword weakly, back and forth.

"I'll kill you!" I yelled.

The Viking laughed. With good reason.

He was crawling forward, I was going backward. I was scared to death. He was at a party. He was having the time of his life. He was grinning like a guy who'd just scored the winning touchdown.

But he'd overlooked one major fact: It's hard to do much with a four-foot-long ax in a four-foot-square tunnel. He jabbed, but I could stay out of reach and even knock his sword aside occasionally.

I heard Christopher cursing behind me. "There's nothing here!" he yelled.

I kept backing up.

"It's, like, a five-hundred-foot drop into the water!"

The choices were not good. But I knew one thing: There might be a ninety-nine-percent chance that a drop that far would kill us all. There was a one-hundred-percent chance we'd die if we stayed to talk things over with the Vikings.

"Do it!" I yelled.

"Oh, man, I should have just let the snake eat me," Jalil said.

I glanced over my shoulder. The square of light was closer than I'd expected. I could see it past Jalil's butt and April's hair.

The Viking took advantage of the distraction. He lunged with the ax. The side of the blade bit into my chest just below my collarbone.

"Just jump!" I bellowed in panic. "Jump! Jump, he's gonna kill me!"

I backed and backed and backed, and suddenly there was nowhere else to back.

The last thing I saw as I fell was the Viking's crestfallen face.

Chapter XV

I dropped rear-first from the air shaft.

My foot caught and spun me so I twisted around facedown. I could see the others below me. I could see the inky water below them. I could see the cut-with-a-knife cliffs all around us.

We were falling.

Falling four hundred feet. The height of a forty-story building. Like jumping off the Golden Gate Bridge, which people did when they didn't expect to survive.

I was going to hit that water and die.

Except that I was still falling. And so was Christopher, who was closest to hitting. We were all still falling. But slowly. Way too slowly. The air felt normal; it wasn't whipping past. I breathed it in short, desperate gulps. My heart was hammering. My deep brain was still convinced I would be crushed by the impact.

But then I saw Christopher hit. He entered the water with barely a ripple. Like an Olympic diver.

Right behind him, April and Jalil. Both with no more impact than if they'd jumped off the side of a pool.

I had time to straighten myself up, to pull my legs up, then extend them again, pointing downward.

And as I did this I happened to see a pinpoint of light shining from between two daggerlike rocks atop the cliff. The light shone, then winked, came on again and, just as I hit the water, disappeared.

My feet hit water. I plunged down, but no more than five or six feet.

For a few seconds the water actually felt good. My wrists were scraped to the meat, my upper chest had been stabbed, and my nose was still a mess.

More to the point, the water cleaned away the rank smell of my own cowardice.

But then, cold. The water was about one degree away from being a big block of ice. I plowed back up to the surface.

"Oh!" Jalil said, sucking in air not two feet from me. "Oh, that's cold."

Christopher and April were not far away.

"Swim for shore," I said.

"Gee, do you think?" Christopher chattered. "I was wondering if maybe we could get up a game of water polo."

I kicked hard to push myself up for a better view. We were in some kind of narrow inlet. The black cliffs rose around us on all sides. We almost could have been in some huge well. I felt I could sense which way the open water lay, but I couldn't see it. The cliffs seemed to hang like curtains in every direction I looked.

I saw a boat. Instinctively I ducked. But that was stupid. Anyone in the boat would have seen us falling. Besides, the boat seemed to be drifting.

"There's a boat," I said. The cold was really attacking my muscles now.

"Leonardo," April muttered through shuddering teeth.

"What?" I said.

"Leo DiCaprio. *Titanic*. Drowned in the icy North Atlantic. Cold like this."

"I didn't see it. Come on, let's swim for the boat."

"You didn't see *Titanic*?" Her incredulous voice followed me as I began swimming hard for the boat.

It wasn't far. I grabbed the gunwale and rocked the boat down so I could look inside. No one. Some stuff tied up with rope and a couple of oars.

The boat belonged to someone. But it was my boat now.

I hauled myself up like I was doing a push-up, then twisted and squirmed until I flopped, wet and frozen, in the bottom of the boat.

I wanted to just lie there and rest, but I hauled my lead-heavy body up to my knees and helped manhandle Christopher up and over. The two of us easily yanked Jalil and April up out of the water.

Then we all just lay there, lifeless, crumpled, arms and legs splayed out, staying as we'd fallen. We knew we should be running or at least rowing for our lives. But we'd been long since exhausted, and nothing adds to weariness like cold.

I hauled my granite-stiff body up and leaned back against the tied bundle. It was soft. I closed my eyes. I never intended to fall asleep, not there, rocking in a twenty-foot rowboat. But I was done for.

I closed my eyes on the black cliffs towering over my head.

And I opened them in World Civilizations. Last period.

"Ahhh!" I sat upright in my desk. My book went sliding off and hit the floor.

Chapter
XVI

"Yes, Mr. Levin?" the teacher, Mr. Arbuthnot, asked me, arching one eyebrow and peering over the top of his half-glasses. "Was that an exclamation of delight at the contributions made by Galileo?"

I grabbed the desktop. I stared at the girl sitting across the aisle from me. I was in my desk. In *my* desk.

I was dry. Warm. I was dressed in jeans and a baggy cotton sweater. I stared at my wrists. Nothing! No blood, no scabs, no scars.

I slapped my hand to my chest. No stab wound.

I touched my nose. Cotton bandages. My nose was tender. At least that was real.

"A dream?" I muttered.

Mr. Arbuthnot had lost patience. "Mr. Levin,

we are rather busy studying the Italian Renaissance. Granted, only two or three of your fellow students are paying attention, but do you suppose that for their sake you could control yourself?"

This was insane. It had all been a dream? No way. Not poss —

My eyes snapped open. Open on Jalil's annoyed face. He was smothering me, his hand clamped over my nose and mouth.

I slapped his icy fingers away. "What the hell are you doing?"

"See?" he said calmly. "No need to yell. Simply shut off the flow of oxygen and a person will wake up."

He sat back, clutching his arms, shivering.

I blinked at him. Utter confusion. A wet April and a wet Christopher glared at me.

"How can you sleep?" April demanded, outraged.

"He has the only pillow." Christopher pushed past me and began untying the bundle I was leaning on. But the knots wouldn't give way to his blue-tinged fingers.

Jalil unfolded his knife, inspected the ropes and cut once. He pulled the rope away, wound it up, and stuck it into April's backpack.

I stared, uncomprehending. I was still dealing

with having been in Arbuthnot's class. Was that a dream? Was this? Both had seemed real. Both had felt . . . complete.

"Clothes," Christopher said. "Warm clothes. Here." He tossed a dull gray wool dress to April.

"I must have dreamed," I said. "I was back home. In class. Last period. World Civ."

"Yeah? Well, your dreams suck," Christopher said. "You could have dreamed anything. You come up with World Civ? Here."

He handed me a skin. Shaggy gray fur. Actually two, crudely stitched together. I wrapped it around myself. I found a belt and cinched it around the waist. Then realized I had the rough garment on upside down. There was no neck hole, but the skins formed vague shoulders.

And really all that mattered to me was that it was warm.

"Okay, does anyone else have a slight problem with this?" Jalil asked. "There just happens to be a boat and no one around? There just happens to be a bunch of warm clothing that just happens to fit us?"

I rose gingerly to my feet, careful not to capsize the boat. I looked around. Bare rock wall plunged straight from the clouds down into the water and probably hundreds of feet farther down. I saw no beach. No place to get out of the water, except for a tumble of boulders where one of the rock faces had collapsed.

"If we hadn't found the boat, we'd have frozen and died," I said. "No way out of the water."

"We were awfully lucky, then," April said darkly. "Way lucky."

"How about the way we fell?" Christopher asked. "Like slow motion. You can't be jumping that far and survive."

"Someone wants us alive," April said. "And I want to thank them."

Jalil shook his head. He was bundled in a sheepskin jacket, fur turned inward. He'd found a matching hat. I would have laughed, only I was wearing a fur coat. And to be honest, I was jealous of the hat. It looked warm.

"Before I thank them I want to know how they did it," Jalil said. "How do you make someone fall slowly? No wires? No parachute? How do you make someone fall slowly?"

Christopher looked like he was trying to work up a snappy comeback. But instead he unwrapped a small parcel that had been with the clothing. He pulled out what looked like it might be a turkey drumstick.

"What? No cornbread dressing?" he said wonderingly. "There's four of these. I don't see any maggots or mildew or anything."

"I'm a vegetarian," April said. "And even if I weren't, I don't think I'd be eating skanky old turkey legs."

"I'd eat a live turkey about now," Christopher said.

"Let's get this boat moving," I said. "Anyone know how to row? How to handle a boat?"

"What's to know?" Christopher asked as he ripped a mouthful of meat from his drumstick.

"What's to know," I muttered. "Figures. I'd better row."

I settled myself facing the stern and fitted the oars to the carved bone oarlocks. I dipped the oars and the boat began to move. It was a sluggish thing, but I felt better moving.

"We need to think about where we are, what we're doing," Jalil said.

Christopher grinned over his drumstick. "Surely you know where we are? We're up a certain well-known creek, but *with* a paddle."

Jalil did not smile. April did. And she glanced at the meat, too.

"Want some?" Christopher offered a piece to Jalil.

Jalil shook his head. "No. I'm waiting to see if

you die first. Salmonella. Botulism. Poison . . ."

Christopher took a defiant bite.

Jalil said, "So, here's what we have. We've been transported to some place that shouldn't exist, but obviously does. We've run into creatures who shouldn't exist, but obviously do. Loki, Fenrir, that snake the size of a derailed Amtrak, trolls. Not to mention Vikings. We jump and fall too slowly, just happening to land near a boat loaded with clothes for three males and one female. And while we're at it: Why does a Norse god speak English?"

I was getting into the rowing. The familiar rhythm was reassuring. But it was causing blood to seep from the shallow puncture in my chest. Not much blood. Not enough to worry about. But it wasn't going to heal with me rowing.

The cliff face passed by, undifferentiated, featureless. I glanced over my shoulder every so often. Nothing visible ahead, either.

I saw April smile mischievously at Jalil. "It's magic. It's all magic." She was baiting Jalil. I guess she knew something about him that I didn't.

Jalil jumped at the bait. "Magic? You mean, what? Something supernatural?"

The word "supernatural" was a sneer.

"Superstitious nonsense. It's for idiots. Horoscopes, New Age baloney, magic, auras, all of it. If something exists, it's part of nature. So the whole idea of something being 'supernatural' is ridiculous. I mean, by definition nature is the sum of all things that exist, so if something exists, it's in nature."

April grinned, satisfied at having provoked Jalil. "So what's your explanation, Jalil? I may be wrong, but that guy back there calling himself Loki looked pretty supernatural to me."

"No. No. See, that's my point. I'm obviously not denying that Loki and all the rest of this is real. I'm just saying that one way or another there will be a logical, natural explanation."

Christopher laughed. "You know, I thought all black guys in the Chicago area wanted to grow up to be Michael Jordan. You want to grow up to be Mr. Tuvok."

"Who's Mr. Tuvok?" Jalil said coldly. "And by the way, all black guys don't want any one thing. Oh, wait: No, we do all want not to be stereotyped by ignorant white trash."

Christopher held up his hands, palms out, miming "no offense." Then he said, "Hey, I basically agree with you. I believe in what I can see and touch and eat and drink and spend. Everything else is bull."

April nodded. "You are so right, Christopher. I

mean, you are so right and so forceful and all
that, you just get me hot. I mean, you really do,
and we're going to die anyway, so just take me
now." She scooted back toward Christopher and
lowered her voice to a husky whisper. "You think
I'm kidding, but I'm not. I want you here and
now."

She was just convincing enough that Christopher made a sort of move to put his arm around
her. She pushed away, laughing slyly.

"Ah, so you just believe in what you can see,
huh? Looks to me like you were ready to believe
in a miracle."

Christopher flushed, gaped, and then laughed.
I gave him credit for that. Lots of guys can laugh
at someone else. Christopher could laugh at himself. You see a lot less of that.

I kept rowing. I was thinking about what Jalil
had said. He had definite beliefs. Me, I was clue-
less. I just knew one thing: All of it involved
Senna.

I was remembering her when we came around
a sharp corner and were, very suddenly, not
alone.

CHAPTER
XVII

The longboats wallowed at anchor, masts bare, empty. Other ships lay beached at the bottom of the crescent-shaped harbor. They'd been pulled up onto a stingy strip of black sand. All together there must have been thirty or forty warships and an equal number of broader-beamed cargo ships.

There was a village to our port side — left, if you're facing the bow. I saw smoke curling up. Through the masts, over the low-slung ships, I glimpsed crude stone houses. I saw people moving back and forth, lots of people.

The black cliffs curved up and behind the village, petering down into a series of upjutting rock teeth. Trees grew behind that dragon's spine of stone. A forest of tall, straight, dark pines rising on a gentle slope.

I noticed some sort of wall, but I couldn't see it

very well, just bits and pieces. Between the wall and the rocks was bare grass. Open space. It had probably been forest once, cut down to build the town.

"Get us out of here!" Christopher hissed. "Before they see us."

"They've already seen us," I said. I nodded toward a man standing on a nearby anchored ship. He stood with his foot on the gunwale. He was resting his hand on a longbow and watching us with a marksman's eye. "I wonder if he's any good with that bow."

"Let's not find out," Jalil said.

April took matters into her own hands. "Hello!" she yelled, waving at the Viking bowman. "Hi, how are you?"

No response.

I kept rowing. A good bowman could hit us from this distance. A really good bowman could probably put a shaft through each of us inside of about thirty seconds.

I felt that shaft. Felt it in my guts, felt it sticking out past my spine. Imagined being able to reach behind me and grab the bloody arrowhead.

"Maybe we should just row away, you know, and keep smiling," Christopher suggested.

My sword was lying in the bottom of the boat. If I could get close enough, maybe . . .

Suddenly, around the back of the nearest ship, a boat only slightly larger than ours came into view. Two men with arms like my legs were rowing it. The boat turned neatly around the sea serpent prow of the ship and came for us.

"We just cannot catch a break," Christopher muttered.

One of the oarsmen stopped and stood up. "Who are you? Why do you come here?"

Three of them now. Four of us. But that was comparing Marines to toddlers. They were armed. They were dangerous. We were four lost fools in a rowboat.

"My name is April," she said, putting out a dazzling smile.

The Viking glared. "Does your woman speak for you?"

"Sexist jerk," April said. But in a whisper.

I backed my oars, killing our momentum. "My name is David. This is Christopher. This is Jalil."

"Strange names."

"We are strangers."

"What manner of men are you? What land do you come from? Are you from the sun-worshipers, the filthy man-eaters?"

"I'm thinking we answer a big N.O. to that," Christopher whispered.

"No," April said, "we're from . . . from north of Chicago."

The Viking stared, not liking the answer. He was deciding. I could see it in his eyes. My life was in his eyes.

Suddenly it was like a light went on in the Viking's head. "Are you the minstrels? King Olaf Ironfoot is expecting a troop of minstrels. He has grown impatient and feared that they have been killed by wild beasts or else murdered."

"Well, worry no more, we are your minstrels," Christopher said quickly, voice shaky. "We haven't been killed by wild animals or murdered, although it's not for lack of people trying."

But the suspicious look was back on the Viking's face. He shot a warning look at the bowman. Out of the corner of my eye I saw the bow come up into its owner's hand. With shocking speed, he drew and fitted an arrow.

"If you're minstrels, give us a song."

I looked at Jalil. Jalil looked at Christopher. We all looked at April. At the same time I bent over just enough to grip the hilt of my sword. Maybe a quick swipe and I could take down the big guy. Of course that still left the bowman.

"I don't know any Viking songs!" she hissed.

"Give him something with lots of killing in it," I said.

"What, Marilyn Manson? I don't listen to that crap!"

"Don't you know anything with killing in it?" Christopher demanded. "Where were you when everyone was into gangsta rap?"

April bit her lip, eyes darting back and forth as she dredged through her memory. "Killing!" she yelled suddenly.

"'Killing . . . killing me softly with his song . . . playing my life with his words . . .'"

I froze. The world froze. She was singing and the Viking was deciding whether we heard the end of the song or never heard anything again.

The arrow would fly. I would reach to stop it, but by the time my hands came up, by the time my fingers began to close, it would be in me, through me, draining my blood in fountain spurts.

But now April was getting into it. The shaky fear voice was giving way to a singing voice that grew stronger and more confident. Her eyes were closed. Her hands were white as she twined them, nails digging into bone.

The girl could sing. Unfortunately, it wasn't what I thought of as a Viking song.

"'I heard he sang a good song, I heard he had a style. And so I went to hear him to listen for a while. . . .'"

I watched the big Viking closely as April's beautiful voice seemed to fill the harbor. His expression remained hard. But then I saw something amazing: The Norseman was crying. I don't mean a little moisture. I mean tears streaming down his scarred cheeks into his greasy beard.

The oarsman behind him was similarly affected. I shot a look at the guy with the bow. No tears, but he was gazing off into blankness now, lost in memory.

I let go of the sword hilt. We weren't going to fight our way out.

We were going to sing for our lives.

Chapter
XVIII

There was more to the village than I'd thought. The architecture wasn't grand or imposing, except for a sort of town hall kind of place that had been built out of whole logs and rose above all the surrounding buildings.

Three piers extended out into the water, with a wharf built of tarred, split logs. Longshoremen off-loaded bundles from wide-hulled merchant ships.

The longshoremen must have been slaves. They were a motley bunch, ranging from the blond, blue-eyed Viking look to smaller, olive-complected men and women to black people, but all with shaved heads. I saw no whipping going on, but a couple of big, old Vikings were roaring away, giving mostly superfluous orders and pushing people around.

Beyond the primitive dock sat warehouses that also looked like they were built of Lincoln Logs. They'd have been right at home in the old West.

Just beyond the far pier and curving away inland was the defensive wall I'd glimpsed earlier, logs set vertically and cut into sharp points. I guessed that it ringed the entire village, but I couldn't see it. I did see a tower, again like something out of an old cavalry movie. Except instead of bluecoats carrying Winchesters, there were bowmen pacing around a parapet and looking pretty alert.

We headed uphill to the town proper. Here the population became more noticeable. We saw a lot of people. More people than could possibly have fit into the twenty or thirty buildings that comprised the village.

And surely this village could not have supported the fleet of ships in its harbor. It was a forest of masts. I counted to thirty and still had only counted a fraction of the ships.

For the most part the men seemed to be engaged in swaggering around, talking in loud voices, and clapping one another on the back. Most were armed. But not all were armed alike. Or dressed alike. After a while you could start to make out differences between what had to be officers and ordinary soldiers.

The officers often wore chain-mail shirts. They carried swords with jeweled hilts or gold-scrolled scabbards. Some carried battle-axes with carved handles and elaborate heads. They had tall leather boots, more luxuriant furs, better-sewn pants. They had attendants, helpers, whatever you call them, who carried their helmets and axes. Squires.

The common soldiers wore simpler clothing and carried simpler weapons. No chain mail. No gold. No engraving. Axes that looked like they came from Kmart instead of a jewelry store. Helmets that could have been banged together out of recycled soup cans.

But even the common soldiers were a loud, swaggering, boisterous bunch. No cringing. No saluting. No groveling. None of what my dad would have delicately called "military chicken product."

I began to notice something else, too. Not all of these Vikings were quite what you'd think of as Norsemen. Yes, the big, blond type predominated heavily, but there were Vikings who looked like they'd just come in from South America, Africa, or China. And a lot who looked less easily identifiable: mixes of Nordic and Asian, Nordic and African. These were as likely to be officers as common soldiers, and all had the same swagger, the same *haw, haw, haw* laugh, the same eager, dangerous eyes.

Blond or brown, these were big, strong, muscular, dirty-faced, smelling-of-sweat-and-charred-meat warriors. They weren't playing dress-up. They weren't putting on an act. These guys killed, face-to-face, ax-to-ax. Everywhere I looked I saw nasty scars, missing eyes, ears, hands, and arms. One young Viking, probably no older than me, had a livid scar, a puckered puncture wound on both cheeks. Someone had stuck a sword through this guy's mouth.

I felt small. Weak. Not something I'm used to feeling. Not something I like feeling. The memory of my own terror was still all over me. It popped up out of nowhere. It was attached to other thoughts the way remoras are attached to sharks.

Of course, not every man was a warrior. I saw unarmed men as well. Some were richly dressed. Maybe businessmen. Others were working. We passed a blazingly hot smithy, open forge aglow, two sweaty slaves working a huge bellows while a hairy, shirtless Viking with shoulders like the front end of my old Buick hammered away, *whang! whang! whang!*

Swords hung from the front of the building, and a nice selection of battle-axes. But hoops for barrels were on display, too, along with nails and woodworking tools.

Our guide — or captor, it was hard to be sure which — led us on past an area where more than a dozen open fires had been reduced to coals. Entire cows, pigs, sheep, and goats were blistering and burning on slowly rotating spits. Vast iron pots bubbled. Fish, some several feet long, others smaller, were sandwiched into iron grids and suspended above the fire.

Maybe fifty women were working this outdoor kitchen, hustling around like any harried bunch of cooks. It was overseen by an immense woman with black hair gathered into pigtails.

"My wife," our guide said genially.

"She's very impressive," April said. "May I ask her name?"

"She is called Gudrun. Gudrun, Man-Beater."

I looked closer and saw the staff she carried. A five-foot-long piece of skinned tree branch. On the end was a doubled fist-sized knot.

"I am Thorolf," he added politely. And then he did something that surprised me, without my knowing exactly why. He pulled out a leather pouch and a rough-cut rectangle of thin paper. And he proceeded to roll himself a cigar.

"Our names, again, in case their oddness may

have caused you to forget, are April, Christopher, Jalil, and David."

"Who is your lord?" Thorolf asked, as casually as if he'd asked what school we attended. But it was a loaded question. A dangerous question, I sensed.

"We're independent," I said, trying to match his casual tone.

Bright blue eyes narrowed at me. He lit the stogie, inhaled, and breathed out a cloud of smoke. "You are free men? Not slaves?"

"Free men," I said.

"You are not from around here," he said. A statement.

"No," I said, keeping it simple.

Thorolf accepted that. Accepted, at least, that we wanted to mind our own business and have him mind his.

"I will arrange for food and drink. King Olaf will send for you when he wishes entertainment. He is in counsel with the other kings and earls."

He led us on to a corral containing forty or fifty stocky, shaggy horses. There were lean-tos around the perimeter of the corral fence. Most seemed to contain hay and alfalfa for the horses. Some contained what you got from horses after you fed them hay and alfalfa.

"You stay there," he said, pointing to a decent, clean little shed, open on one side. "Food will be brought. And drink, eh? Eh? What point in food if there is no drink?"

He stomped off, blowing clouds of cigar smoke into the frosty air.

"Tobacco!" Jalil said excitedly. "Hah."

"It bothered me, too," April said. "But I didn't think it was the right time to bitch about second-hand smoke."

Jalil waved his hand impatiently. "Who cares about smoke? The man was smoking tobacco. A Viking!"

We all stared pretty blankly. I was busy trying to see a line of retreat if things got bad.

"Tobacco is a New World plant. So is corn. And tomatoes. They were stewing up corn and tomatoes back there. None of which any real Viking would have."

"That's what you focus on?" Christopher asked. "You focus on tobacco and corn? The man's a living, breathing Viking, speaking English and living practically next door to Loki's happy little family, for God's sake. Why wouldn't he have a stogie?"

"It just proves it's not a dream," Jalil said defensively. "I might dream about Vikings, and since I don't speak Nordic they'd have to be

English-speaking Vikings. But I'm not dumb enough to have a Viking firing up a panatela. And I don't know why I'd come up with Asian Vikings. Black, maybe."

"Just proves it's not *your* dream," April said. "Maybe it's my dream and I just think it's kind of . . . exciting . . . all these big, burly men and all."

A woman appeared quite suddenly, carrying a tray. Without a word she set it down on the ground and walked away.

We took a look at the tray. A loaf of dark bread. A single, big bowl of soup. A hunk of rank cheese. Two deep-cut bowls. One water, and the other . . .

"Beer!" Christopher said, delighted. "Hey, maybe this is a dream. My dream!"

"I'm thinking maybe getting faced isn't a great idea," I said. I don't drink. My personal choice.

"Say what? After the day we've had? This is the best excuse for getting hammered I've ever even imagined." He took a deep, defiant swig of the beer and glared at me over the rim.

April laughed and took the bowl from him. "I'm guessing the drinking age here is about three," she said. She took a sip and spat it out on the ground. "Okay, let's try the water."

We broke up the bread and wolfed it down. It was excellent. The soup was even better, despite having to dig the chunks out with our fingers.

"Food is freaking magic," Christopher said. "I mean, after a day of hanging around the castle walls, being terrorized by insane mythical gods, you need some food. Food and *beer*," he added, looking defiantly at me again.

I calmly took a drink from the water.

We heard an explosive guffaw. I spun left and saw Thorolf. He was hysterical. I mean, laughing like he could laugh himself to death. Tears streamed down his cheeks.

We'd made the man cry twice in an hour.

"Come, come," he managed to gasp. "The king has called for you. Oh, you really are minstrels! Drinking the washing water and leaving the beer! Ah-hah-hah-HAH!"

CHAPTER

XIX

"We don't exactly have an act," April muttered.

We marched through the pushing, shoving, happily drunk throng. The crowd grew more and more dense as we approached the large building that dominated the center of town.

"Make way, make way!" Thorolf yelled, pushing common soldiers aside, roughly but without malice, and shouldering past officers.

The proportion of officers grew as we progressed. So did the general level of drunkenness. I was a good head shorter than the average guy we passed, a head and a neck shorter than a lot of them. And most of them were armed.

Suddenly we were shoved out into an open space. I hadn't even noticed when we'd passed within the great hall, but now I could see.

It was like a model version of Loki's throne room. Timber walls that had been roughly plastered instead of Loki's stone. A high, wood roof supported by massive beams.

Shields, all scarred, many with holes, hung from the top of the left wall. Along the right were various flags and banners. War trophies, I assumed. The shields and banners of enemies who hadn't done too well upon meeting the Norsemen. Like something you'd see in a museum. Only these didn't represent some long-ago, forgotten battle. Some of the bodies represented by these banners and shields still lay rotting on misty fields. Widows and orphans still living remembered the men who'd fallen behind these banners.

In the center of the room was an open hearth the size of a small swimming pool. Smoke rose to a hole in the roof. The smell stayed behind: the smell of burning meat, joining the smell of sweat and beer and smoke.

"It's like a frat party," Christopher said, in a shout that could barely be heard above the level of voices all around.

Back from the fire, behind a clothed table sat a dozen or so Vikings. These were rich men, powerful men: silver brooches, lush furs, polished leather, chains of silver baubles around their necks, elaborately filigreed silver goblets, silver-handled knives sticking out of the piles of meat before them.

Some of the men at the table looked like punks. Drunk, glaring, mad-at-the-world, don't-make-me-kick-your-ass punks. Sadists. Psychos.

But for the most part they were a sober, bright-looking crowd. They were swilling beer and something that came in smaller glasses, but they still looked clear-eyed enough.

Then I recognized a face I knew. At the far end of the table, ignored by everyone, was the old man who had sacrificed the sheep.

He looked at me. I looked at him. We both knew we'd seen each other before. I had to work to start breathing again.

At the center of the table was a black man chewing at the edges of a slab of pink meat on a silver knife.

Thorolf pushed us forward. "My king! The minstrels are here," he said in a bellow that was normal conversational speech in this crowd.

"They had better be good," King Olaf Ironfoot warned. He jerked the meat-laden knife toward one of the other Vikings to his left. "My good friend King Eric the Grim says his sword is hungry for blood."

This evoked quite a bit of guffawing by all but

Eric, who glared and said, "Would I dirty my sword with these . . . these gamesters? Better to throw them into the fire and hear their fat crackle in the flames, as the sun-worshipers do!"

Now an argument erupted. Another Viking said, "That's not the sun-worshipers. My second wife was a princess of the sun-worshipers. They did not burn men, they cut open their chests while still alive and drew out their still-beating hearts."

This was accompanied by hand gestures and by rude asides from some of the others at the table: "Princess, my arse, she was a slave girl with nice —"

"They burn them, too!" Eric said, punctuating his statement by pounding on the table and making a burned pig jump. "They burn them and eat their bones!"

"Are you saying I am a fool? That my second wife, mother to my eldest son, would dare lie to me?"

Olaf held up a placating hand and even put down his knife. "Worthy kings, worthy kings. There are four minstrels here. Enough for you, Eric, to burn, and for you, Hedrick, to cut out their hearts."

Another fabulous witticism from Olaf and the place erupted in *haw, haw, haws* and "What did he says?"

"Come, minstrels. Juggle, jest, or recite the poems composed by your betters. If you amuse me you will be well-rewarded. And if not —" He looked around, building to the big joke. "If you do not, then we must in the spirit of fairness cut out your hearts . . . and then roast you."

The last time I'd tried to entertain anyone had been the ill-fated poem where Christopher had made everyone laugh.

This was going to be worse.

What passed for silence descended. In other words, there was a sort of lull in the mayhem.

"April! Sing something!" Christopher said through gritted teeth.

"I —" she stammered. "I —"

The look in Olaf's eyes grew darker. He wasn't laughing anymore.

"Give us a poem!" he roared in a voice that rattled the roof timbers.

I opened my mouth. "Twas brillig, and the s-s-slithy toves did gyre and gimble in the wabe. All mimsy were the —"

"Do you seek to mock me?"

He wasn't Loki, but he was doing a good impression.

At this moment it was Christopher who saved us. I don't know what moved him. I don't understand the brain that could do what he did next.

But at that moment he not only saved us. He gave us a hit.

He stepped forward. He clenched his fist. His knees buckled, but he caught himself before he hit the floor. And in a loud voice edged with hysteria, he sang:

"M-m-mine eyes have seen the glory of the . . . the mighty Viking lords, they are trampling out the vineyards where the grapes of wrath are stored. They have loosed the fateful lightning of their terrible swift swords, the Vikes are marching on!"

He went through the "glory, glory, hallelujah" chorus with a few changes and then stopped suddenly.

The Norse kings were gaping. The crowd was silent. And then Olaf, his dark eyes ablaze, said, "What do you call this manner of poem?"

"Um . . . a song?" Christopher said in a soprano squeak.

"A song! Give us more, give us another verse. Only start back at the beginning."

"There's a second verse?" Christopher asked me, his eyes desperate.

Starting at the beginning was easy enough, and Jalil, April, and I all joined in, more or less tunefully belting out the chorus, but how was

Christopher going to come up with a second verse?

"We jumped aboard our longboats and we sailed upon the seas, and we slaughtered all who fought us and we did just as we pleased, 'cause we're crazy Viking warriors and . . . and . . ."

". . . and we never beg for peace," April jumped in.

"The Vikes are marching on! Glory, glory, hallelujah!" we all sang. "Lordy, how we'll stick it to ya. Glory, glory, hallelujah, the Vikes are marching on!"

Pandemonium. Foot stomping, fist pounding, yelling, bellowing, roaring approval. Some of the drunker ones were trying to repeat the lyrics, struggling to catch the tune.

Christopher shot me a grin. "We *own* these guys."

And that's when the crowd parted and four massive trolls walked in.

CHAPTER XX

"Trouble," Jalil whispered.

Olaf curled his lip. "Well, my good trolls, what brings you here to a hall of men?"

This was apparently too subtle for the trolls. They stared blankly, confused. I looked for a way out. Reaching any exit would involve getting past a hundred armed Vikings.

Helpless. Trapped. Nothing we could do. I'd soared on hope, and now I was yanked back to reality. Four lame kids in a land of mad killers.

I saw the old man who'd done the sacrifice watching me. A glint of humor? Or at least curiosity?

"Come, come, good trolls," King Olaf said again. "Why are you here? What do you want?"

The leader of the group comprehended this. "I

am Gatch. We come from Great Loki. He seeks four who . . ." He searched his memory, pig eyes rolling up. "Great Loki seeks four who were his guests and are lost."

I had begun to think the Viking kings were at best primitive warriors and at worst drunken fools. But when I shot a fearful glance at the head table I saw a dozen very alert, very intelligent faces.

Remember that if you live, I told myself. *Don't underestimate these men.*

Olaf considered the trolls while he calmly munched his slab of meat. "Great Loki has . . . lost his guests?"

He wasn't calling the troll a liar. But he wasn't even half fooled.

"Yes, O mighty king," Gatch said, ducking his big rhino head.

"Are you sure these guests did not escape?"

The troll answered hotly, "No one escapes Great Loki's castle! It is guarded by loyal men and mighty trolls."

Olaf nodded reasonably. "That is certainly true. Yes. Why, if Loki's prisoners were ever to escape, Great Loki would look foolish, eh? And good friend troll, you are not calling Loki a fool, are you?"

All four trolls shook their heads. No. No, they sure weren't calling Loki a fool. But they weren't blind, either. They kept glancing at the four of us.

"Those are Loki's guests," the lead troll said defiantly.

That was laying it on the table. Showdown time. I tensed up, searching for a sword I might grab. But I noticed that hands were on swords now. The babble of voices was dead still. Olaf whispered his next statement.

"These are my minstrels," Olaf said.

"They . . . they have the same faces as Great Loki's guests."

"Are you calling me a liar, friend troll?" Olaf smiled as he said it. But even the trolls weren't dumb enough to buy the smile. If Olaf so much as raised a finger, an awful lot of swords and an awful lot of axes were going to start flying. The trolls knew it.

"Great king . . ." the troll leader began, then ran out of words.

Olaf stood up. He was a large man, even by Viking standards. I won't say he could have wrestled one of the trolls, but he'd have given it a shot. "All men know why we are gathered here," he announced in a loud, politician's voice. "We gather here to go a-Viking, as our fathers did, as their fathers did, even in the generations of the Old World before the gods brought forth Everworld. And as all our fathers before, we will take to the sea in our ship and visit terror on our foes!"

Lots of foot stomping, then total silence again.

"Only this time, we go for a new purpose. To collect the ransom demanded by Loki. An impossible ransom to collect, were we not carrying a mighty weapon!"

Everyone but us must have known what the weapon was because Olaf might as well have been introducing Michael Jordan to a Chicago boosters club. The place went nuts.

Olaf weighed the applause, let it go on for a while, then continued. "Then we will pay the ransom to Loki so that he may release from unjust captivity the All-Father himself, Odin One-Eye."

I saw Jalil's eyebrows go up.

So, I thought. *These weren't Loki's men at all. Or at least not all of them.*

"I, Olaf, who some call Olaf Ironfoot because my own natural foot was eaten by a dragon — a dragon who will never more trouble a peaceful village —"

Lots of murmuring and approval, sort of a collective "You got that right." Dragon killing was approved of by all, except possibly the trolls, who may have gotten Olaf's underlying message of "Look, I killed a dragon, so don't mess with me."

"I, Olaf Ironfoot, have said that I will lead this expedition, and I have sworn to pay the ransom demanded by Loki." He leaned down over the table, going face-to-face with the troll. "Go to your master Loki and tell him this: He needs us to destroy the sun-worshipers who ally themselves with the Hetwan. And this we will do. But I am not Loki's vassal. And I will not be questioned by his foul creatures."

The trolls hesitated. But not for long.

"Loki's guests are not here," Gatch said.

Olaf held his hands out placatingly, the genial host again. "Exactly what I've been telling you."

The trolls walked away, shoved a few guys just to act tough, and disappeared. The room breathed again. I breathed again.

"Hetwan," Jalil whispered to me.

"Yeah. I heard." At least one Hetwan had been with Loki. And it sounded as if that creepy alien spoke for the head Hetwan. Things were going on here that were over my head. Not my concern. My concern was simple: Keep Olaf happy. Olaf happy meant me alive.

"Now give us the song again!" Ironfoot commanded. "More verses!"

We sang. I'd have sung anything for the big Viking.

Chapter
XXI

We sang the "Battle Hymn of the Vikings" about twenty more times till the whole drunken, reeling assembly was singing along with us. Then April sang "Killing Me Softly" again, and it was a mass weepathon. Burly, violent men just boo-hooing and letting the tears run down without shame.

This was not a bunch of guys worried about acting tough.

They started tossing us slabs of meat: goat, horse, I don't know what they were. We ate the meat, even April, and quaffed water, to the vast amusement of all. We expanded it into a whole routine. We'd lift bowls of beer up like we were going to take a drink and then pause . . . and the whole Viking host would hang there, poised, ready . . . then we'd turn up our noses and grab the water instead.

Jerry Seinfeld on his best night has never cracked up an audience like we did with our water-drinking routine. The women and slaves would come crowding in to watch.

"We're a hit!" Christopher said. "If these guys had cable we'd be getting our own HBO special by the end of the week."

The Vikings partied till what had to be three A.M. But by then slaves were patiently disentangling heaps of passed-out bodies, then hauling them off on stretchers. The great hall reeked of stale beer, vomit, urine, wood smoke, tobacco smoke, meat, and sweat.

We were passing out from exhaustion by the time Olaf himself finally slumped facedown on the table, signaling the end of the party. They carried the big black Viking off on a section of the table.

A nearly sober Thorolf came to collect us. He marched us out of the town and into the forest.

It was a forest from a Grimms' fairy tale. A forest of black trees and blacker shadows. Distant wolves howled, plaintive. Nearer, sometimes so close I felt I could reach out and touch them, glittering eyes blinked, watched us, considered us, lusted after the marrow in our bones.

Thorolf seemed unafraid. But he kept a firm grip on his ax, and once raised it from his shoulder, feeling the weight, sending the message.

"Nothing like a ten-mile hike on no sleep," Jalil grumbled.

"Where are we going, Thorolf?" April asked, her voice raspy from singing and from breathing smoke.

"You are to stay at my farm till the fleet departs tomorrow if the wind is fair," he said. "Olaf Ironfoot said you were to be well cared for."

"Guess he's a music lover," I mumbled.

Thorolf smiled. "Ironfoot loves a good entertainment, it is true. But still more, he loves to show all men that he is not Loki's vassal."

So. Olaf knew full well that we were the ones Loki was looking for. And in sheltering us he was jabbing a finger in Loki's eye.

"An extra bargaining chip," Jalil said. "Loki's demanded some kind of ransom for releasing Odin. Olaf doesn't trust him. Figures if it gets down to hard bargaining he can throw us on the pile as a sweetener."

That killed some of my affection for Olaf.

Thorolf looked at Jalil with troubled eyes. The thought had not occurred to him. But now that Jalil had mentioned it, Thorolf wasn't exactly laughing it off.

"The ways of kings and chieftains may be different from those of ordinary freemen," Thorolf allowed.

We marched on, tensed for a sudden attack, expecting to turn the next curve and find our way blocked by Fenrir himself. We were on something that might have been called a road, but it was dirt and narrow, with the forest beginning abruptly on either side.

Looking up, I could see occasional hints of gray, dawn sky overhead. But I was so bleary, so far past exhaustion, that I wasn't doing much sightseeing.

At some point Thorolf led us off the road, along a much less traveled path. Here the forest gentled down into white-trunked birches, with open spaces and even pale, ghostly flowers.

After another interminable walk, we emerged very suddenly into the open, into earliest morning sunlight and green and blue.

A long, gentle, sloping field opened before us. It was covered in grass so green it seemed unreal. A rocky, snow-streaked peak loomed above in the distance. The sky was deep blue, fresh with morning sunlight.

We saw a farm, although at first we didn't notice it. It seemed to be a single building added to many times, expanded in all directions. The walls were low and dark, with few windows. The roof was covered in the same brilliant grass that covered the slope.

A fenced enclosure contained a single horse. Along the slope, in various little patches of white fluff, were grazing sheep.

The sunlight woke me up — a little, at least. I noticed Thorolf taking in every detail, the sharp landowner checking to see that all was well.

As we approached, Gudrun Man-Beater appeared in a doorway. I guess it was the front door, although concepts of front and back seemed iffy on this building.

She laughed on seeing her husband with the four of us.

"I have guests," Thorolf said, grabbing his wife and giving her a ferocious hug.

"I have eyes," Gudrun said. "I see them. They can stay with the cows. Are you hungry?" This last directed at us.

"No, ma'am," I said. "Just tired."

"It is tiring work, entertaining kings," Gudrun said.

"And more tiring still, escaping Loki's castle," Thorolf said.

Gudrun blanched. Her lip trembled and she glanced away in a particular direction.

Toward Loki's castle.

"They are under Olaf Ironfoot's protection," Thorolf explained.

"Yes, but are we?" Gudrun said darkly. "When Ironfoot has taken you and the other men away, we will still be here. With Loki's creatures and priests and evil men everywhere."

She looked darkly at us. We were not exactly welcome guests. But that didn't stop her from shoving a small loaf of bread off on each of us and detailing a yawning slave girl to show us to an empty cow stall.

It was a musky place, but clean. The cows were being milked by an old woman who muttered to herself as she yanked the udders. She didn't look up as we passed by.

The slave girl showed us the stall. Hay. I hit it facedown and was asleep before I could take a second breath.

"When it happens, David, will you save me?" a voice whispered.

"Yeah," I said. "But sleep. First, sleep."

When I woke the electric red numbers on my bedside clock said 3:21 A.M.

CHAPTER

XXII

Clock?

I jerked up out of my bed. Covers! Sheets!

I threw them back. I had nothing on, no T-shirt, no warm fur tunic, no dirty running shoes.

My wrists. Normal! No scars.

I fumbled for the light switch and snapped it on.

My room!

I froze, staring. No, no, no. This was a dream. This wasn't real. In the harsh light it didn't even look real.

"Oh, man," I muttered. "Something here is messed up."

I climbed out of bed, slowly, carefully, like I might break something. I went to my closet and searched for my Radiohead T-shirt. The one I had been wearing.

It was gone. So was the cutoff sweatshirt.

My running shoes, gone.

Everything I'd been wearing was gone.

I just stood there, totally lost. Was this the dream? Was that the dream? Were they both dreams and April was right that I was a lunatic locked in a padded cell somewhere, imagining I was me?

I grabbed the phone. Jalil. I'd call Jalil.

And ask him what, at three in the morning? "Hi, Jalil, are you having my same nightmare?"

Senna. She was the key.

I dressed as quickly as I could. Down the stairs. Silent. I looked in my mom's room. The door was closed. So this was a different night, not the same night.

Out into the dark street. Dawn was a long way off. Here it was dark; there it was bright morning. Maybe.

I walked fast, boots loud on the sidewalk. It was chilly. Damp, but not rainy. I walked past normal houses with normal fences and hedges and lawns. Some entirely dark. Others with a porch light burning. In one I saw the blue light of a TV. Some insomniac up late. Or early. Whichever it was.

Senna's house was eight blocks away. Her folks

had money. They were on this little private street right down near the beach.

I trotted a little. I wasn't tired. But why not? I'd been exhausted in . . . in my dream? In the other place? In bizarro Vikingland.

Senna's house. It had a high privacy hedge all around the street side. On the beach side it had a stone fence. Easier to go over the fence.

I scrabbled up and over it and landed on their manicured lawn. No lights on. I knew, though, which was Senna's window. April had said her room adjoined Senna's.

It was on the second floor at one end of the house. Extending out beneath it was a wrap-around screened porch. The supports for the porch roof were thick beams, pedestaled and ornate.

It wasn't an easy climb, but it wasn't impossible, either.

It occurred to me that I was acting crazy. By anyone's standards. But I had to know. I had to know right then. As long as someone didn't see me and call the cops. Senna wouldn't mind.

Probably.

Nah, why should she? Some guy she's just started dating comes creeping into her room in the middle of the night? Man, she'd scream and have her dad and stepmom throw me in jail.

I had lost my grip on definitions of normal. I was back in a world of logic and reason. Or if not reason, then at least consistency, predictability.

No stopping, not now, too late. I was committed. Climbing. I had to know, had to. Sleep would never have come, anyway. I couldn't have Everworld burning away in my brain and not know, know for sure if I was sane or mad.

I crept along the porch roof. I found the window. I tried it cautiously. It was unlocked.

I slid it up with infinite care. Inch by inch.

Then I reached inside and parted the gauzy white curtains. Was she there? Was she in her bed, warm, waiting for me? Would she wake, surprised but not alarmed, ready to give way to the moment, draw me down into her arms, stretch her body against mine?

I swallowed. Which Senna was I looking for? Which dream of Senna?

"Senna?" I whispered.

No answer.

Then, "It's me. David. Don't be scared."

I stuck my head inside.

"I wondered if this would be your first move," a female voice said.

A small light came on. April had her hand on the lamp.

"She's not here," April said.

I looked at her. She looked at me and slowly nodded.

"Yeah," she said. "It's real."

Chapter
XXIII

Senna's bed was a double. The room was plenty big for it. A down comforter was folded, all puffy, stuffed out of the way in a big wicker basket. The bed wore only a thin cotton blanket, two pillows.

Her desk was missing the computer almost every student's desk had. The mahogany surface was polished. Schoolbooks, notebook, pens, and pencils.

I leaned over to open a drawer, feeling I had no right, but feeling spiteful, too. It was locked.

The walls were decorated with a small number of framed posters. Framed posters, generic vintage advertising posters, nothing she'd have chosen. Decorator-chosen. No thumbtacked posters of favorite bands, no photographs of friends taped to a dressing table mirror.

No dressing table mirror. No mirror at all.

"Senna disappeared three days ago," April said in a whisper.

"Three days? What do you mean, three days? It was today. Yesterday, I mean."

April nodded, an action that set off a cascade of auburn hair. "It seems like yesterday here and yesterday *there* aren't the same day. Just to confuse things further, I don't know how long I've been here. I was asleep. But search your memory, David. You'll realize you remember being at school yesterday while we were in Everworld."

I stared at her. Probably I looked a little nuts. But it was a lunatic world. The weird thing was, she was right: I did remember going to school the day before. I remembered both: Loki's castle, the Viking feast . . . and getting up and going to school like any normal day.

But the normal part of my memory, homeroom, the gym, talking to some guy named Tony about whether I'd change lockers with him because he wanted one closer to most of his classes — all that, all that everyday, day-in-day-out stuff was like remembering a still photograph. The Everworld part was in vivid color, full-motion video.

"Is that a bathroom through there?" I asked, and without waiting for an answer, tried the door, flicked on the light. It was private, not connected to any other room.

No medicine cabinet, no mirror.

There was a wire bin on a shelf. I looked in. Toothpaste, a brush, a comb, Band-Aids, matches. No makeup. Matches.

"Tell me you've figured this all out," I said to April.

She formed one of her patented half smiles. "Not me. I've figured nothing out. Except that I don't think any of this is a dream, even though it should be. I woke up in my room next door. And I had memories of knowing that Senna had disappeared. I had memories of us being down at the lake, watching her out on the pier. And memories of my folks asking whether I knew what had happened to her."

"They must be worried out of their minds."

"You'd think that, wouldn't you?" April said, eyeing me shrewdly. "We have the same dad, different moms, you know. Everyone's kind of vague about what happened to Senna's mom. I mean, you know, I kind of filled in the blanks, but no one ever just came out and said that she ran off. So maybe you could figure my mom, Senna's stepmom, wouldn't care all that much, but my mom's not that way. She treats us both the same. At least I think so."

I led the way back into the bedroom. "Wait a minute. I'm losing this here. You're saying, what? You have memories of the last two days and you remember your folks noticing that Senna was gone. But neither of them is worried?"

"They act worried," April said.

"Emphasis on 'act'?"

"Yeah. Act. As in not real. As in concealing some other, truer emotion."

"What emotion?"

"Relief."

We both just kind of looked at each other. This was way deep. Way deep for David Levin. Way over my head. One day there was three days here. We — me and April for sure, maybe Jalil and Christopher, too — were not missing. We were still here. And there. Living our lives in both places.

I pressed my palms against my head and April laughed a quiet laugh. "Head exploding?"

I put my hands down, feeling sheepish. "Yeah. Major exploding head. Like I felt when I was in that physics class before I bailed out. I don't think that way. I mean, I do okay thinking in a straight line. Point A to point B to point C. You start talking about a lot of 'if this, then that,' I lose it."

"The question is: Will the 'real world' us remember that we were here, sitting here, talking about Senna?"

"You assume that we'll go back to Everworld?"

She shrugged. "I assume that when we wake up there, we'll be back there."

"So this is a dream."

April seemed to be searching her memory. "Something someone told me once: 'Maybe dreams aren't in your head. Maybe dreams are memories of another universe.'"

"Some New Age guy?"

"Senna. I had a nightmare once. Woke up screaming. I was maybe ten, eleven. My dad came in and said, 'Don't worry, dreams aren't real. They're just neurons firing randomly in your brain.' As soon as he was gone, Senna came over. Told me it wasn't in my head, it was real, but real in a different way, in a different place. It wasn't exactly comforting."

I remembered the dream of her coming to me. Kissing me. Calling me names she didn't like to say. I remembered the coldness of her, and the greedy way she'd told me I would always be hers. And I remembered what followed, what I felt, and what I would give my life to feel again.

I scanned shelves of books. School assigned reading. I don't know what I expected to see. The room was a blank. It was devoid of personality. It could have been a hotel room.

"Senna's not a comforting person," I said belatedly. "So now what?"

April sighed. "Damned if I know." She sat down on the bed and absentmindedly stroked the blanket beside her.

"It's like no one lived in this room," I said angrily. I'd wanted some clue, some explanation. Senna had given me nothing. Again.

"She didn't give much away," April said. Then, "You know what's stupid? I woke up thinking I needed to get in some serious studying on chemistry. There's a test tomorrow. But guess what? No chemistry book. Also no backpack. It's all over there."

I nodded. My own real-world memory told me I had a paper due. It was ludicrous. Tomorrow would either involve me making excuses to my teachers, or waking up in a Viking barn next to the cows. Or both. Or neither. Or . . .

I sat down beside her. She was real. I was real. This room was not. Every piece of it, every detail was real, from some store or catalog, all of it merchandise, all of it matter, but in the aggregate, all together, it was a fake.

"I wish we could load up on some firepower and take that back with us," I said. "I don't know if you can hurt Loki with a nine-millimeter hollow point, but I'd like to try."

"You're such a boy," April said. "Why not wish for a tank while you're at it?"

Her laugh drove the weirdness away for a moment. "Not a bad idea," I said with a smile. "An M-1 Abrams tank would be the perfect way to travel in Everworld."

"Good lord, you even know the tank's cute little name."

She was awfully attractive. I felt it suddenly. I mean, she was close, we were whispering, sitting on a bed, and we were both scared little puppies, despite all the calm talk. She was very beautiful, April was.

"You know —" I started to say. Then I changed tack. "You know, before yesterday, the night before, I was with Senna."

"With as in *with*?" April asked in pretended shock.

"No, no. Just with. She said . . . I mean, she knew something was going to happen. She told me so. Something awful. I thought she was nuts."

April wasn't smiling anymore. The charged moment was over. She looked deadly serious. "What do you mean, David?"

"I mean, she said, 'Something is going to happen.' And then —" I hesitated. Somehow it was just between me and Senna, what she'd said. And it would sound so insane. "Never mind."

"Uh-uh," April said. "No. We're all in this. That was me hanging by my wrists, right alongside you. Tell me."

"Yeah. Okay. She . . . she asked me if I'd save her. 'Will you save me, David?' That's what she said."

April's green eyes went cold. "That bitch. She's done it again."

"Again? What again?" I asked. But I asked it of the cow whose white face was looking down stupidly at me as it munched the hay around my ear.

"Damn it!" Christopher yelled.

He turned his head and looked at me furiously. "You woke me up. Why did you wake me up? I was back home. I was just about to carry out a serious refrigerator raid. My mom made a cheesecake! A strawberry cheesecake, and I don't mean one of those things from a mix; the woman can make cheesecake."

Then he looked at me again, more dubious. "David? Are you spooning me?"

To my abject horror, I was. In the night — actually day, but it was dark in the barn — in our utter exhaustion, I had cuddled up with Christopher.

I pushed him away and jumped to my feet.

April and Jalil stuck their heads around the corner, looking into the stall.

"Oh, you're up?" Jalil asked. "We've been up for a few seconds, but we didn't want to disturb you two. Frankly you . . . well" — he said with a not-at-all-innocent grin — "you looked like you might want some more time together."

"That is just so funny, Jalil," Christopher said, climbing to his feet.

"I thought so," April said.

Christopher brushed straw from his jeans. "So let me just ask: Anyone else have, shall we say, interesting dreams?"

"I called you, David," Jalil said. "Woke your mom up. She was pissed. She didn't seem to want to get you to the phone."

"I wasn't there, anyway," I said. "April and I went to look in Senna's room."

"She's missing," Christopher said. "Everyone at school has been talking about it."

The cow nosed me, pushing me aside so she could reach the hay I'd slept on. The milking was long since over. Dim exterior light penetrated the barn from the far end, where the door stood open.

It was day. Day here, anyway. Maybe back in the world it was already a week later.

I walked toward the light.

"Parallel universes," Jalil said.

"What?"

"I think that's what it is. How else are you going to explain it? We're here, we're there, simultaneously. Only not, because time here and time there are running at different speeds."

"It's magic," April said. "Enchantment."

"Magic, my ass," Jalil said.

We stepped out into brilliant sunlight. The grass was a green fire. The sky looked like that blue-sky wallpaper you get on Windows computers: perfect, with a perfect mix of fluffy white clouds.

Most of the cows were off on the upslope, munching grass. Cows in one loose gaggle, sheep in another. A stream I hadn't noticed earlier tumbled and leaped down the slope — whitewater, but far too narrow and shallow for even a kayak.

"Hell of a coincidence having two different universes where so much is the same, don't you think?" Christopher pointed out. "Sheep and goats and cows and grass, and the sky is blue, and the water runs downhill, and the local big shots are all mythical gods, and, oh, by the way, everyone speaks English? Very Earthlike for being a parallel universe."

"The Hetwan are not Earthlike," Jalil pointed out mildly. "Neither are the laws of physics. We fell too slowly, but gravity seems the same here as always. Loki changes size whenever he wants, wolves talk, and a giant snake calls Loki 'Daddy.' That snake can't exist, you realize. No way. Not on Earth. Not in our universe. Neither can that wolf. Animals are a certain size for a reason. That wolf, that big? He should have elephant legs to carry the weight. You increase height and length, you increase weight geometrically. You'd need a different design. You can't have some tiptoeing wolf that's the size of a Seismosaurus. Laws of physics, man. Laws of freaking physics, which do not change anywhere in the universe."

"Anyone else notice anything weird about that one horse? The one grazing off by himself?" April asked.

I squinted. April must have good eyes. But when I squinted harder, I saw it. The horn. The single horn, like a ten-inch spear, that stuck straight out from the horse's head.

"Okay," I said as calmly as I could. "That's a unicorn."

Jalil nodded. "Yep. That's a unicorn."

"What's keeping the fairies and leprechauns and the Keebler Freaking Elves?" Christopher demanded. "Any minute now some little toad-boy with a shamrock hat is going to pop up out of the grass and say, 'Always after me Lucky Charms.' I want to go home. I want my mommy. Or at least her cheesecake."

I spotted Thorolf. He was coming downhill from the nearest sheep. He was walking in giant steps. Happiest guy in the world, from the look on his face.

"The ewe is pregnant and the wind is fair!" he bellowed.

I glanced at Jalil. "Say what?"

He made a "search me" face.

Thorolf galumphed on over and slapped me on the shoulder. "The ewe is pregnant, hah-hah-hah, I knew Ildric's ram would do his duty by us. She'll have a fine litter come spring."

"Oh," I said, trying to sound interested. "So . . . baby sheep, right?"

He stroked his beard thoughtfully. "I must make a sacrifice to Frey before we sail. I can't leave something like that to Gudrun. She'll decide to be thrifty and offend Frey with a paltry sacrifice."

"Sail?" Christopher asked. "'We sail.' You mean you and the other Vikings."

Thorolf looked at Christopher, perplexed. "And you as well, of course."

"We have to sail somewhere?"

Thorolf tilted his head indulgently, like he was dealing with not-very-bright children. "You are free to sail or not, as you wish," he said. "But these are Loki's lands, now that he rules the castle. And when Olaf Ironfoot has moved on with his host, the priests and creatures of Loki will soon find you."

"Ah," Christopher said.

Thorolf clapped a big hand on Christopher's back. "You don't fear battle, do you? Ah-hah-hah!"

"Me, no. Love battle. Who are we, who are we battling?"

"The sun-worshipers, of course. Crafty, cruel, and hard men," Thorolf said. "They slaughter prisoners like pigs, making sacrifices of thousands at a time. Though they tell tales that they first adore them, feeding them delicacies by the bucket and wine by the barrel. And, ah, the women . . ."

"The sun-worshipers?" April asked.

"Yes, yes. We go to seize a ransom for the All-Father. We must free wise Odin. With Thor lost to us, who else will save us from the Hetwan?"

I shrugged. "I don't know." I'd been wrong. The Hetwan were becoming my problem.

"These sun-worshipers. Do they have another name?" April asked politely.

Thorolf nodded. "All peoples have more than one name, child. The sun-worshipers are also called the Mexica, the blood-drinkers, the man-eaters, the Aztecs."

"Aztecs? We're going to hop in a bunch of Viking longboats and go kick butt on some Aztecs?" Christopher asked incredulously.

Thorolf mistook that for enthusiasm. "We will trample out the vineyards where the grapes of wrath are stored, ah-hah-hah!"

XXV

The village was a swarm of activity. Shaven-headed slaves were rushing back and forth, mostly shuttling enormous loads down to the dock. There they dumped their burdens off into boats rowed by more slaves. The supplies moved out to the ships, all to the encouraging bellows of Viking petty officers.

It was afternoon, with the sun already dropping from its peak. It wasn't hot. I had the feeling it never really got hot around this place.

Nevertheless, out on the boats I saw Viking crews stripped to the waist, trouser legs rolled up. They were coiling ropes, checking the caulking between the strakes, shinnying up the masts to check the seating of the single spar. They hauled on stays and went over the oars looking for cracks. They attached new sails and supervised the slaves who were manhandling pallets of bread, entire sides of beef, live sheep, live chickens, and barrels of what might be water or beer down into the shallow holds.

It was a picture of purposeful, serious, directed activity.

"Wow. Mass confusion," Christopher said.

"Uh-uh," I said. "Only if you don't know what you're looking at. I'll tell you something: These boys have done this before. These guys are pros."

The ships, on closer examination, came in several sizes, and no two were identical. Each had the almost-matching stern and prow that would allow the boat to reverse without turning around, the same single mast and square sail. But on some, the figurehead blazed with silver and gold. And some were quite long and large: I could count twenty-five oarlocks a side. That presupposed fifty rowers, when needed, plus petty officers, officers, and at least one guy to handle the big starboard-mounted steering oar.

I did not see the longboat with Loki's symbol, the one that had carried the old man to make the ritual sacrifice. But it would have been easy to overlook in the crowded harbor.

"That is our ship," Thorolf said, pointing to a boat of average size lying well out in the water. "She is called the *Dragonshield*. She is one of Harald Goldtooth's ships. He has three, and the *Dragonshield* is his flagship. Her figurehead was carved and inlaid with gold by dwarves."

"Of course. Dwarves. Had to be dwarves," Christopher muttered. "What looney bin is complete without dwarves and elves?"

"There are very few elves around these parts," Thorolf said sadly. "Elves are found to the south, though once they lived nearby in greater numbers. Much has changed, and not for the good. We were fortunate to be given a bench on Harald's ship. Since Loki came and strangled Earl Jens, may that good man have been carried swiftly to Valhalla, we have been allowed no ships in this land. No ships but the tribute ship." He spit on the ground. It was a statement of his feelings about the tribute ship and Loki more generally.

A rowboat nosed up to the pier and Thorolf jumped in, moving like an experienced sailor, taking the roll easily. He reached up a hand to me.

I ignored it and jumped across, landing on a vacant bench, catching my balance almost as easily as he had. I saw an eyebrow rise. A sailor knows a sailor.

Together we got Jalil, April, and Christopher into the boat. The slave oarsman rowed us out into a thicket of small boats that reminded me of the Dan Ryan Expressway at rush hour.

"We saw a unicorn back on your farm," April said.

"Yes, yes, we see unicorns there from time to time. They say that unicorns may only be handled by virgins," he said with a sly wink at April.

"Kind of makes you regret that homecoming dance, huh, April?" Christopher said brightly.

April batted her eyes. "You shouldn't listen to rumors."

"You know what they say about rumors: They're always true."

At that point we came around the sheltering point out into more open water. I saw the castle. The very wall where we'd been hung by the wrists. I had a dark, nasty feeling about those massive stone walls. I had seen a small part of the horrors contained in the castle and in the tunnels that cut deep into the black cliffs.

My blood was on those walls.

"Thorolf," I began, as casually as I could, "have you ever heard of a girl named Senna? Some say she's a witch."

Thorolf glanced over his shoulder up toward the castle, a nervous reaction. "Don't talk to me about witches! Do you want to curse this entire voyage?"

Jalil shot me a look. "You know, we may have enough on our hands without worrying about Senna."

"We're getting ready to sail away, who knows how far?" I said. "She may be here. We may be abandoning her."

"She may be *there*," Jalil argued. "After all, if Lo . . . if the Big Creep lost her, what's to say she's anywhere around here?"

"If he's looking for her, maybe we should stick close to him. He finds her, we find her."

Jalil shook his head. "That's fine, except for one little problem: He finds us, we're dead. Dead, we aren't much use to Senna. Or anyone else."

April said, "You know, David, maybe things aren't as random as you think. Maybe we're doing exactly what we have to do."

"Yeah, the Great Cosmic All is guiding our steps," Christopher said, mock-serious. "Karma, dude. It's all, like, karma."

I looked again at the castle. And then at the village. I was looking for something. A sign, maybe. Hoping for an intuition to guide me.

But all I had was a memory of a dream. Senna, calling me names that made her angry. Names that might someday be mine.

Maybe a hand was guiding me, and all of us. Maybe, even, it was Senna's own hand. Life's so much easier if you think that way. So much easier to blame some unseen force.

I closed my eyes and felt the last of the dream, the moment when she had softened, become warm, and pressed her body against mine.

That was the Senna I would find. But Jalil was right: I'd have to live to do it.

CHAPTER
XXVI

We reached the ship. The sides were not much higher than our rowboat, but it was still a chore getting the three landlubbers up and over.

"Harald Goldtooth and his sons, Sancho and Sven Swordeater," Thorolf said. He nodded to midship, where the crew was rigging a striped tent.

Harald Goldtooth was easy to spot. When he grinned — which was not often — you saw two flashes of gold right where his canine teeth had been. I'd seen him the night before at the feast. He glanced at us, decided we were not important, and went back to discussing business with his two sons. One of the sons was the young Viking with the stab wound through both cheeks.

I was guessing he was the one called Swordeater.

"Sancho?" Christopher asked. "That's a Norse name?"

"There has obviously been some inter-marriage, Christopher," Jalil said. "You did happen to notice that King Olaf was a brother, didn't you?"

"You sure he's not just really tan?"

Suddenly, a horn blast. It echoed through the harbor. Then again. And a third time.

A roar went up from a thousand throats. On shore, women waved good-bye. But there were women aboard, too. Evidently some Vikings brought their wives, or at least their close personal friends.

Harald Goldtooth stepped out of the tent just long enough to give a curt, businesslike nod to the officer who must have been his captain.

The captain in turn nodded to the guy I assumed was the mate. I had no clear sense of what ranks and functions there were aboard this ship. No one was wearing a uniform and I saw no insignias of rank.

"Man the oars!" the mate bellowed, and there followed a wild tramping and pushing and shoving as men ran to their appointed posts.

Thorolf left us standing, feeling stupid and out of place. Four dorks from a different universe.

"When does the steward show us to our cabins?" Christopher asked.

I walked over to the empty bench, sat down, and worked the long, heavy oar into the oarlock as I'd seen the crew do.

The mate strode over. "You're cargo. You don't need to row."

"I'll row," I said.

The man laughed. "You'll foul the other oars. Go away. Stand with your woman and the other minstrels."

It was a test. At least that's how I saw it. "If I foul another rower, I will stand with the others," I said.

"Up oars!" the mate yelled in response. All the oars came up out of the water. A sense of anticipation filled the air. Excitement. This wasn't a crew being driven against its will. There were grins and nods and exchanged winks.

"STROKE!" a new voice hollered, and all the oars hit the water at the same moment. I kept my eyes glued on the man in front of me. He wasn't big, but his bare back was nothing but rippling muscles.

He moved, I moved.

"Up and STROKE!" The bos'n — for lack of any better term — called the rhythm. The ship began to make way, amazingly easily. Not that the rowing would be easy after an hour. But for now it was more a matter of catching the precise pace, the exact flow of synchronized movements.

The cry of "stroke . . . stroke" was replaced by a drum, pounding hard on the start of each pull, tapping gently on the return stroke.

I pulled hard, putting my back into it. Thorolf was three benches up from me on the other side, doing the same. There were fifteen of us to a side, thirty men pulling in unison.

And all around us, visible as I rolled forward at the end of a stroke, were ships. Some larger, some smaller, all cutting the water, all moving. It was an awesome sight. An awesome spectacle that I was a part of. Something no one had seen in the real world for centuries: a Viking fleet putting to sea.

STROKE with the drumbeat, pull, pull, pull, then lift, roll forward, stretch out, way out, then STROKE and push with your legs, thigh muscles burning, and the narrow, shallow-draft ship would leap through the water.

"Harald Goldtooth!" a rowdy voice called out from off the port side. "Harald Goldtooth! Do you have women rowing that slow, diseased-pig of a boat? Should I send some of my true, hearty men across to help you before those weak-limbed, venereal-diseased old women you call a crew faint from their exertions?"

His crew gave him a roar of approval, followed by shouted obscene suggestions relating to all of us.

Harald yelled back, "Edrick, you senile, effeminate dog, Thor himself could not blow the wind that could speed your filthy wreck of a ship faster than the *Dragonshield*."

This, of course, was the signal for our crew to taunt and ridicule Edrick's crew.

"My white mare against your best bull!" Edrick shouted, laying out the bet. "First to pass the line of the point!"

Yeah, it was all juvenile. Like junior high school with swords. But it worked. We'd only been pretending to row. Now we rowed. The drumbeat accelerated and we hauled oar, yelling like idiots on each pull, the Vikings egging one another on.

My hands were soon blood-raw. My back was screaming. My legs were on fire. My arms were lead. I'd probably never be able to unbend my fingers again.

But all second thoughts, all doubts, all dreams and memories of dreams were set aside as my world honed down to the rhythm and the strain.

It was a dumb, energy-draining race. I was on my way to a battle that was none of my business, surrounded by simple, illiterate men who were no part of my universe, on a mission from a lunatic mythical god.

And it occurred to me then that at that moment I was as happy as I've ever been in my life.

Just beyond the point we caught a following breeze. The Viking ships were great for their time and place, but they weren't much good at sailing close to the wind. They could tack — move back and forth at angles to a wind that was against us — but only slowly and clumsily. Any weekend sailor in the real world could have sailed circles around these ships.

And the Viking ships had no weapons, aside from the men. A ship like the *Constitution*, a War of 1812–era ship armed with cannons, could have blown an infinite number of Viking ships out of the water.

But this was a ship designed eight hundred years or so before the *Constitution*.

Which made me wonder. How long had Everworld existed? When had it formed, if that's what had happened? How many local years had passed without the Vikings ever learning to use fore and aft sails? Or at least multiple masts?

The breeze stayed fair for all that afternoon and evening. Once under way, there wasn't much for me to do. I could row well enough, but I didn't know how to trim a square sail, and no one was going to put me on the steering oar.

Christopher and Jalil and I were given a few inches of deck as a bed. They rigged a tarp that shielded us from most of the spray, but it was going to be a hard, cold, wet night.

April slept under the tent. The back half belonged to the women — wives and mistresses. Harald, his son Sancho, and a couple of the higher-ranking guys slept there. Not much better off than us peasants, but better enough that it made Jalil grumble.

Getting to sleep wasn't easy. I knew what sleep would mean. So did everyone. We made plans to get together on the other side.

But it wasn't that easy. I fell asleep, lulled by the rise and fall of the ship under me and by my own deep physical exhaustion.

I slept . . .

"Grande latte and a no-whip Venti Mocha," the cashier called.

I stared at her. "What?"

"Grande latte and a no-whip Venti Mocha," she repeated.

I stared at the espresso machine before me. I stared at the stainless steel container of foamed milk in my left hand. I stared at the customer, who was staring at me.

I reached down and grabbed a handful of my dark green apron.

Starbucks. Where I worked three nights a week. I was at work.

Now the cashier was staring at me, too.

"Grande latte and a no-whip Venti Mocha," I repeated faintly. I started to make the drinks. The motions were automatic. Flicking the coffee from the grinder, twisting on the steam, pumping the chocolate syrup for the mocha.

"Is that skim?" the customer asked me. He was a middle-aged guy with a gray ponytail.

"Do you want skim?"

"Yeah, make it skim."

I changed milk containers and began to steam the skim milk.

What else was I supposed to do? I was at work, and it was a good job for someone my age. I was sixteen and the manager had stretched the rules to let me train as a *barrista*. The guy who makes the drinks.

It paid better than Mickey D's, and the humili-

ation quotient was lower. I worked three six-
hour shifts, earning eight-fifty an hour plus a
share of the tips. I needed the hundred and
twenty bucks a week I cleared after taxes. I had
college to think about. Not to mention a car from
this decade.

This was in my head. All that rational, sensible
stuff. It was in my head right next to the crazed
voice yelling about Vikings.

"What flavor are those biscotti?" the customer
asked me, since the cashier was busy with the
next customer.

I felt like screaming, "How the hell do I know
what flavor the lousy biscotti are, you ponytailed
freak? I'm asleep on the deck of a Viking longboat
on my way to a war!"

But I knew the answer. I mean, somehow I
knew what flavor biscotti we had.

"Amaretto and chocolate chip," I said.

The guy turned up his nose.

"Grande iced cappuccino, two tall cappucci-
nos," the new customer said.

"One Grande iced capp, two tall cappuccino,"
the cashier repeated for my benefit.

I flicked coffee. I tamped it down. I punched
the button.

I should call Jalil. That was the plan. Once we

were over, we'd all hook up, call one another, get together, try and make sense of everything.

No time now, though. I was at work. You couldn't just walk out on work. This was a good job. Anthony, my boss, was a good guy. I had a duty.

A duty? A duty to make coffee for snotty yuppies? How was this my life? How was making coffee my life?

As soon as I was done with this next customer, I'd make a call. Jalil first. He'd told me his number. They were unlisted, so I'd have to remember.

This was crazy!

"Here you go, sir. Grande skim latte, Venti Mocha, no whip cream." I worked the tops on and handed the drinks over.

Ka-ching. The cash register drawer opened and closed with a bang.

People sitting at tables, sipping drinks. The room warm with wood and soft lights. Bags of coffee all lined up, stocked up. Shelves of cups and coffeemakers. Someone needed to restock the —

I grabbed my head. This was crazy! This was —

A foot tramped down on my outstretched hand. One of the crewmen, moving aft to tighten a stay.

I blinked and looked around. The ship. Snoring Vikings all around. Jalil and Christopher closest by. Jalil snoring. Christopher, eyes open, looking up at the stars.

I was exhausted. Tired in every muscle, every bone.

I drifted back to sleep.

CHAPTER
XXVIII

RrrrRRRRrrrrRRRRRrrrrrRRRRR.

I released the key. My car. I was in my car. Morning. Something had just happened here, here in the real world.

I searched my memory. My mom. That was it. She hadn't done my laundry. No clean shirt. I had to wear some pathetic, raggedy thing from, like, three years ago.

Why did I care? Oh. Yeah. We'd all had dinner together the night before. Me, my mom, this guy she was seeing. Eddie. That was it, Eddie. She wanted Eddie and me to be friends, to get along.

I knew she was thinking about getting married. I knew it, although she denied it. The final step was getting me and Eddie so we could stand each other.

It would be heavy lifting, that would. He

didn't like me, and the reverse. He was an assistant professor of Romance languages at the university.

RrrRRRRrrrrrRRRRRrrrr.

A shirt that didn't fit and made it look like I thought I was going golfing, and the memory of a huge fight with my mom the night before, and now the car wouldn't start.

I climbed out, raised the hood, and then kicked the front fender till I thought I'd broken my foot. I cursed the car and then moved on to cursing life in general.

Then, calmer, I unscrewed the air filter and leaned over to look down inside the old-fashioned carburetor.

From the carburetor, cold salt water sprayed.

I opened my eyes. The ship had caught a freak wave on the beam. The spray had slapped me awake, but only partly. I opened my eyes and closed them, wondering whether I'd ever be able to fall back to —

The four of us. Jalil, April, Christopher, me. All sitting cross-legged on the grass. Outside the school. Books open on our laps, sandwiches in wrappers, small bags of chips. Kids all around, lounging, talking, joking, eating.

Lunch. Outside the cafeteria, out on the common. It was a nice day. Not night, day. Not Starbucks, not my car, school.

"You two must have woken up," April said, looking at me and Christopher.

Jalil jerked his thumb at me. "No, he just crossed over. You can tell by the confused 'where am I?' look on his face."

"I'm here," I managed to say. "Someone stepped on my hand, woke me up. Christopher's looking at the stars."

Christopher made a face. "I am not looking at the stars, I am right here looking at the three of you. Just because he . . . me . . . the other me . . . isn't here, doesn't mean I'm deaf, dumb, and blind and you have to act like I'm some senile old man. He . . . Everworld Chris . . . popped in yesterday evening, so I got a memory update. I know about the Viking ship and us . . . you, whoever . . . being on the way to start trouble with freaking Az-freaking-tecs."

"Both versions of him are equally annoying," Jalil said to April.

A second later, Christopher frowned. His face confused.

"Meeting called to order," Jalil said sardonically. "Other Chris has joined us."

"This is beyond nuts," Christopher said. "Normal me can't tell if he's losing his mind or what."

"There is no normal you," I said, an attempt at a joke. I never had gotten my car going that morning. Yes, that morning. I'd ended up taking a city bus because the school bus had come and gone.

"Let's talk fast," April said. "I'm sleeping back under the tent with the women. Someone will wake me up any second."

"Hey, try being out in the open," I said. "What are you complaining about?"

April made an amused face. "I'm with the wives and the girlfriends, and these Vikings aren't exactly discreet. Or even civilized. I'm getting my sex education class here. And I managed to make matters worse by handing out Advil to Harald's wife, who was having cramps, and now he's enjoying himself because she's feeling better, and the two of them want to give me a goat as a thank-you gift. I'm trapped in the middle of *Love Secrets of the Norsemen*. Not to mention that in the dark a couple of these guys have accidentally-on-purpose plopped down on top of me."

"Except for that last part, I'd trade places with you. So. What do we talk about?" Christopher asked brightly. "You think the Bears will change quarterbacks?"

"How do we stay here?" April demanded, showing no interest in joking. "How do we hang on to this, to being here? How do we stop getting dragged back to Everworld?"

Jalil nodded in agreement. "That would be Issue Number One."

I started to say something. Then stopped.

"We can't just stay asleep over there, can we?" April asked, knowing the answer.

"No," Jalil said anyway. "I don't think the Vikings have discovered sleeping pills."

"This was fun, in an insane kind of way," Christopher said, "but I have a life. Okay, not much of one, but better than the life that involves getting killed by Aztecs."

"There must be a way," April said. "Not to . . . look, I don't want to sound like a ditz, but my friends are acting weird around me. Like they don't trust me anymore. It's all this stuff. I mean, of course I'm different than I was. Look at what's happening to me!"

Her voice rose to a near shriek. She took a couple of deep breaths and tried to form her face into its usual lines.

"It's like being that bag lady downtown, the one who talks to voices. I'm living this nice, normal life, but in my head I have memories of being in Everworld, and then when I slip back across, it's like this second personality, like me but not me, takes over. This is the textbook definition of insanity. I feel like me, only not. I'm here, only not."

"'There's someone in my head, but it's not me,'" Christopher sang. "Sorry. Suddenly I was channeling Pink Floyd."

I remembered the fight with my mom. Freaking out and kicking my car. More emotion than I usually show. Less in control than I usually am.

April was right. We were living through something that was very close to insanity. Maybe it was insanity. How would you know?

"I want to be home," April said.

Christopher nodded.

Jalil shot a look at me, questioning. "How about you, David?"

I started. I'd been off in my own thoughts, still assimilating the memories of the last couple days. This was all taking place in a single night's sleep. But Starbucks had been last evening. An hour ago there, twelve hours here.

"Senna," I blurted. "There's still Senna. I want to find her."

"True love," Christopher sneered. "Here's a thought: Find another girlfriend. Senna's gone. Even if she weren't gone, she's trouble."

"No. I want to find her. I'm not giving up till I do."

"Kind of a moot issue," Jalil said wearily. "Since we don't know how to stay here, how to escape Everworld."

"Yeah, well, if that's what we want to do, I think the answer is probably over there in Everworld," I said.

"If?" April echoed, staring hard at me. "If?"

I snapped awake.

No one had stepped on my hand. No splash of cold water. I simply woke up. Jalil and Christopher slept. Presumably April, too, back with the women.

I was relieved.

XXIX

Sven Swordeater was there by the rail. I wasn't sure if I was allowed to be around him or not. But mostly the Vikings seemed like a fairly democratic bunch. As long as you didn't screw up. Then this wiry little guy named Jospin would come over and kick the hell out of you.

I got up, moving carefully so as not to wake Christopher or Jalil. They would still be back there. Sitting on the grass, nibbling Doritos and asking themselves how they could stay there.

I'd still be there, too. Part of me. That me. But they'd know that I had crossed back over. That I was in Everworld again.

I went and stood, leaning on the rail, and looked up at the stars. Different stars, I was pretty sure. No North Star. A moon, but larger and more pale.

Sven was doing pretty much the same. Hanging and looking and, I guess, thinking.

When he spoke, it was with a heavy speech impediment, like he had a mouth full of sandwich. I was surprised he could talk at all. I could see the scars, even in starlight.

"My father says you escaped from Loki's castle."

No point denying it. "Yeah. The four of us," I said.

Long silence.

"My father says you come from the Old World. The world of before."

I sucked in a deep breath. "Yes, we . . . um, excuse me for not knowing, but do you have some title I should use when I talk to you?"

Sven smiled his hideous smile. "No. Harald is lord on this ship, and should he fall then Sancho will take his place. I am only Sven. Tell me about the Old World."

"It's very different," I said. "More like . . . I don't know. More complicated, maybe. Lots of machines. Flying machines and cars. It's hard to describe. It's mostly peaceful, at least where I'm from. No swords or armor. We have guns instead. And, you know, TV, movies, books."

Well, David, I thought ruefully, *that should paint a pretty clear picture.*

"It's very different," I added lamely. "Tell me about this place. Everworld."

"It's very different," Sven said without missing a beat. We both laughed.

Silence again.

"Things are changing," Sven said after a while. "Many things. For many centuries we tended our fields at planting and harvest, sheared our sheep, and bred our cows and horses. Twice a year we would go a-Viking. We raided along the coast of Atlantis — until they agreed to pay us a yearly tribute. And then we raided up the great Nilus River to take the gold and silver of the Egyptians, and through the swamps and fens to find the wondrous steel made by the Coo-Hatch. We took slaves and women and all manner of riches. And of course we traded peacefully when that was profitable: our fish and wool for Dwarvish swords, our wood for Greek pottery."

"Sounds interesting," I prompted, while my brain was busy going, *Atlantis? Coo-Hatch?* I glanced over, wishing Jalil or Christopher would wake up so they could hear some of this.

"There was a balance in this world," Sven said. "And then came the Hetwan."

"I saw one of them," I said. It came out without me thinking about it. A sudden blurt.

All at once the friendly chat was over. Sven

spun, grabbed my arms, and yanked me close. "You saw a Hetwan? Where? Where?"

"In Loki's castle," I said.

"By the gods," Sven whispered, appalled. "By all the gods of Asgard! Father! Father!"

Sven and I were no longer friends. He dragged me, half stumbling, toward the stern, yelling, cursing, calling for his father to wake up.

Seconds later I was standing in front of Harald Goldtooth, Sancho, Sven, and half the ship.

"You're sure you saw a Hetwan?" Harald demanded.

"Yes. Yes . . . my lord."

"Neither man, nor dwarf, nor nymph, nor elf, nor any other creature of the Old World? But not like the Coo-Hatch or the Ett, either, but standing as a man stands, and with wings, and with —"

"With three little insectlike arms that are always moving, like they're snatching food out of the air," I finished. "Loki called him a Hetwan. I think he was, like, the representative for some guy named Ka Anor."

Not a sound from any of the men and women there. I swear that hearts stopped beating. The water gurgled down the side of the ship, the sail sighed as it swelled, but not a word.

"We have been betrayed!" a man said, quickly hushed.

"What did Loki say to this Hetwan filth?" Harald demanded.

"He . . . well, he was basically apologizing and threatening. The Hetwan was mad because . . ." I didn't know how to go on. Should I mention Senna?

Jalil made the decision for me. "Loki tried to remove someone from our world and bring her here. He sent Fenrir. He succeeded in grabbing this person, but somehow she got away from him, or he lost her. That's how we ended up here. We were carried along in her wake."

Harald looked to both his sons, then at each of us. "I tell you now, minstrel, that if you lie to me I will kill you."

Said quietly. Said without anger. Said with absolute seriousness.

I believed him.

"Who is this person that Loki took from your world?"

I pressed my lips together, firm. Not this time. I wasn't giving Senna up. We didn't have to answer. You don't lie if you don't answer.

Christopher didn't feel the same.

"Who is she? Good question. Loki kept calling her a witch."

No one laughed. No one rolled their eyes. These men took that word very seriously.

"What did Loki want with this witch?" Harald asked.

"We don't know," I said.

Harald's sword was out and pressed against my throat before I could twitch. I felt cold steel, a coldness that reached down deep and froze my insides.

"He's telling the truth!" Jalil yelled desperately. "He's telling the truth! He doesn't know. Not really."

Harald looked hard at me. "Then what does he suspect?"

"We think Loki may want to use her somehow," April answered for me. "We . . . we don't know how. You have to understand, we had no idea Everworld even existed. This is all new. All of it. In our world there are no Vikings and no Loki."

Harald was not offended or surprised. "Of course not. When Everworld was born, the gods left the Old World and came to this new place. And they carried their people with them. Zeus and his children, Huitzilopoctli and his foul brood, Odin and his own. All the gods."

"A new universe," Jalil said under his breath. Then, "Why did the gods create Everworld? Why did they come here?"

Someone standing behind Jalil swatted him in

the back of the head. It wasn't malicious, but it wasn't gentle, either. "Harald asks the questions here," a man's gruff voice admonished.

Thorolf. It hadn't occurred to me that he might feel responsible for us. And if we offended, he might suffer.

Harald shook his head, considering, suspicious, but not quite ready to call us liars or spies. "Everyone back to your duties," he said at last, dismissing us.

Grumbling Vikings went back to sleep. April looked like she wanted to hang out with us, but it wouldn't do for us to look like we were conspiring.

I went back and lay down again. But I didn't sleep.

CHAPTER
XXX

The sun rose on a Viking fleet spread across miles of ocean. We were sailing east into the sun. Assuming that the sun rose in the east here. Assuming it mattered.

Christopher was in line to use the head. This amounted to a short platform with a hole in it. The platform hung out over the sea. I'd used it the night before. It was a good idea to hurry: The sea had a tendency to rise up and come shooting like a fire hose up through the hole. Which woke you up in a big hurry.

There was no privacy, male or female. Which took a little getting used to, and explained my own preference for going at night.

Breakfast was salted fish that had been steeped in fresh water to leech out some, but not nearly all, of the salt. There was bread, still fresh after only a day out of port. And apples. Small and wormy.

I saw Jalil writing in the notebook from April's backpack. I went over to stand by him, not wanting to pry. He saw me and held the pad so I could see. He was using an unlined divider piece to sketch a map. It showed the outlines of the inlet containing Loki's castle and the village. The detail was surprisingly good.

"Might as well get to know the place," Jalil said.

He had also covered at least one page with tiny handwriting, a description of what we'd seen so far. What we'd learned.

"You writing a book?" I asked.

"More or less. A record. We don't know how long we'll be here. How long till we find a way to escape. Maybe we learn something and don't know its significance till later. Maybe there are clues." He shrugged.

I turned toward the bow and caught a shot of fine, cold spray. It made me grin. "You hate all this so much?" I asked him.

"Hate it? No. I think it's the most amazing thing that has ever happened to me. But that's not the point, is it? I have a life. I have family. Friends, although they can get along without me."

"They aren't getting along without you," I pointed out. "You're there. You're there and here."

"Yeah, that's not too strange," he said. "Anyway, that's my life, man. Back there. Back in my own universe. That's my life."

"Yeah. Good life," I said sarcastically. "You work, where? Burger King?"

"Boston Market."

"We'll both go off to college, get degrees in something or other —"

"Business major, minor in journalism," Jalil said.

"Whatever. So you do what with the rest of your life?"

He didn't look like I was getting to him. "Report on business. You know, *Wall Street Journal*, CNN, CNBC, something like that."

"Get married, have kids. Buy a nice car. Buy a house. Water the lawn. Shop with your wife. Watch TV. You ever think about that? Going to work every day, kissing someone's butt, someone's, it doesn't matter whose. Some boss you have to tell, 'Yes, sir, brilliant idea, sir!'"

"Maybe I'm the boss," he said with a small smile.

"Maybe you are. So it's someone else kissing your butt. Is that better? I mean, high school is four years, and it seems like forever. You work for thirty, forty years. Forty freaking years getting in the car, driving through traffic, dealing with b.s., driving home, and taking the kids to buy sneakers?"

I realized April had come over. How long she'd been listening, I didn't know.

"And you don't want all that?" she asked me.

"Maybe. Someday," I said. "I don't even know if I'll go to college, but my mom's looking at an MBA for me, and I go along, mostly. Why? Because I care about business? No, because everyone's on me about my future. Gotta get the grades so you can get a good college so you can get a good business school so you can get on with some big firm where you shuffle papers and tap on a keyboard and that's it, man, that's your life till you get old and wonder what the hell you did with your life. That's not life. Not for a man, anyway."

April cocked an eyebrow. "The way you describe it, it doesn't sound like life for anyone. That won't be my life. You leave out all the good stuff: friends and family. Kids. The things you love to do."

I waved my hand, dismissing it all. "There used to be adventure. You know? Going west in a wagon train, or going to war, or exploring someplace no human being had ever been before. Now what do we have? Look at Sven. Look at that guy. He's my age. Look at his life. Then look at mine or Jalil's or yours."

April barked out a laugh. "He can barely talk because someone rammed a sword through his mouth."

I nodded. "You know the difference between him and me? We're both about sixteen. But he's a man. And I'm a boy."

April made a face, angry, dismissive, frustrated. "What is it with you guys? Is it the testosterone? You know, David, it's the dawn of the twenty-first century, and you live in the richest, most powerful nation on Earth where there's almost no one starving and no one enslaved and no one invading to murder and pillage and rape. And finally, finally, after thousands of years of men slaughtering men, women, and children over nonsense, we have a few places on Earth where there's a little peace, a little decency. A few places where most people get to be born and live their lives without total horror being rained down on them, and your reaction is, 'This has to stop!'"

Christopher had wandered over, drawn by the sound of harsh words, I guess. He laughed. "Don't blame me, April. I'm a lover, not a fighter. Would you like a demonstration?"

April and I stood glaring, both angry, not angry at each other, not really, but glaring at each other because neither of us could find a real enemy to take out our frustrations on.

"Come on, peace," Jalil said. "As bizarre as it sounds, we're on our way to a war between Vikings and Aztecs. Probably not much point having a little battle of the hormones between you two."

April and I backed away, but it was a phony peace. We were making nice for Jalil and Christopher. And because we looked like idiots in front of the men.

The breeze had gone slack, and Harald reluctantly ordered the men to their oars. I went to my bench and rowed and wondered how much I believed what I'd said.

I noticed Christopher taking a bench toward the bow. One of the crew had smashed his hand up the day before, and Christopher took his place. He fouled the oars a few times till he got the rhythm.

Harald called for a song and April obliged. She sang "Blue Skies." I think she faked about half the words, but the Vikings thought it was great. Other boats rowed closer, keeping station with ours.

The calm didn't last long, a couple of hours.

And then we got more wind than the landlubbers wanted. But it was a sailor's breeze, the big square sail bellied out, the bow slicing the waves, sending up explosions of spray.

The wind held through the night. I fought sleep. But sleep came anyway, and I crossed over into p.e. in the middle of a scratch basketball game. I wanted to quit the game but I couldn't because you don't just quit, even though no one cares but the one jerk who wants to prove he's some hardcore jock.

I went through p.e. and my last two periods and made it home, where my mom had made veggie lasagna for dinner and we watched some sitcom and she laughed and told me I should laugh, too, so I did.

None of it mattered. Had it ever mattered? If it ever had, it didn't anymore. I was far away from it. Real seemed unreal. Familiar was strange. I'd gone to sleep in living color and woken to black and white and all the shades of gray.

This wasn't it for me, not anymore. My world wasn't about condescending teachers and hypocrite parents and "Why don't you take out the trash?" and "Where's that two-thousand-word paper, Mr. Levin?"

I'd lived sixteen years' worth of shiny malls and dark school hallways and narrow homes and

TV blaring and smiley face e-mail and don't do drugs, don't do sex, don't smoke, don't eat junk food, don't don't don't because your boring, boring life, your robot march from kindergarten to grammar school to junior high to high school to college to work to the condo in Florida to the grave where you'll slowly decay for all eternity, should be nothing but leafy green vegetables and happy thoughts and G-rated lyrics about puppy love.

I knew where I was. I was aboard a Viking ship on my way to battle. I wasn't here, I wasn't in my chair in my living room, watching two-dimensional images of people pretending to be other people. I was asleep, and all this was a memory.

I hooked up with Christopher later that night and we talked about school, and some girl, and some team in some game that neither of us cared about.

We went our separate ways, unable to figure out how to relate in the now-strange universe where we'd lived our entire lives.

I went for a walk over to the big Borders store. I decided if I was going to sail the seas of Everworld, I'd see if I couldn't make some improvements. I looked up a book on the history of sailing, trying to figure out what I could do to enhance the sailing characteristics of a Viking long-boat.

She was in the coffee shop. Sitting at a table.

I saw her and the world, the brightly lit world, swirled around me.

Senna. Sipping tea from a paper cup.

CHAPTER
XXXI

"Senna?" I whispered. "Senna?"

"Yes, David. It's me."

I couldn't talk. Not for what felt like a long time. I just stood there, staring, swaying back and forth a little, like I might fall over.

"You're not here," I said. "Everyone says you're still missing. It's been days. You're not here."

She smiled a cool, easy smile. "I'm here," she said. "For now."

With numb fingers, I pulled out a chair and sat down hard. "What the hell is going on?"

"Lots of things are going on," she said.

That made me mad. "Don't jerk me around, Senna."

She sipped her tea carefully, like it was too hot. "There's going to be a battle," Senna said.

"Yeah, I know. I'm there, thanks to you."

"Stay out of it," she said. "When the moment comes and you see a chance to run away, run. Run and keep running."

I flushed. "I don't think so."

"This isn't your fight, David. It is a single battle in a war that will spread, inevitably, throughout Everworld. Great forces are at work, I know that now. Greater than I could ever have guessed. But I still need you, David. I still need you to be my champion. Not to die in battle."

She put her hand on mine. It felt real. The way my body reacted felt real.

"Loki does a very good impression of you," I said harshly.

"Does he?" She leaned into me. And kissed me. "Run, David. Run away."

And then she was gone. And the people at the next table were carefully not looking at me. The way you ignore a lunatic in a public place. Only I had seen her.

I woke in Everworld to a cry that has dragged many sailors from their sleep down through the ages.

"Land! Land!"

Chapter
XXXII

Not just land. Not some bare cliff or tree-covered point of land.

The sun was rising, bright and buttery yellow, as if we'd been traveling south for weeks and months rather than east for two days.

We were approaching the mouth of a wide river. Numerous small craft plied back and forth, primitive even by Viking standards.

I saw no warships, no ships at all that would merit the word. Nothing that would sail out to challenge us as we stood in toward land, menacing, closer and closer, silent and deadly.

On the left bank of the river was what might have been a fishing village. It looked not very different from the Viking village but was more sprawling, a collection of mud and thatch huts without defensive walls or a definable perimeter.

It might almost have been picturesque, except that it was totally overshadowed by the city on the right bank. Not a village, a city.

The city looked ancient and modern all at once. The walls of shining white stone were perhaps a hundred feet high. I saw no towers. It wasn't a castle built for defensive war; it was a wall raised against the jungle that pressed in all around the wall, a sea of dark, almost black-green that flowed down from distant mountains. Green, unbroken green, as far as the eye could see.

The city rose beside the river, from the edge of this jungle, a brilliant, blinding Escher print rendered in color. Since the town sloped uphill, I could see some of what was beyond the walls: straight-as-a-ruler streets lined with white stone buildings and tile roofs.

Here and there at intervals, pyramids rose, peeking over the wall. They were stepped, not smooth. Two or three times the height of the walls. And these pyramids would have seemed fabulous and incredible, except that one pyramid made the others look like foothills next to Mount Everest.

It rose so high I think it could literally have touched the clouds. It was so vast, so monumental, I wondered that the ground could support it. The entire rest of the city, every stone in build-

ings and walls, could not have built a quarter of
that mountain of rock.

Down the center of the pyramid was a broad
stairway, steps shorter than the step-back construction of the pyramid itself. A rust-red stain
ran down the top third of the steps.

"The city of Huitzilopoctli," Thorolf announced with satisfaction.

"We're attacking that?" Christopher asked.

"That is what we must do, yes. There lies the
ransom demanded by Loki. There, atop the great
pyramid, within the temple itself."

"What is the ransom?" April asked.

"The head of Huitzilopoctli."

"Say what?!"

"Isn't he a god?" April pressed. "You can't just
chop off a god's head, can you?"

"Mere mortals? No. A mortal may not kill an
immortal, as anyone knows who has heard the
sagas and eddas, the great poems and tales,
knows. But we have a . . ." He hesitated and
frowned. "Perhaps I will leave that unsaid."

I heard Sven Swordeater's thick, mangled
speech coming from behind me. "Tell them, good
Thorolf."

Thorolf grinned. "Great Thor is lost to us, we
know not where or how, but his hammer, Mjolnir, is not."

We all stared stupidly, having no idea what this might mean.

"King Olaf Ironfoot has the hammer of Thor," Sven said. "Mjolnir carries the power of Thor's own mighty arm within it. With Mjolnir we may kill Huitzilopoctli as Thor slew the frost giants."

So that was the weapon Olaf had bragged about. Thor's hammer.

Christopher turned to April. "Nurse Ratched, I'll take my medication now."

A new level of activity broke out aboard the ships as we glided toward landfall. Men sharpened their swords and axes. Officers went over their chain-mail shirts, carefully checking for any small defect. The archers laid out their arrows, trimming the feathers, filing the iron arrowheads.

I asked Thorolf for a sword. He didn't argue, but he didn't have a spare: He wasn't a rich man, he protested. Besides, he preferred an ax.

It was Sven who armed me. He sent his man for a sword and had the servant buckle it around my waist.

"I have no mail shirt for you, nor any helmet, nor shield," Sven said.

"Thanks for the sword," I said, trying not to feel too much like an idiot amateur.

"The Aztecs fight with spears and swords of obsidian. Our iron blades will break theirs, and their shields are like cutting through cheese. But be careful of the throwing spears. They are very quick with their throwing spears."

The guys on the shore weren't standing around idly as we approached. They'd have had to be blind not to see us, and they weren't blind.

We heard distant horns echoing from the city walls. Tiny human figures could be seen racing along the wall.

But an hour went by, with us almost ashore, before a column of troops, fantastically arrayed in bright turquoise and crimson feathers, came trotting out of the main gate down toward the puny sand beach where we would land.

We were in the river's current now, so we went to the oars, moving with surprising ease upstream.

Closer, closer, closer.

My heart more and more in my throat.

Jalil stood beside me as I rowed. "This is a real war, David," he said. "This is for real. These guys are going to be hacking one another up here."

I nodded, conserving energy.

"This isn't our fight, man. This isn't about you hating your life or whatever. This isn't about some macho pose. This is real, serious, screaming and dying war."

I shot him a quick look. He sounded like Senna. *Run away, David.*

"Question for you, Jalil," I rasped out between strokes. "You see those guys on shore?"

"You have a point to make?"

"You figure those guys know we're not Vikings?"

He bit his lip. I don't know why, but it made me glad to see Jalil was scared. I'd have been more scared myself, only I was focusing on rowing. And focusing on what had happened when I'd gone up against Loki. Focusing on maybe wiping that out. Maybe putting that behind me.

Or maybe getting killed. Blade biting into me, cutting me, tearing me open, my insides spilled out into the sun.

I had to focus to keep my grip from tightening to a panic cramp on the oar.

"Screw it," Jalil said bitterly. "If I'm getting killed, I'm inflicting some pain first." He went off in search of a weapon.

I had a sudden, clear image of a spear thrusting right through my body. Right through my stomach. First the point pressing against cloth and ripping through to flesh. The wound widening as the spearhead flared out. The blood seeping out around the black stone blade. The spear pushing through my internal organs, out through my back, between the ribs. Pierced through and through. Impaled.

It was an image from dreams I'd had since I was six. Impaled. Helpless.

I missed my stroke and felt the oar behind mine whap hard, sending an impact up to my hands.

For once Jospin didn't come over and scream bloody murder. I guess he was focused on battle, like everyone on that boat. Like everyone on all the longboats.

The beach was close now. I could see individual faces of the wall of soldiers facing us. I could see sun glinting on black spears.

"Take in the sail!" a voice roared. Crewmen, already expecting the order, shinnied up the mast, while others hauled on ropes.

"Archers!"

"Oars up!"

Then, a scraping sound that shook the ship.

We were beached. Beside us were other ships, the ship we had raced. Carved prows hit the sand.

It was going to happen!

Right now, it was going to happen.

"Fire!"

A dozen bowstrings twanged, a dozen arrows flew from all around me, and dozens more from the other ships. Ships were still coming in, still landing, and arrows flew, flew, flew.

The first Aztecs began to die, howling, screaming, tugging at arrows that stuck in their shoulders, bellies, legs, groins, necks, eyes.

"Arise!" Harald bellowed, appearing at the bow of the ship and waving his sword in the air. The Vikings leaped up, grabbed their shields, gripped their swords, and began a sustained, bloodthirsty roar.

"Attack!" Harald cried, but some of his men hadn't waited.

A huge, blond Viking leaped to the sand, screaming like a madman, screaming in throat-tearing rage, insane, uncontrollable. Berserk. He landed, stumbled, caught himself, and went barreling toward the Aztec line.

Then it was pandemonium. I couldn't have resisted if I'd wanted to. A mass of men all around me, running, climbing onto the gunwale, leaping, falling, staggering, running, pushing.

All of us shouting, all of us pulsing with adrenaline, all mad and scared.

It was electric. I can't find another word. It was electric! My body tingled, my brain was somewhere else, I wasn't David Levin anymore. I wasn't me, an individual; I was lost in the mass madness. Raw screaming fury, I ran.

We roared into the Aztec line. Spears thrust at me, dodge! Ah! Stab me? I'll chop your head off! I'll kill you, kill you, kill.

I raised my sword high over my head, shot wild looks left and right, panting, gasping, as my heart refused to let up and let me catch a breath.

Eyes locked on me. Dark, deep-set, ferocious eyes. I saw him. Saw him lunge with the spear, quick as a snake. The black spearhead aimed right at my stomach.

I twisted right, swung my elbow forward, caught the spear point on its flat side, and felt it slice through my shirt and graze flesh. I swung back, left elbow twisting toward the Aztec's face.

He was unbalanced, leaning forward. I caught him on the side of his head. He staggered. He fell facedown in the sand at my feet.

Another spear, this one wide. I swung my sword down and cut into the Aztec's helmet. I didn't see what happened next, didn't know if I'd injured or killed the man. Too much was happening all around me, yelling, cries, grunts of effort as men swung heavy weapons.

From the center of the line of battle there came a new note, a roar of triumph, laughter! And moans of despair.

And suddenly I saw him: Olaf Ironfoot. He stood alone, tall, wild, bellowing. In his hand was a massive hammer with a short handle, just enough to grip.

He swung the hammer into the head of an

Aztec. The warrior didn't just drop, he flew. It was as if he'd been hit by a truck. He tumbled across the sand into his brothers.

"The hammer of Thor!" Thorolf cried.

The Viking army began to chant.

"Mjolnir! Mjolnir!"

The Aztec line broke and ran.

They ran and we were on them, stomping over the wounded, screaming ourselves hoarse yelling, "Mjolnir! Mjolnir!" Me as insane as the rest, as caught up in the frenzy of slaughter.

We chased the Aztecs as they ran for the walls of their city. Across the sand onto paved road.

And then I felt a shadow.

I looked up. A cloud? No, darker than any cloud.

The sun had risen behind the huge pyramid. It almost seemed to be sitting atop the pyramid. And from that sun, at the top of that monstrous pyramid, a shape appeared.

Huitzilopoctli.

He was shaped like a man. Blue, the blue of the sky late on a summer day. His face was striped horizontally with bands of blue and yellow. Around his eyes were glittering white stars, stars that seemed real and hot and explosive.

Iridescent feathers grew from his head, spreading down across his shoulders and back. In his left hand he held a disk, a mirror that smoked and burned. In the right hand was a snake, a twisting, writhing snake that breathed fire and almost seemed an extension of his hand.

His other hand, the one that held the mirror, dripped red. It dripped red and you knew, knew deep down, that it could never, would never be wiped clean.

Huge! How could he be so big? How could his shadow fall on me all that distance away?

And how could his shadow reach inside me, down to my soul?

I had felt dread in Loki's presence. This was different.

This was the heart and soul of evil. This was corruption and filth and torture and madness.

This was Huitzilopoctli, blood-mad god of the Aztecs.

Run away, David, I heard Senna's voice in my head. *Run away.*

Lost and Found?

Closer. Walking. Then creeping. Tiptoeing. Holding my breath, cursing the noise of my rumbling stomach. I was gonna get killed for being hungry. Maybe they had food. Cookies. Beans. A nice leg o' human.

The fire was definitely fire. Small. That was good. It was a fire built for one or two, maybe three. Not a whole army. Closer. Pushing the leaves aside, trying to see what there was to see. A hint of something near the fire. Couldn't see. Eyes straining, aching from the squint, head pounding with the tension.

I was lower, hunched over. *Don't see me, don't see me. Let me see you, but don't see me.*

No! This was wrong. Whatever was out here in the middle of nowhere might be scared, too. Jumpy and armed, a bad combination. If I crept up, snuck, seemed to be attacking, it was all over. . . .

I stepped into the clearing. A neat, circular space, walled by close-packed bushes and saplings and weeds.

In the center, a small fire.

Sitting by the fire, legs crossed, arms resting palms up, face worried, eyes staring into the fire, was Senna Wales. . . .

EVER WORLD

LAND OF LOSS

CHAPTER

I

In the real world the Vikings never fought the Aztecs.

This was not the real world.

I had a sword in my hand. My fingers were so tight around the hilt that blood was seeping from my cuticles.

My breath came in shallow gasps. So little air I should have passed out. Knew I should breathe but couldn't, couldn't make my chest relax enough, couldn't unknot my stomach to let the air come in.

My body was a series of vises, vises on vises, all twisted tight, tight till the bones cracked and sinews and muscle screamed.

I was running. Legs stiff, like a puppet. It probably looked funny. Big, bounding, awkward steps with knees that alternately locked and collapsed.

Widen out the picture and I was just one scared fool in a mass of thousands. They were all around me, ahead of me, behind me, on either side. Big, bearded, indifferently armored, helmeted, ax-swinging, sword-waving, screaming, yelling, running, running and falling and climbing up to charge again, always yelling at the top of their harsh voices.

Up the beach. Over warm sand. Feet losing three inches of slide with every step. Sand sucking at you, trying to stop you, trying to keep you from this suicidal rush. But all around was the madness. Men in the lunatic rage of combat. Hungry for murder. Thirsty for the blood that would drench the sand. Not their own, of course, never their own, because what fool ever goes to war expecting that he will be the one to die? The movie in your head has you as the hero, bravely whacking away at the bad guys. Courage without the sight of your own intestines spilled out in the buttery sunlight.

That wasn't my movie. I'm not a romantic.

I ran. David ran. He was beside me, a few feet away; we wobbled one way or the other, back and forth, nearer and farther. On David's right, hanging back, sensible person that he was: Jalil.

April? Back on the boats. Back on the Viking

longboats that had been beached like so many confused whales all down the strand.

She had a pass. She was a girl. She had a uterus, so she didn't have to fight, couldn't, not according to the Vikings. So she was on the boat. Safe? Not if we lost. But if we won, yeah, safe, out of it, sipping bad Viking ale and eating roasted lamb and watching us as if she were in a skybox at the Super Bowl, thinking what damned fools we were.

If I'd had room in my head for any emotion beside fear I'd have felt jealous. But fear was filling every wrinkle and knob of my brain. Fear soaked through the gray matter that at other times concerned itself with passing tests and getting girls and avoiding speeding tickets and coming up with clever one-liners that made everyone laugh.

Ah-hah-hah, that Christopher is so funny. Man, he's funny. I mean, he really is.

That's me, funny, funny, Christopher.

Want to know what's funny? Funny is a high-school junior surrounded by sweat-reeking wild men, waving a sword and rushing at a bunch of Aztecs. That's funny.

Aztecs. Mexica. Those were their official names.

Flesh-eaters. Blood-drinkers. Man-burners. Heart-thieves. The Vikings have all kinds of names for them. The Vikings think the Aztecs are a bunch of crazed psycho killers in the service of an evil god. And it's not like the Vikings are a bunch of Altar Guild Ladies from the local Baptist church.

The Aztecs were ahead of us, in a line. They looked ludicrous.

They wore feather headdresses, they disguised themselves as eagles, they disguised themselves as jaguars, they carried shields made out of sticks. Their swords looked vicious enough, like the snouts of sawfishes. But then you realized they were just hardwood with sharp chips of black rock embedded in the edge. Not much use against a steel sword, even the rusty, dented, tin-can things the Vikings use.

But the Aztecs had another weapon: short spears they flung with the aid of a notched stick. We'd been warned about those.

So that's where I was. Running toward a solid wall of Aztecs on a mission to chop off the head of their god Huitzilopoctli and bring it back to Loki so that he'd free Odin.

"Makes perfect sense," I muttered through chattering teeth, bounding stiffly, sliding and trying to keep from falling on my own sword.

Suddenly, from down the line, the big black Viking king named Olaf Ironfoot started yelling, "Mjolnir! Mjolnir!"

We hit the Aztec line. Two lines of men slammed together, literally, physically, so that you could hear shields grinding on shields and chests against chests and swords and axes all flailing wildly.

I was behind David. Some Aztec swung at him. David ducked. Then he drove his own sword into the feathered man and lurched away.

The Aztec fell. Not dead. Yet. But with blood and something black coming through the hands that clawed at his belly.

There was a sound coming from me, a noise, a moan, like a wounded animal, repetitive, wordless. Coming out of my throat and me having no control, no choice but to make that sound.

I was muscled aside by Thorolf, a Viking who'd taken charge of us. Thorolf was yelling, bellowing, roaring, swinging the big ax he carried up over his head and bringing it down like he was Abe Lincoln splitting rails.

I was down!

Sand in my mouth. Wind knocked out of me.

What had happened? Was I cut? Was I hurt? I dropped my sword, rolled onto my back, slapped myself frantically with my hand, looking for the wound. Couldn't see. Something in my eyes.

Blood!

I'd been hit in the head. Was I dying?

Feet stamped the sand all around me. A kick. I rolled over on my side. Dizzy. Wiped the blood out of my eyes. Fingers grazed a cut on my scalp.

Sickness washed over me as I realized I had just touched my own skull.

I'd never seen what hit me. And now I was in the rear, the Vikings pushing on, pushing the Aztecs back. Steel weapons versus obsidian and wood and bone.

"Mjolnir! Mjolnir!" the Vikings bellowed till it became a constant background roar, loud as a CTA train rushing by, almost drowning out the cries of rage and pain.

Mjolnir. The hammer of Thor.

The Aztecs were on the run! Back toward the tall, golden walls of the city they called New Tenochtitlan. Back toward the distant, stepped pyramid that towered above those walls.

I made it to my feet, tripped, staggered, caught myself, stopped, and went back for my sword. Blood was in my eyes again, my hand so wet with it that I couldn't clear my vision.

"Mjolnir! Mjolnir!"

David was gone. Jalil, barely visible, just his head, surrounded by Vikings twice his size.

Could I go back to the boats? I was injured, wasn't I?

Then I saw a Viking, an Asian guy, with a short, obsidian throwing spear sticking out of his upper thigh. He was staggering forward, yelling like all the others.

"Guess not," I muttered.

Besides, we were winning. The Aztecs were on the run. And as long as I didn't run too fast I probably wouldn't catch them.

I saw a flash of David. Just his head. He was stopped. Staring.

And through the Vikings, like an ice-cold wind, the terror blew.

The cries of "Mjolnir!" died away, replaced by the low, animal moan that men make when they are afraid, deep-down-inside afraid. I knew that sound. I'd been making that sound.

I'm tall. Taller than David or Jalil. Not as tall as a lot of the Vikings, but tall enough that from the back of the mob, standing on a slight rise in the sand, I could see the pyramid.

It was impossibly, absurdly high. Like it had been drawn by an artist with no sense of perspective.

Atop the pyramid, on the flat platform, was a temple. An open building on the front side and yet dark within, despite the bright morning sun.

From that temple stepped a creature out of a

madman's nightmares. He was huge! Almost as tall as the temple itself, and somehow, in defiance of all logic, his shadow fell across us.

We must have been half a mile away, but his shadow fell across us, across me, the darkness, the cold reaching deep inside me.

He was mostly blue, with broad, horizontal yellow stripes across his face. The blue was the blue of a late afternoon sky. The yellow was the yellow of unpolished gold. There were burning stars in his eyes, a burning mirror in one hand, a monstrous green snake in the other.

Huitzilopoctli. Aztec god.

We had come, armed with Mjolnir, to cut off his head and deliver it to Loki.

"Not happening," I said.

Huitzilopoctli grew wings, fabulous rainbow wings that spread wider than a thousand eagles.

He flew from the top of the pyramid and swooped down toward us.

Impossible, of course. Nothing that big could fly. It violated the laws of physics, that's what Jalil would have said.

Impossible anywhere in the universe.

Only, this wasn't the universe.

This was Everworld.

CHAPTER

II

Everworld.

Somehow, someway, for some reason, the old gods of Earth decided to abandon the real world. We didn't know why. Just knew that the gods of the Norsemen and the gods of the Greeks and the gods of the Aztecs and the Inca and the Egyptians and all the endless panoply of immortals, all decided they'd had enough of the real world. Our world.

They moved. They built themselves a little space-time condo. A separate universe.

They brought all the creatures of myth and legend. And they dragged a healthy number of humans across with them, because, hey, what's the point in being a god if there's no one around to kiss your immortal butt?

For a while, I guess, everything was fine. I have to guess because I don't know. I don't know much.

But somehow, into this combination Asgard-Olympus-Boca Raton, this cosmic retirement home for gods of war and love and wine and mischief and death — and no doubt pizza, for all I know — strangers crashed the party.

Immortals. Gods. But not human gods.

Then all hell broke loose. And now, somehow, don't ask me, there was some god-eating god from some dark armpit of the galaxy who was scaring the eternal pee out of the human gods.

Ka Anor. Not a nice creature. So I gathered from the fact that Loki, who isn't exactly a cheerleader himself, is scared by him.

Why was I there? Because of a girl named Senna.

Senna Wales. A freaky piece of work, but with a B-plus face and an A-plus body, assuming you're not one of those guys looking for eight pounds of silicone. Smart. Weird. Sexy. Inscrutable.

Man, I was hot for her.

Then it all went sour. Don't know why. She was like a spider who'd wrapped me up in the silk web and was ready to finish me off, and me wanting to be finished off, and then, nothing.

Next I see her, she's with David.

And yet, I was there that too-early morning, down by Lake Michigan, called there by a voice that only my deepest brain heard. I was down there watching, me along with Jalil and April and David, when the world went "tilt."

A wolf the size of a tractor trailer broke through from somewhere that was definitely not a suburb of Chicago. Broke the barrier of our comfy, cozy little universe and snatched up Senna in his jaws.

We were dragged along in the backwash.

Next thing we know, Senna's gone, we're face-to-face with a pissed-off Loki and a bunch of trolls, and Loki wants to know what we've done with "his witch." Senna.

Long story short, we escaped and got in tight with some Vikings who were about to leave on a mission for Loki. A mission to kill Huitzilopoctli and bring his head home as a trade-in for the freedom of Odin One-Eye, boss god of the Norsemen.

And it gets weirder. Because we aren't all the way into Everworld. We're there as long as we're awake. Go to sleep and we slip back into our old lives in the real world.

In and out. Back and forth. Cutting assembly

and groaning about the homework and checking out the visible panty lines one minute, being chased by murderous trolls the next.

It's a lunatic life.

Dangerous, too.

CHAPTER

III

Huitzilopoctli flew, swooped down on us like a gigantic bird of prey, and the Vikings fell back.

Instead of looking ahead to see backs, I was seeing faces now. Worried, frightened, disheartened faces. It wasn't a stampede. More like a hand that had reached out and touched a hot stove and yanked back almost instinctively.

The Big H looked like any one of his warriors. More feathers. Larger. And blue, of course. But it wasn't what you saw of Huitzilopoctli that scared you. It was what you felt.

There are people you meet, people whose eyes you happen to look into and right away you know. You know that they are apart from the basic humanity that more or less unites us. You know, without knowing why, that you're seeing a person whose pleasure comes from the pain of others, someone whose entertainment is gloating at the terror of others.

Beneath the shadow of Huitzilopoctli's wings you didn't have to look at him to feel the evil. It invaded your mind. Like an acid, it ate away your defenses and seeped into your soul.

I started to run. A hand grabbed me.

David.

"We can't run," he gasped, looking feverish and wild.

"Why not?"

"It's what *she* wants," he said.

She? I said something like "forget you," only several shades more intense. I didn't know who *she* was. I didn't care. I tore loose of his grip. A big Viking slammed into me, knocked me down on my back, and kept on running.

The Aztecs, emboldened by their god, counter-attacked. They made a weird, trilling scream as they came on.

I tried to stand up. Too many fleeing bodies all around me. Legs, knees, feet hitting me, heedless. My head was still bleeding.

David grabbed me again. Crouched next to me. We were a boulder in a stream.

"I think she's with him!" David hissed. "Senna! She's with Huitzilopoctli!"

"I don't give a damn!" I yelled.

"Stand fast with Mjolnir!" Olaf Ironfoot bellowed, suddenly now just a spear's throw away. "Mjolnir!"

"We still have the hammer!" David said.

"Are you nuts?!" I shrieked. I told him where he could stick Mjolnir.

"If we go for the boats they'll cut us to pieces," David said. "We won't be able to get the boats off the beach, and if we try we'll be exposed and helpless. They'll have us by the rear. We have to hold our ground!"

Somehow that calm, cool assessment, that military judgment penetrated my panic. He was right. We couldn't run for the boats, the Aztecs would be all over us. They'd massacre us at their leisure.

I let David yank me to my feet.

"Come on!" he cried fiercely.

The glory-hog moron. Like the two of us were going to turn this disaster around.

I pushed David aside, sucked in the first real breath I'd taken in twenty minutes, and yelled, "Are the Vikings all women? Are you all cowards?"

That little insult slowed approximately no one. Not one of the big men said, "Hey, he's right, what are we, a bunch of wussies?"

They kept right on past. I could see the Aztecs

rushing toward us. They were smiling. Smiling and waving their Stone Age weapons up at their lunatic god, who swooped low, spreading his own private cloud of doom in his wake.

"The song!" David yelled. "Give them the song!"

I knew which song. The Vikings believed we were minstrels. We'd obliged them by coming up with a song that just made them crazy.

I looked at David and actually laughed. It was a sad, barking little laugh of despair, but it was a laugh.

He was right. You can't retreat with nothing but ocean and the mouth of a river behind you. We had to win this battle. Or die.

"Mine eyes have seen the glory of the mighty Viking lords!" I croaked in a harsh voice that would have gotten me ejected from a middle-school talent show.

"They are trampling out the vineyards where the grapes of wrath are stored. They have loosed the fateful lightning of their terrible swift swords, the Vikes are marching on!"

David had joined in, too. And man, were we pathetic. Like ants putting on a show of defiance just as someone's lowering a size-thirteen Ecco boot on them.

And yet . . .

And yet, about three Vikings slowed down. Thorolf was among them. Jalil was with him.

"Sing, Jalil!" I said.

We sang, the three of us. The Aztecs rushed on. The Vikings kept running. Only not as fast.

For a long, horrible moment the battle hung in the balance, hung poised on the edge of a rout and slaughter.

The ragged Aztec line was rushing. The Viking line was pulling back.

In the few yards of no-man's-land that separated the two armies stood Olaf Ironfoot. All alone. Just him and Thor's hammer

About ten feet behind him was our little knot composed of three quivering teenagers and a handful of Vikings all yelling a mangled version of the "Battle Hymn of the Republic."

And swooshing by overhead like some kind of gigantic, satanic piñata, the feathered Aztec god who lived on human hearts.

We sang, because we were dead meat and we'd have tried anything, anything to stay alive for another eight seconds.

"We jumped aboard our longships and we sailed upon the seas, and —"

Suddenly, a new voice chimed in. Big Olaf and

his big baritone. He threw back his head and yelled the words up at Huitzilopoctli while he brandished Thor's hammer.

"— and we slaughtered all who fought us and we did just as we please, 'cause we're crazy Viking warriors and we never beg for peace, the Vikes are marching on!"

People do strange stuff in battle. You take a human and pump him full of adrenaline and, in the case of the Vikings, a lot of beer, and you never know what's going to happen.

The Vikings stopped running.

We sang and they stopped running. They turned. They hesitated. Then Sven Swordeater, a kid not much older than me, yelled in his muffled, mangled speech, "Follow me!"

And all down the line of battle other Viking lords yelled, "Follow me!" And the line surged back up the beach, back toward the Aztecs.

Olaf exploded in insane laughter. He drew back his arm and let fly with Mjolnir.

The hammer flew. The stubby little handle and the cinder block of steel flew. Up and up, farther, faster, harder than was possible. I mean, it was like that hammer had a rocket backpack.

Mjolnir flew toward Huitzilopoctli.

IV

Huitzilopoctli carried no weapons, at least not in the conventional sense. In one hand he had a sort of smoking mirror. It was round, like a discus or a squashed Frisbee. It was maybe ten feet in diameter.

In his other hand was a snake. The snake was a brilliant, shocking green. The snake wrapped back over Huitzilopoctli's shoulder. Its tail disappeared in the god's iridescent feathers.

Mjolnir flew. Every head craned back to watch it. Every eye, Viking and Aztec, watched.

There was a sound like a thousand-pound bullet slamming into a million pounds of raw beef.

Mjolnir hit Huitzilopoctli in his left arm. Hit him just above the elbow. The hammer broke through flesh, shattered bone, ripped the arm off, and sent it spinning slowly through the air.

Ten thousand voices wailed.

The arm, as long and thick as a subway car, fell. The Aztecs beneath it scattered. But it's tough to run in sand.

The arm landed with a terrific impact that sent shock waves to weaken knees and ruffle hair. A dozen Aztec warriors lay crushed.

And let me tell you, this wasn't some fake, unreal arm. Huitzilopoctli may have been a god, but I saw splintered white bone, as thick as an old oak tree.

Mjolnir inscribed an arc through the sky, then came racing back to Olaf's waiting hand.

The Vikings roared.

The Aztecs wailed.

Huitzilopoctli said nothing. He swooped around, slowed, then, as both Vikings and Aztecs fell back, making room, he landed. Just stopped flying, put down his legs, and landed. He was about the height of a five- or six-story building. Maybe ten times as tall as Olaf. Fifty times taller than me because I was hugging the sand now.

One huge, sandaled foot planted itself just a few dozen feet away.

Jalil's face was in the dirt beside mine. He shot me a look. "We can hurt the foot," he said.

I assumed he was babbling. But David was nodding agreement.

The Aztec god's big toe was as big as all of me. But yeah, a sword would hurt it. Had to hurt.

"Who are you, human, that you come to trouble me?" a voice demanded. A huge, rolling voice devoid of emotion, devoid of even the possibility of emotion.

Olaf looked nervous. He spoke up bravely enough but he sounded like a Chihuahua yapping at a tank. "I am Olaf Ironfoot!"

"Who sends you against me?"

"I come to free Odin One-Eye from unjust captivity in the dungeons of Loki!"

I don't know if Huitzilopoctli was stumped by this or thought it all made perfect sense. I couldn't see his blue-and-gold face. Couldn't see the burning supernova eyes.

"You have a brave heart," Huitzilopoctli said. The word "heart" sounded like an obscenity.

The snake on his shoulder lunged, quicker than any human eye could follow.

The green fangs closed around Mjolnir.

Olaf jerked the hammer back and tried to swing. But the windup was short. His arm was being blocked by the snake. Mjolnir flew, but ineffectually.

The magic hammer circled back to Olaf's hand.

Huitzilopoctli threw the smoking mirror. Like a Frisbee. It skimmed out and then, just like Mjolnir, circled back, spinning at impossible speed just a few feet above the sand.

Olaf jumped. Straight up. A high jump.

Not high enough. The mirror sliced off Olaf's one real foot. It clanged against the iron foot. It careened off, still spinning, and into the Viking ranks.

The deadly, ten-foot-wide disc sliced men in two. I don't know how many men. A lot.

Sven Swordeater was sliced in half, right at the belt. The top of his body slumped to the sand. His legs remained standing. He landed on his side. I could see him staring at his still-standing legs.

Olaf was on his back. Crippled. He threw Mjolnir but the throw was weak and wild. It flew past Huitzilopoctli's head, ruffling a few bright red feathers.

The Aztec god reached down with his good hand.

"Now!!" David cried.

He was up, I was up, Jalil was up, Thorolf was up, all of us running madly for the near foot.

I got there first. I held my sword stabbing-style, drew it up, arched my back, and down, down, down! The point sliced into the foot. Thorolf's ax, David's sword, and Jalil's all bit deep.

Nothing!

No blood, no cry of pain, no agonized reflex.

Huitzilopoctli lifted a helpless Olaf Ironfoot off
the sand. He held him by the legs and used the
jaws of the snake to hold the top half.

He broke Olaf in half and swallowed the king's
still-beating heart.

Chapter
V

The Vikings broke and ran. No good. As David had predicted, they were caught trying to shove the boats off the beach.

I don't know how many died in the massacre that followed. Thousands, I guess. I don't know how many were taken prisoner. I was. David was. Jalil? April? We had no way of knowing in the mad chaos.

It took all the rest of the morning and into the afternoon for the Aztecs to round everyone up. Meanwhile, we sat in the sand. No food. No water. Hot, with the slowly sinking sun blistering the open wound on my head.

Finally, with evening coming on, they marched us into New Tenochtitlan in columns, armed Aztecs all around us. We stumbled with the weariness of the defeated through huge gates, onto streets laid out and cobblestoned with mathematical precision.

Women and kids came out of the houses to taunt us. Throw things at us: ashes from the fireplace. Bones. Feces. It wasn't pretty.

I tried to look around and see if I could spot Jalil or April. I hadn't seen either of them. But it was a sea of heads, big, tall Vikings with their heads down, but still tall enough to screen Jalil or April.

David was beside me. He was looking around, too. Looking for a way out. David, the insecure hero-wanna-be. This was all some kind of macho party for him.

Me? I wanted out, too. But I wanted out of it all. I was done with Everworld. I was ready to go home, stay home, sit in my desk at school and do my homework and take my quizzes and call the teachers "Sir" and "Ma'am" and rush straight home to tell my mom I loved her and tell my dad he was my hero.

That was the direction of my escape: home. The real world.

But David was busy sizing up the walls and the defenses and the proud, happy, cocky Aztec warriors.

Down along broad avenues we trudged. Neat, spotlessly clean adobe and stone buildings rose on either side of us. Businesses, I suppose, shops. And some houses. Some of the buildings were three stories high. All were crowned by deliriously happy Aztecs waving palm branches and throwing poop.

"They don't throw food," a voice said.

I jerked my head around.

"Jalil! Where have you been? David, Jalil's here, man. Didn't see you, where were you?"

"Hanging back," he said calmly. "I wanted to see if you guys were in any special trouble first."

That kind of annoyed me. But this wasn't the time to complain about Jalil's tendency to look out for himself.

"I don't see anything yet," David muttered. "But you know, they'll probably party all night. Get faced, pass out, maybe get careless . . ." He dodged a flying turd. He dodged. I didn't.

"They aren't throwing food," Jalil said again.

"You were hoping for watermelon and fried chicken?" I snapped as I wiped the stuff off with my sleeve.

"You know, you turn into a real redneck when you get stressed," Jalil said with a smirk.

"What about food?" David asked. "So what?"

"So, if you're looking to pelt the losing army with stuff, you go and dig out the garbage, right?

You hit them with apple cores and . . ." — he rolled his eyes toward me — ". . . chicken bones and watermelon rinds. But these folks aren't throwing food. Not even scraps. And look at them. The civilians, I mean."

I looked. Looked more closely, I mean.

"Skinny," I said.

"Malnourished," Jalil said. "Borderline starvation. The soldiers are well-fed, but the kids and the women are not. Plus, do you see any old folks?"

I didn't. And I didn't like where Jalil was going.

"Huitzilopoctli eats the hearts. Who eats the rest?" Jalil asked.

It was bad walking through a crowd of people who looked at you as an evil invader.

It was worse walking through people who looked at you as lunch.

They walked us past the base of the mountainously tall pyramid. Huitzilopoctli was nowhere in sight.

The pyramid reeked. The stench was intolerable. It made you hold your breath.

It wasn't hard to guess the source of the smell. The steps of the pyramid, from top to bottom, were covered with a dried crust many inches thick.

Blood.

I looked up those stairs and imagined how much blood it would take, and how quickly it would have to be spilled, for it to run all the way down from those heights.

I wanted to go home. I wanted that very badly.

CHAPTER VI

"Well, this isn't all that bad," I said. It was an hour later. We, that is to say me, David, Jalil, and about two thousand of our closest Viking friends, were all locked in an enormous room. The ceiling was maybe twenty feet over our heads. The walls so far away they'd have been a ten-minute walk. Massive pillars, each as big around as a sequoia, held up the ceiling.

Up there, interspersed between pillars, were grates to let in air and light. The light was fading fast. It was already as dark as my basement at home. People walked across the grates. Probably stopped and looked down at us. I couldn't really tell.

The Aztecs were better builders than the Vikings. That was for sure. The Vikings were at the log and straw stage pretty much. The Aztecs were into the great big Toyota-sized stones form of building.

And the Aztecs cared about the simple things in life. Recessed into one wall were a series of stone cubicles with toilets. You did your business, yanked a chain, and they flushed.

And they had baths. Centered in the vast hall, low-slung square vats of warmish water.

The Vikings, naturally, had no interest in the baths.

I guess no one in that room had much interest in anything. The Vikings were quiet. None of their usual boisterousness. None of their bragging. No one calling for a poem or a song or a tankard of ale. No one threatening to split anyone open with an ax.

Just glum, downcast faces. Not surprising. Everyone knew. Everyone knew what was coming for us. Didn't know when, but we knew we were going to be marched up the stairs of that pyramid, where the priests would stretch us back over the stone altar and expertly cut out our hearts while our blood ran rippling down the steps.

Couldn't think about that. Couldn't. It made my stomach heave, my heart miss, my throat clench.

"Wouldn't mind washing the crap off my head," Jalil said.

I breathed. I'd stopped when that hideous image popped into my head.

I held out a hand, palm up, inviting. "Go for it. Doesn't look like there's going to be a fight over the hot water."

Jalil looked nervous. So did David.

"Locker-room willies all over again, huh?" I mocked them. "Afraid the big, mean Vikings will laugh at your . . . equipment?"

"It's a jail," Jalil said. "You realize that, right? No women? Bunch of guys looking for the weak ones so they can . . ."

"I'm not sitting here with crap smeared all over me," I said. "I'm taking a bath."

It was a small expression of courage. But I needed to do something besides sit there and imagine what it would feel like to live for those last few seconds staring up at my still-beating heart.

Like Sven Swordeater had gaped stupidly at his own legs.

Like . . .

Breathe. Breathe. Don't show the fear.

"I'd prefer a shower," I said, trying unsuccessfully to sound nonchalant. "I've never been a bath person. But I guess I'll make do."

I began to strip off my clothes. The Norsemen did not seem especially fascinated. One glanced up, I suppose to see if, as an outlander, I had something unusual, say a tail.

Naked, I climbed up into the bath. I settled in slowly because right about then it occurred to me that the baths might not be baths.

But no, my bare feet found smooth stone. The water rose around me as I shivered down into it. There was something semiliquid, like melted wax, in a woven-leaf dish. I stuck a finger in and smelled.

"Soap," I said. "Kind of flowery, but it's soap." I began to carefully wash the matted gash on my head. I didn't have any Bactine but I could at least get it clean.

"What do you do?" the curious Viking asked gruffly.

"I'm taking a bath."

He shook his head. "Your comedies will not lift many hearts today, friend minstrel."

I scooped up some of the mango-smelling goo and lathered it into my hair. Jalil was next to climb in. Then David. Three all-American kids with a lifetime of soap and deodorant jingles playing in their heads. We were in the third circle of hell, but determined not to smell bad.

I lay back and closed my eyes. I knew I wasn't ready to sleep. But I could lay back and think of something other than the horror I'd seen that day.

I could think about lying on the couch, watching the tube. I could think about playing tag football in the park down by the lake, using the pull-up bar as a goalpost. I could think about me and a few buds catching the train and heading down to Chicago on a hot summer day and wandering around Navy Pier with our shirts off, looking for girls, looking for fun, looking for trouble.

I could think about something besides the impossible monster that would soon be feasting on my heart.

No. I couldn't. I couldn't think of anything but that. Nothing but pictures of the brutality I'd witnessed. And the things that might have happened or even be happening to April.

Had Senna known? When she dragged us into this, had she known what it would be like? Had she known she'd be dragging her half sister into this? Me, Okay. Senna and I were done, but what about April? They lived together, for God's sake.

I opened my eyes and looked around. David was deep in thought. Jalil, too.

I wanted to ask them. They wouldn't know the answer, but didn't we have to at least think about it? Ask ourselves what we were doing there? Jalil would at least have some kind of theory. Something more profound than my own simple belief that we were screwed, screwed, utterly, irretrievably screwed by Senna Wales.

"So how do we get out of here?" David wondered, his head pinkish-white with lather.

"On a plate, surrounded by potatoes and carrots," I said.

He shot me a dirty look. "How do we get out of here?" he repeated.

Jalil looked blank. I looked blank. I was tired. Exhausted. The warm water made me want to sleep. To sleep was to escape back to the real world.

"We have more than a thousand of the toughest warriors anyone ever saw," David said, looking around at the Norsemen.

"We have squat," Jalil said. "They don't work for us. We're minstrels, remember? No one promoted us to generals."

"Hope April's okay," I said.

Stupid! Don't think about April again. Don't think about April. Don't picture what might be happening to her.

Breathe.

"She's probably okay," David said. "Her. And Senna."

I exploded. Don't know why, I just blew up. "Senna can die for all I care! Senna can be Big H's next meal for all I care! Forget Senna! She's the stupid head-case who got us all into this!"

Breathe. The vise was around my chest, squeezing the air out of my lungs, the blood out of my heart. I could feel my heart. It was right there, in my chest, under the ribs, under the breastbone, my God, they would split me open like a chicken, chop through the cartilage, my heart, beating, arteries pulsing, the blade, the serrated obsidian blade would sever the veins and arteries and my heart would . . .

I would scream. I would scream and beg and they wouldn't care, wouldn't hesitate, I was nothing to them, nothing to the blood-crazed god who would eat my heart.

Breathe. Breathe.

Breathe.

"Okay, look," David said in a low voice. "It's bad. As bad as it can be. But we have to deal with it as well as we can. There has to be a way out. Has to be."

Jalil laughed with no trace of humor. "David, the blood on that pyramid? Tens of thousands of people have gone up there to lose that much blood. Tens of thousands. Maybe hundreds of thousands. They probably all thought there was a way out."

I climbed out of the tub.

Breathe, Christopher. Breathe.

Chapter
VII

Driving up the middle, shirt off, ball bouncing up to imprint its pebbly surface on my hand, Nikes slipping on the polished wood surface. A hand shot out, tried to snag the ball. No way. I shouldered him aside.

The basket right in front of me, wide-open . . .

Memory flooded my brain. Vikings. Aztecs. Olaf split open like a chicken, Sven sliced in half.

Huitzilopoctli.

I lost the ball. It bounced away. One of the "shirts" snagged it, turned, and started driving down the court.

"What the hell happened to you, Hitchcock?" the coach yelled.

My fellow "skins" glared at me.

"Hamstring," I said, reaching down to hold

my leg. I limped off the court and sat on the bleachers.

I was back. Somehow I must have finally fallen asleep in Everworld. Hard to imagine. I'd been lying there on clean straw beside dirty men, staring up into blank darkness and trying to think about anything, anything besides that pyramid.

But I had fallen asleep. It was the only way I could possibly be here. Back in the real world. It's the way it worked. We didn't know why. Fall asleep in Everworld, you woke up back in the old life, the old body, with two intact sets of memories: the dull, ordinary details of another dull, ordinary day of school and home and more school. And you had the memories of the other side. Memories that were not so dull.

It, like the real me, the normal me, the me that didn't attack Aztec gods with Viking swords, got a little update every now and then. And vice versa. Like I, we, both of me were tuning in to CNN every once in a while and learning about what was going on with the other self.

Oh, interesting, I see I got a B-plus on the chem test.

Oh, interesting, I see I'm about to have my heart ripped out to feed Big H.

Well, thanks for the update. Good luck getting to third base on your date Saturday!

Thanks, and good luck to you in escaping from cannibal hell. See ya!

The others. I had to find the others. But there was still another ten minutes before we were supposed to hit the showers.

Somehow, somehow, I didn't know how, we had to stay here. We had to not go back.

Maybe there was some copy of me over there, too bad. As long as I, Christopher, the brain, the memories, the thoughts, the sense of humor, the nasty, self-interested creature called Christopher, isn't there, I don't care. Huitzilopoctli can eat my heart. As long as I'm not there to see it.

"Coach!" I yelled too loudly.

"What do you want, Hitchcock?"

"I need to see the nurse. Need a couple aspirin or whatever before this swells up."

"Uh-huh. You are the laziest human being I've ever met."

"Can I go?"

"You're no good to anyone here," he said.

I took off, careful to hobble as I went. Once in the locker room I showered fast, slipped on my clothes, and went looking for David.

Instead, I found April. She was in the hall, heading for the library.

"Oh, man!" I yelled.

She nodded, cautious. Amused, too.

I grabbed her arm and pulled her aside, practically shoving her into a locker.

"Where are you?" I hissed.

"Um, right here?" She pried my fingers loose.

"No, I mean on the other side. Where are you in Everworld?"

She shrugged. "Last I knew we were still on the longboat, heading for an attack on the Aztecs."

"You haven't fallen asleep yet," I said. "Either that, or . . . or I don't know," I finished lamely.

"How'd it go?" April asked.

"What?"

"The battle."

"We didn't exactly win," I said, trying to keep my instinct for sarcasm under control.

"Is anyone hurt?"

"Of us, no. Not yet. Although you, maybe, we don't know where you are. Sven's dead. Olaf's dead. And the rest of us are being held, pending the removal of our freaking hearts, after which we will be barbecued and served up buffet-style with coleslaw and baked beans!"

I had failed to control my sarcasm. I was nearly screaming. I was spitting on her with each percussive sound.

"Where am I?" April demanded, scared.

"We don't know. But you were back with the boats which, trust me, all belong to Huitzilo-poctli's happy crew now."

Her face was pale. The huge green eyes grew more huge.

"Oh, my God. They could be . . . I could be . . ."

"Entertaining the Aztec warriors? Yeah."

CHAPTER

VIII

She looked sick. That had been a harsh thing for me to say. I do that when I'm scared. I take cheap shots at people. Not one of my more attractive personality traits.

"What if I've been killed?" she asked. She put her hand on my arm.

She's a babe. Any other time I'd be doing a nice tingle and thinking, *My backseat or yours?* But I knew better. This wasn't a romantic touch. This was a "tell me it's all going to be okay" touch. I couldn't tell her it was okay. It wasn't.

I said, "Not to sound cold, April, but if you're dead over there, cool. That means we can survive dying over there. Believe me, with what's happening to me over there, I'd love to find out death isn't fatal."

She nodded. Slowly. Still looking sick. "And if

it is fatal? I could, what, drop dead any second because of something that's happening to me in Everworld? Something I don't even know about?"

"Have you seen David or Jalil?"

It took her a few seconds to respond. She was far away. I thought for a minute she'd snapped back. You know, that the Everworld April had arrived. But then, no.

"I saw Jalil in class. Just now. He didn't give me a look or anything. Are you sure both of them are alive?"

"Last I checked. I think I'd have woken up if someone came along to drag them away."

"What do we do?" she asked.

"Oh, gee, I don't know, I guess we go to our next class and wait to see if . . . I don't know. I don't know! This is bizarre. How do you make sense of this? How do you figure your life out when you're late for a class *and* about to be sacrificed to a pagan deity? I don't know which life to lead. Any second now I could wake up and boom, I'm back there, and then I, the me who's left here, I go around like you're going around now. Waiting to find out what happens when they cut the heart out of Everworld Christopher."

That vise was around my chest again, tightening, tightening.

"I wish I would go to sleep," April said. "Then at least I'd know where I was."

A teacher passed by right about then. She must have overheard part of what April said. The teacher shook her head slightly and walked on.

"We keep this up, pretty soon we'll be dead over there and in a looney bin here," I said.

"We need to find David," April said.

"What's he going to do?"

"I don't know. Something. I hope."

I was kind of hurt. April had just dissed me without meaning to. David would do something. Me? What was I good for? Not much, I guess.

The bell rang. Doors all down the hallway flew open. Kids exploded out of their classrooms, yelling and talking and laughing and running and swinging their backpacks up onto their shoulders.

David appeared. Jalil was with him.

"Are you here or there?" I snapped.

"I'm asleep," Jalil answered. "David's not."

"Come on, let's get out of here," I said.

"I can't cut last period!" April protested.

Suddenly, I was back in a dark room full of smelly men. "No!" I yelled.

Jalil jerked awake. David? Gone. Not in sight.

I looked around, trying to see what had awakened me. There were Aztec warriors making their way through the flopped-out throng.

A half-dozen heavily armed warriors. And two characters who looked like Pig Pen from Peanuts. All grown up, and still refusing to bathe.

They wore black. Probably. It was hard to tell what color their long robes might have once been. Their hair was long, matted, sticking out in dreadlocks, hanging in greasy strands.

Their faces were blackened. Not black black, because unlike the Vikings, who had evidently welcomed all races to their happy little Looney Tunes world, the Aztecs were all identically copper-skinned and black-haired. These guys were black not from melanin but from soot and cinders and a complete aversion to soap.

I'd only thought the Vikings smelled. The Vikings were walking, talking Clinique sales-people compared to these two. The Vikings were dirty by accident. These two had made a career out of being filthy.

The reek was intense, powerful, hideous, and disturbing. It was the reek of body odor and dirt and fungus. But most of all, it was the stench of dried blood.

The two walking sewers, and their escort of well-groomed warriors, picked their way gingerly through the snoring bodies.

From time to time they would point at one of the Vikings. Then the guards would rouse the Norseman, not unkindly, and pass him along, unescorted, to the far end of the room.

"Priests," Jalil commented.

"What are they doing?"

He slid his eyes sideways to look at me. "Choosing up teams for the big volleyball tournament. How would I know what they're doing? I'm as ignorant as you. Almost. But if I was to guess, I'd say they're ordering off the menu."

The priests kept coming. Should we sidle away? Or would that draw attention? It was like some awful version of the old classroom game: Keep the teacher from calling on you.

Jalil and I pretended to go back to sleep.

Breathe, Christopher, I told myself.

"These two," the priest said. "Young. Their hearts will be tender and unblemished."

CHAPTER IX

I could have said, "No! Not me!" I didn't.

I stood up. Shaky. Numb. Like I couldn't quite feel my own body. Maybe I was trying to convince myself I wasn't really here. Maybe I wanted to believe that I was back there, back in the world, back in school, in a familiar hallway, standing by lockers, talking to my friends, far away, not here.

It couldn't be real. Could not be.

I stumbled, a step behind Jalil. The warriors were almost gentle in their treatment. Respectful, even. Not just to us but to the Vikings as well.

The Vikings went along like sheep. We did, too. But I guess I expected more from the Norsemen. They just hung their heads and shuffled along.

"Where's David?" I asked Jalil.

He shook his head.

"Figures he would find a way to hide out," I said bitterly.

We were outside. The moon cast a blue glow over the city. Golden adobe walls and terra-cotta roofs and volcanic black cobblestones were all blue and silver, shadows and darkness.

The air was humid. Jungle air. Warm, even at night. Thick. But there were no mosquitoes. Strange. Maybe Huitzilopoctli had banished them. Maybe he didn't want any competition for the blood supply.

I did see rats, or something awfully much like rats, scurrying across our path, trundling along the bases of walls.

They marched us along the street in near silence but for the shuffle of feet. Maybe two, maybe three hundred of us, guarded by no more than twenty warriors.

"Not many guards," I whispered to Jalil.

He nodded. "They're armed, we're not. But it's not like they're carrying shotguns or machine guns. One guy with a stone sword can't stop ten times his own number."

It was weird. We could have taken the guards down. We didn't. No one but us even seemed to be thinking about it. The guards themselves were laid-back. Relaxed.

"Come on," I said. "No one said we have to keep up." I jerked my head subtly.

Jalil caught my hint. We started walking a little more slowly, letting the Vikings flow around us. Maybe I was looking for David. Maybe I was just looking for an opportunity. Something. Anything.

What we found was Thorolf. He's a picture-book Viking: big, big arms, big chest, big beard. An older guy. Middle-aged. Not a kid. But we liked him. Thorolf was about as close as you could get to a mellow Viking.

"Thorolf!" I whispered.

"Yes, it is me. More the shame."

He didn't look like himself. Not the bluff, loud, backslapping, guffawing guy we knew.

Then again, I wasn't exactly myself, either. Imminent death will do that to you.

"Thorolf, we can take these guys," I whispered. "There's hundreds of us. Just a handful of them."

He looked puzzled. "We are prisoners."

"What Christopher is suggesting is, maybe we don't have to stay prisoners," Jalil said.

Thorolf kept on looking dumb. "We lost the battle. Their power was greater than ours."

"Yeah, we were there, dude," I said. "We know who lost and who won. But that was before. Right now we outnumber these guys about ten or fifteen to one. Bada-bing, bada-boom, we take them down, run for the gate, make it to the boats, and haul butt."

"Their god is too powerful. Even Mjolnir wielded by Olaf Ironfoot could not defeat him."

"Maybe Big H — Huitzilopoctli, I mean — maybe he's asleep. I mean, it's night, right?"

Jalil jumped in with his usual "I've figured it all out" tone of voice. "If there are still warriors in this society it can only mean that Huitzilopoctli limits his involvement. I mean, why would those guys still be training and practicing and making weapons and so on, if all they had to do was dial up Big H every time they ran into trouble?"

"What he said," I urged Thorolf, pointing at Jalil. "Come on, man. Give the word. Let's take these guys out!"

"Give it up."

David! He was just a few paces behind us.

"Oh, so nice of you to join us," I said, torn between relief and annoyance.

He shrugged. "I didn't go anywhere. I've spent the night trying to get some of these guys to work on an escape. No luck. Not happening."

We sidled back from Thorolf to join David.

"They don't get it," David explained. "For these guys the battle was it. The last word. They bring Mjolnir, the Aztecs bring Big H, everyone's brave and heroic, our side loses. So that's it. Now they're prisoners. The end."

Jalil nodded. "I was afraid that was it. Fatalism."

"Fatal is right," I muttered.

"It's a fatalistic outlook," Jalil went on, probably soothed by the sound of his own brain churning. "It's what comes of believing that great supernatural powers control your life."

"Yeah, well, great supernatural powers do," I said. "Or didn't you happen to notice the big blue guy with the snake on his arm?"

"No. Bull. I'm not saying Huitzilopoctli isn't real. I'm just saying he doesn't seem to be able to keep his people fed. And anyway, Olaf knocked Big H's arm off with Mjolnir. So he's not invulnerable."

We had reached the end of our march. We had gone around what looked like the back side of the pyramid. There was a large building there, four stories tall, with no windows and a single large door. The door was open, a rectangle of golden, welcoming light.

The head of our column started through.

"Now or maybe never," David said.

"The three of us, alone?" Jalil said. He shook his head. "You ask me to commit suicide before I can be murdered? Uh-uh. There may still come a better chance."

I hesitated, waffling between the two of them. Then, I heard a strange, incongruous sound. The sound of a female voice giggling.

"There may be a better chance," I said.

We reached the doorway. Stepped through, behind the first hundred or so Vikings.

Inside there was a line of nine priests. A Supreme Court of dirt, crusted blood, and odor. Several of them had knotted cords of thorns passed through their tongues, lips, cheeks, ears. Some of the thorns were an inch long. There were lacerations from pushing the thorns through the flesh. Sideways, in some cases. Some of the priests had ears that looked like the fringe on a buckskin jacket.

The Aztec priests took their body piercing very seriously.

At one end of the room was the best buffet table I'd ever seen. Huge mounds of bananas, mangoes, brilliantly red tomatoes, and something that looked like cactus with the prickles removed. It was like the exotic produce section of the supermarket, times ten. There was roasted corn and roasted potatoes. Eggs in a dozen different sizes. Whole pigs. Whole . . . some other animal. There were pottery jars full of beverages. Flowers. Pastries. Tortillas. Beans.

It was a brunch at the Aztec Hyatt Regency.

But, as hungry as I suddenly was, the food was only the second most interesting thing about the room.

Because behind the line of priests were women. Young, attractive women. A lot of women. At least one, maybe two for each prisoner. A lot of pretty, underfed women, most as skinny as Courtney Cox, many with faces painted yellow, and very little clothing between them.

"Our farewell party," Jalil said mordantly.

He was right, of course. The Vikings had mentioned this aspect of Aztec behavior. For the Aztecs, feeding your heart to Huitzilopoctli was an honor. (One they themselves tried hard to avoid.) They figured the human sacrifices should be in good shape, well-fed, and happy. They were going to stuff us full of food and booze they themselves didn't have enough of. All to make us fit for Huitzilopoctli.

The Aztecs were giving us a nice send-off. But still, a send-off.

And yet, I thought, *if you gotta have your heart ripped out, you might as well enjoy the last few hours.*

Chapter X

"Eat up," David said. "But stay away from the women."

"Yeah? How about, forget you?" I said. I grabbed a fried plantain and a piece of what was probably ham. Maybe ham. There were two attractive women draped around me, clinging, hands reaching here and there with very pleasurable effect. "Did someone die and make you God, David? Must have missed that."

"Is that ham any good?" Jalil asked.

I took a big, ripping bite and chewed it in David's face. "Yeah, it's very tasty. Wish I had some yams to go with it."

Jalil nodded. "That young lady on your arm there? That's what she'll be saying about you: tasty. Wish she had some yams to go with you."

Jalil was right. Later, tomorrow or whenever,

this skinny girl would be gorging herself sick on my left calf, ripping at it with her tiny white teeth, smacking her lips, enjoying the crispy, crunchy, fire-roasted skin. . . .

"Get away," I muttered. I gave her a shove. Not a harsh shove. Not as harsh as I ought to give someone who was thinking of whether she'd have me broiled or fried.

She shrugged and took her friend off with her.

The Vikings, needless to say, were not even slightly restrained. All around us was a TV evangelist's vision of hell: gluttony, drunkenness, and more different types of wanton behavior than you see on Cinemax late at night.

My vision of heaven. If you left out the part where they cut out your heart and eat you.

"You know what?" David whispered to Jalil and me as we huddled together like the three biggest losers ever to blow a cool party.

"What?" I moaned, unable to stop myself from looking around at everything I was missing.

"I don't know if anyone has ever tried to escape from the Aztecs, but I know one thing for sure: If anyone ever did try, they didn't try during this particular phase."

Jalil nodded. Even he looked wistful. "Guess not, probably. Most are like Thorolf. They figure it's fate."

"So we book?" I said skeptically.

"Yeah," David said, putting on his crud-eating, fear-nothing, James Bond grin.

Save me from insecure jerks with hero fixations. I looked at Jalil. Jalil was a prickly, self-serving know-it-all, but he wasn't trying to prove to the world that he was Conan the Barbarian.

"Now or maybe never," Jalil said.

He looked sick. I nodded in approval. I trust a guy who looks sick when he's getting ready to do something suicidal. If I'd had a mirror I'd have seen one sick face looking back at me. Ninety percent of the trouble in this world comes from guys who think they have something to prove.

"You know what we do?" I suggested. "We walk right out the door."

David nodded. "Yeah. Like we're going outside for a smoke or to take a leak."

"Cool and calm," Jalil agreed. "Then, when they try and grab us, we run. But where? Which way?"

"Out of this city," I suggested. "Into the jungle."

"April," David said.

"We can't help April dead," I said harshly.

"We all go home together, or no one goes," David said. "Us, April, Senna."

"Yeah, whatever," I said.

"Not the jungle. Down the shore," Jalil said. "Down the beach, that's a footrace. Maybe we can win. But into the jungle, that's about animals and bugs and quicksand and being chased by guys who know the jungle a lot better than we do."

Made sense to me. I jerked to my feet very quickly. I didn't want to have a deal with David doing a big "Let's go, team!" thing.

I wiped my sweaty palms down my pant legs. "I would trade my mother for an Uzi," I muttered.

The three of us walked through the wild, drunken, gulping, pleasuring crowd. We looked like a trio of missionaries who'd stumbled into Caligula's New Year's Eve party.

Legs stiff-casual, arms jerking with a pathetic, overdone display of nonchalance, we headed for the door, still open to the warm night air.

Two guys made up with eagle feathers and craft-show eagle hats stood there, arms crossed over their hairless chests. Closer. Closer. My eyes strained for the first sign that the two eagle knights would whip out their obsidian swords and hack us to death.

"Laugh," David whispered tersely. "Talk."

"Ah-hah-hah-hah!" Jalil said.

"Yeah, you are so right!" David yelped with idiot enthusiasm. "The Cubbies are going all the way this time. Hah-hah-hah!"

"You're killin' me, that is so funny!" I said with the kind of phony cheer you usually reserve for visits with Great-aunt Whatever at the old folks' home.

Closer. Closer. Nothing. No movement. No reaction.

I grinned at one of the guards. "Great party!"

He reached for his sword hilt.

I swung. Big, dumb right-hand aimed straight for his chin. I missed his chin and caught him in the side of the head.

Swung again. Caught air.

The sword was out. The second guy was moving fast. David slammed into him, knocking him back against the doorjamb.

My guy whipped his sword in an uppercut that swished a millimeter from my chin. I fell. I kicked. A little of both. My foot caught shinbone.

I slammed on my back, wind gone. Jalil swung on my guy. Connected with his ear. My guy staggered. David was all over his guy, swarming him with short punches, staying in close, gasping like a beached fish.

I crawled, tried to fill my lungs, staggered up just as my guy went down. I snatched his sword from his weakened grip and took a wild swing. Obsidian flakes caught in his collarbone. I yanked the sword out.

All this with no yelling. No cries of alarm. Grunts of surprise and effort and pain.

"They don't box," David said, panting.

His victim's face was a mess from a dozen hard, short jabs. The guy hadn't even managed to draw his sword. The guy looked like his brain had been knocked into next week. Confused, stupid.

"Let's haul," Jalil said.

Into the night, running, sneakers on flagstones bouncing weird, UFO echoes off the walls. My heart was hammering. Huitzilopoctli would hear it! He would hear my heart and come to take it from me.

I still had the heavy, awkward sword.

"Which way?" David asked.

It was dark. Not civilization dark. This was no-streetlight dark. Middle-of-the-woods dark. The moon was behind the clouds. We could easily lose one another in this dark. And we had long since lost our way.

Then, not fifty feet away, we saw her.

She shone as if the moon were sending down a single, tight, floodlight beam just for her.

Senna.

Senna wore a long robe with a hood that was folded back to show her hair and face.

She said nothing. We stopped.

"Senna!" David cried.

She turned and began to move away. Walking quickly, almost seeming to glide.

David started after her. Jalil grabbed his arm.

"No," Jalil warned.

David shook him off. "She's trying to lead us to someplace safe."

Senna had stopped, still fifty feet away. Waiting. Silent.

"This feels bad, man," I whispered. "Why doesn't she say anything?"

"Doesn't want to wake up the whole neighborhood," David said.

Suddenly, from back in the direction we'd come from, an uproar. Loud, male voices.

"You know a way out of this city?" David demanded of Jalil and me.

I shook my head. "But I don't trust her."

"I'm going with her," David said. He started walking.

Jalil and I looked at each other. All either of us saw was the whites of wide-scared eyes.

"This is bull," I said.

"Yeah," he agreed. "But we have to stick together."

"She's the cause of all this," I argued. But already I was in lockstep with Jalil, following David, following Senna, feeling like, *Oh, God, it's just getting worse, and I wouldn't have thought that was possible.*

The uproar of angry voices grew louder behind us. I quickened my pace. Senna. Senna would show us the way out. *Yeah,* I told myself, *sure, yeah, she'd get us out of this.* Senna was our friend. Senna was one of us, freaky, yeah, but one of us, from the real world. I'd made out with her, after all, we'd been close, I'd gotten to second base, that had to count for something.

So why was she shining like a dashboard saint? Why was she silent? Why did she keep her distance?

Down a darker than dark street, she led us, led us with her own eerie light. Led us on with a feeling of dread that mixed with hope and left the dread all the stronger.

I so wanted to be home.

A turn. Down an alley. David stopped. We caught up with him. The three of us stared down that alley. Nothing. No Senna. No way out. Dead end.

"There must be a way out," David said. "She went somewhere. A doorway. We have to find it."

A rush of sandaled feet on stone. I spun around. A dozen warriors. More coming. The escape was over.

"She wants us dead, man," Jalil said. "She wants us dead."

Hard to argue with that. Because we were sure dead now.

CHAPTER
XII

The first time I really noticed Senna was at a pool party at her house. Not Senna's party, of course — she'd never do anything so normal.

It was April's party. April and Senna are half sisters. Hard to believe they share any DNA at all.

April has all the charm, all the flirty smiles and the knowing winks and the deep, rich laughs. April is like her name: she's springtime. You're around her, you start feeling that maybe life is okay, maybe there's nothing to worry about, maybe you'll get into the great school and get the great job and marry someone like April and still party with your friends when you're thirty years old.

Not that she's even slightly airheaded or giggly, it's not like that. It's just that April makes you think she's been out the door, had a good long look at life, and decided it's safe. She's not idiot-happy. She's wise-happy.

Senna would not be like that. It's not that she's depressed like some whiny chick singer with an acoustic guitar. Depressed is boring. Senna is not boring.

Senna is the night to her half sister's day. She's that night where you're wide-awake and the energy inside you is making you drum your fingers and hitch your shoulders and bounce your leg impatiently. Senna's the night you cruise the streets, driving slow, eyes so alert, so hungry for something, something dangerous and sexy.

Senna's a magician, always promising to reveal, always hiding what's important. Confusing, obscuring, misleading.

Walk along this dark alley with me, Christopher. Why? I won't say. I'll only smile. And when you ask whether there's anything to fear, I'll say, "Yes, Christopher. Wasn't that what you wanted?"

She'd been at school, of course. But it's a big school. Lots of girls. I hadn't noticed her. Why? I have a theory. I think I didn't notice Senna because Senna didn't want to be noticed. Not by me. Not yet.

But at that party, April's pool party, Senna had wanted me to see her, to focus on her, for my mouth to go dry, for my arms and legs to feel weak.

Strange, freaky girl. Never underestimate the dark side of the Force.

I'd always been the one in charge in previous relationships. I'm a big, glib, smart guy. I'm an expert at holding people at arm's length, at using wit to manipulate the distance between us.

I wasn't in charge with Senna.

She walked around the pool, one of those wrap-around skirts drifting open, a drink in one hand, the other hand resting just below her navel, a thumb hooked in the waist of her skirt, like a guy would hook a thumb in his jeans.

I made some dumb joke through the cotton in my mouth. She made a smile. I asked her if I could have a sip of her drink. She said no. I asked if she was there alone. She looked at me. Appraising. Serious. "I don't know," she said.

Stupid, the things you remember sometimes, huh? Stupid, the things that can fire up your imagination. A thumb in a waist, a refusal. A look that challenged me and made me realize instantly that I would fail the challenge.

Senna.

I never loved her; I knew, from that first moment I knew she'd betray me. But, good lord, I had wanted her.

As for her? I'm not as dumb as I may act sometimes. I knew she had no real interest in me, as me. You know? I knew she was looking down at me the whole time, not impressed. Not reached. Not touched. Not by me. Not really.

See, I knew she was using me for something, setting me up, making plans for me, me as a pawn, me as a tool, me as something she could pick up or put down as she chose.

Here's the sick thing? When she stopped seeing me I was a wreck. Not because I'd ever thought she would love me or sleep with me or be mine, all mine.

I was crushed because I'd felt her closing in, the predator to my prey. And I wanted her to destroy me. I guess I felt like in that moment of destruction, I would really know her. Understand something.

Now she had destroyed me. And still I knew nothing.

No Aztec love party this time. No food. No babes. A locked room. A toilet, no bath. A big, thick wooden door and stone walls and guards outside. The three of us sitting on our butts on stone, knees on elbows.

Maybe no one had ever tried to escape from the Aztecs before. That didn't mean they couldn't adjust.

"Had to be a mistake," David kept muttering. "She didn't lead us down there to trap us."

"You know, this faith you have in Senna is really romantic and touching and all, but you're a damned idiot!" I raged after about his tenth time. "She leads us all into this lunatic asylum to begin with, and next time we see her it's to lead us down a blind alley. So how about you get your head out of your butt, David? 'Cause here's a clue: She's not Snow Freaking White, and you aren't Prince Charming."

"Not the next time," David said.

Jalil sighed. "What?"

"I've seen her before this. After the lake, before this."

That got my attention. "Say what?"

"I saw her on the other side. In the bookstore. At least, it was, I don't know, like a vision."

"Your fantasies are not really all that relevant," Jalil said dismissively.

"It wasn't a fantasy. She was there. She told me there was going to be a big battle. Told me to stay out of it."

I swear if I'd had that sword back I'd have laid it into the dumb jerk's head.

"Heard her again, in my head," David said, staring down at the floor. "When the battle started. She said 'Run away. Run away, David.' She's not trying to kill us. She wants to save us."

"Hey, David. You're a Jew, right?"

"Half Jewish," he said.

"Yeah? Well you know the word 'schmuck'? Did I pronounce that right? 'Schmuck'? Or maybe you'd prefer a good old-fashioned Anglo-Saxon word, you —"

"Back off," David warned.

"Back off?" I yelled. "Back off? You hold out on us, you lead us after that evil chick, down that alley, so now here we are, trapped again, waiting to die —" My voice broke.

I put my head in my hands. I wanted to cry. I guess I did. How could I be there? How could I be there, waiting to die?

"I want to sleep, man," I said.

"That'd be good," David said. "Cross over, maybe get in touch with April. Find out where she is, how she's doing."

"We may not want to know," Jalil said.

"Can't sleep anyway, man," I said. "Can't sleep. In a couple hours . . . What are we going to do?"

"Had to be a mistake," David mumbled into his hands. "Senna didn't set us up. Had to be a mistake. We were too slow. She didn't have enough time. Probably our own fault."

David muttered about Senna. Jalil sat there talking to himself, spinning theories about Everworld, trying to figure out logically whether dying here meant death in the real world, or whether death here would merely bring us freedom from this awful place.

For a while I made responsive grunts to Jalil.

Then I stopped listening. David had his delusion. Jalil had his. David's world was somehow going to be about him playing hero. Jalil's world was going to somehow, somehow make sense. He was trying to keep his little house of logic Legos standing.

Me, I had no delusion. I just wanted to live. I just wanted to go home. What I had instead was imagination. Terrible thing, imagination is. See, without imagination you can't picture every horrible detail in advance. Without imagination death is just death. With imagination, death is detailed. Detailed and specific and so real.

No one slept. Hours dragged. Hurry up, get it over with. Hurry up and die.

Turn off my brain! Turn off the feeling, the so-terribly-real feeling of being grabbed by strong hands and bent back, back over the altar, the sight of filthy priestly faces intent on their work, as indifferent to me as a butcher is to a hog.

Obsidian knife rising.

Stomach muscles screaming.

Heart beating, oh, beating, beating, the bare skin of my chest vibrating with each desperate rhythm.

Feeling the jagged-edged knife cut.

Seeing the hands, the filthy, blood-caked hands diving into my own chest . . .

No.

No.

The door opened. Brilliant sunlight made me squint, made me cover my eyes.

No.

Chapter
XIV

The three of us stumbled outside. Out into clean, pure sunlight, still low on the horizon.

The Vikings were being assembled in the street. Hungover. Hair twisted. Beards matted. Dried vomit on their clothes. Exotic fruits and legs of lamb stuck in their belts and pockets, you know, in case they got hungry waiting to be eviscerated, in case the wait to die worked up an appetite.

I spotted Thorolf. As much a wreck as the rest. Eyes blinking owlishly. Expression resigned, defeated.

The other Vikings I'd known by name were gone. Sven Swordeater. Olaf Ironfoot.

"I don't see April," Jalil said.

"Maybe she's okay," David said. "She was with the boats. Maybe she's okay."

"Or dead," I grated.

The guards started us all moving. There were more guards today. I guess our example made them nervous.

We shuffled along, foot after foot, making a noise like some gigantic sack of dirt being dragged through the streets. Shuffle and stumble and mutter and glare. What a proud, brave bunch we were. I hated the Vikings. I hated us. Hated myself. Most of all I hated Senna.

So bright. So sunny. Bad things didn't happen on sunny days.

Down the street. Onto the vast, open plaza. They waited there, silent, impossibly silent, a thousand, ten, hundreds of thousands! Thin, gaunt, staring black eyes in deep sunken sockets, staring at us as we stumbled past. Staring at us. Staring at the food some of the Vikings carried.

All of New Tenochtitlan was turned out around the base of the pyramid, back at a safe distance, standing clear, holding in neat lines in neat rectangles, men, women, silent children. All bright and dark at once.

Soldiers, better-fed, taller, stronger, arrogant in ludicrous feathers and animal hats, were in front in a single file that outlined the masses.

We stopped. Like train commuters who'd reached a turnstile, we milled in disorder. Up ahead, not far enough ahead, too close, the priests were shoving the beaten men into a double line. Two by two, up the steps.

The pyramid was steps on steps. The basic construction, the blocks themselves, formed narrow, steep steps. But a broader, gentler stairway had been layered over this, still steep, but not so anyone would be likely to fall. To our left a central stairway of sorts, for more-than-human feet and legs. I could have climbed those stairs, too, but it would have been more climbing than walking.

Ahead of the three of us I saw the first rank of Vikings climbing. Up they went, the head of the snake that extended up out of the mass of victims.

They climbed, and the priests shoved, and suddenly it was my turn, suddenly filthy hands grabbed by biceps and shoved me into place, like an impatient first-grade teacher lining up the kids for a fire drill.

Jalil was beside me. David behind.

First step. Oh, God, we were climbing. Oh, God.

No.

Lift foot. Put foot down. Thigh and calf muscles work. Lift foot. Put foot down.

Oh, God. I was climbing. Had to stop. Had to stop! Had to stop!

Lift foot. Put foot down. Thigh and calf muscles work.

Legs shaking, quivering from the effort. Stomach wanting to heave. Heart . . . heart . . .

No!

Lift foot. Put foot down. Thigh and calf muscles.

I squinted to look ahead. Sunlight blinding. So far above us, but already too close. The head of the line was reaching the top. The black-robed priests waited.

We'd just go back over, that was it, Jalil was right, we'd die here, but we'd be back over there, laughing about it all, wondering if it was all just a dream, laughing, all of us together going, "Man, was that weird or what?"

I tripped.

David, behind me, put a hand out to steady me. Thanks. Thanks, David, wouldn't want a bruise, wouldn't want to fall and hurt myself. Oh, God, we were climbing.

The line stopped.

Then he appeared. Huitzilopoctli.

CHAPTER
XV

Huitzilopoctli stepped out of his temple and stood there, legs spread wide, towering over the dozens of priests.

"His arm," Jalil croaked. "Didn't heal. Still gone. He has limits. He can be hurt."

I snorted in absolute contempt. Jalil still believed he was going to think his way out of this. Was he out of his stupid, stupid mind? Didn't he see?

He looked at me. Our eyes locked. Yeah, he saw. He knew he was just making noise to drive away the panic. He knew.

Four priests came hustling out from offstage. They carried a turquoise pillow, holding it up for their evil god like they were offering him a mint. From that angle I couldn't see what was on the pillow, but then Huitzilopoctli reached down and raised a tiny, toylike Mjolnir.

It looked ridiculous in his massive hand. And I guess he thought so, too, because he held it up, displayed it for all to see,

Silence.

Then, Huitzilopoctli laughed.

And everyone in the plaza below us laughed, too. I had forgotten them. But hearing that echo of laughter I twisted my head around and saw the spreading crowd. They seemed so far down.

The effect on the Vikings was what you'd expect. Mjolnir was as much magic as they had. And now it was Huitzilopoctli's toy. They'd flashed the cross at a vampire and had the vampire laugh.

Then, having milked the desperate, near-hysterical laughs, Huitzilopoctli lay Mjolnir back down on the pillow. The priests hustled Mjolnir away, and the blood-mad god stepped back into his temple.

The line began to move.

I couldn't see the first killing. Or the next or the next. They were cut off from sight by the heads of those before me and the angle of the steps.

I couldn't see the first forty or sixty or a hundred killings. But at that point I began to see the stream. The sludgy, slow-moving stream of red that trickled and poured and congealed its horrifying way down the steps to our left.

It was blood over blood. The wet and fresh over the baked and crusted. The higher we climbed, the thicker the crust. The higher we climbed, the quicker the stream.

And then came the bodies. They rolled down. Stopped. Were kicked and shoved by lines of sweating priests.

Bodies untouched, except that in each there gaped a black-red wound, a hole where a heart had been.

Lift foot. Put foot down. Thigh and calf muscles.

Stop! Stop! Stop!

Lift foot. Put foot down.

Why couldn't I stop? Stop! Run! Run away!

Lift foot . . .

So close now. A sound. Oh, no, no, no, no. The sound of knife in flesh. The grunt of pain. The grunt of effort. The sound of wet scooping . . .

A line of women arrayed up the steps. A dozen. Hoods, cloaks, faces half-shaded.

Not looking at us, we were dead! No . . . one looking. Looking hard. Green eyes. Red hair.

April!

A dozen steps above us. She moved her head so slightly, side to side. "No," she signaled. Quiet.

Quiet? Why? To save her? To keep her from being found out? Screw her! No, no, no, Christopher, die a man, die a man. Help her live. Be a man.

I nudged Jalil. I met his eyes then carried his gaze over to her.

I twisted back to see David. He'd already spotted her.

The sound of blade on meat.

The ripple of blood trickling slowly in the heat.

The smell of it.

I looked at April. Silent, she mouthed a single word.

"Mjolnir."

CHAPTER
XVI

"What?" Jalil whispered to me.

"The hammer," I said.

April was just ahead now, we were almost abreast of her. Her robe parted ever so slightly. I saw pale flesh.

I saw steel.

"You up for this?" David asked softly.

Up for it? I was shaking in every muscle. I was drenched in my own fear sweat. I was ten minutes from having my heart cut out and fed to a creature that couldn't possibly exist.

"I like it better than the alternative," I managed to say.

"On three. One."

Lift foot.

"Two."

Put foot down.

"Three!"

I jerked my quivering muscles, broke from the line, and went for April like she was a lifeline and I was a drowning man.

Robe open!

Sword! Ax! A long knife! Viking weapons. Steel!

Hands fumbling, grabbing, missing, heart, gasping, heart, had it! My hand closed on the haft of an ax with a two-foot handle, a curved blade on one side and a pickax on the other.

"Go for the top!" David yelled, and I didn't need encouragement. The four of us plowed through and around the Viking line, onto the blood-slicked steps, running, leaping, scraping knees, climbing, up and running, running across the platform, the foul, reeking platform.

A Viking stretched out on the black altar, priest on his hands, priest holding his legs, knife high in the air, poised over a bared, blond-haired chest. Thorolf.

The knife man gaped, outraged, like I'd just farted in church and giggled about it. I ran straight at him. He was still gaping when I swung that ax. His head kept the expression as it rolled down the steps.

No soldiers! Priests, black, filth-encrusted, their flesh mortified by thorns. They ran, confused, then came rushing back.

"Damn it, Thorolf, get up!" I yelled.

I swung my ax at the line of priests. Jalil and David jabbed at them. What a surprise: The priests were not exactly profiles in courage.

They backed up again, yelling, praying, screaming, mad and scared and worried that things had gone suddenly strange at their little picnic.

"The hammer, you idiots!" April yelled. "Get the stupid hammer before he comes!"

I saw the hammer. Still on its cushion, atop a platform like an auxiliary, backup altar. I knew who April meant by "he."

The temple was impossibly tall above us. Open, yet dark. He could be just inside, watching, laughing, ready to come for us, ready to take over for his priests and murder us himself.

I jolted toward the hammer. David sword-whipped a warrior who'd come rushing up.

A sudden blow. I was down, breathless! What?

A priest had plowed into me. I jumped up, kicked him, leaped over, and ran, racing Jalil for the hammer.

The mass of priests charged at last. Too late!

The cushion. The hammer.

My fingers closed around the stunted handle of Thor's hammer.

The priests stopped. Stared. Babbled to one another in renewed confusion. That was okay, because the four of us were pretty lost, too.

"The Vikings," Jalil gasped, winded. "Show them the hammer."

I raced back to the edge of the platform. I held that hammer up in the air over my head. I yelled at the top of my lungs, "Mjolnir! The hammer of Thor! Come on, you bunch of babies, let's kick some Aztec butt!"

An excellent speech. A real cinematic moment.

Only I realized that the Vikings were no longer looking at me. They were looking behind me.

I felt the flesh on my back creep.

Slowly turned my head, slowly my eyes, all in slow motion, molasses. Towering over me. His one remaining hand clutched a dripping red mass. Red stained his mouth and chin.

I spun, kicked my leg out, whipped around, and like a pro pitcher throwing out a runner, I let fly with Mjolnir.

The hammer flew.

Huitzilopoctli just had time to look down before Thor's sledge hit him in the feathery loincloth.

The hammer came sailing back toward me, but I was too gone to notice. It sailed past.

Huitzilopoctli grunted. He got a "now I'm going to kill you!" look on his blue-and-gold face.

Then, slowly, slowly, he crumpled. Like a guy who's standing on his bike pedals when the chain breaks, he crumpled.

"Look out! He'll crush us!" April yelled. She jerked me aside.

David and Jalil ran. I ran. April ran.

Huitzilopoctli yelled out in agony.

He fell.

The Vikings roared to life.

The Aztecs moaned.

We were over that platform, around the side of the temple, and heading down the far side by the time we heard Big H hit the steps.

"April?" I gasped.

"Yeah?"

"I am your slave for life."

Chapter

XVII

No sleep, coming off battle, coming off an aborted escape, coming off that awful march up the side of that hideous pyramid. We were exhausted. Beyond exhaustion.

We wandered, lost in the streets of the city of Huitzilopoctli for an hour before we located a gate.

An hour during which time the sounds of combat and pillage and depredation grew louder, then fainter, then louder again.

Mjolnir had woken the Vikings out of their slumber. They had no swords or axes, but a thousand or more Vikings in the middle of a city is serious trouble anywhere. And they had Mjolnir. The breeze carried that cry to our ears.

"Mjolnir! Mjolnir!"

The Vikings historically didn't draw sharp

lines between killing soldiers and killing innocent civilians. I didn't care. Anyone who wanted to eat me wasn't innocent.

I ran. We ran, footsore and exhausted. Out of the gate. Out of that evil, evil city.

"The beach," Jalil said. "Still our best bet. The Aztecs will be busy with the Vikings now. We don't need anacondas and jaguars."

No one argued. We ran right back the way we'd come, away down across the battlefield. All the dead and wounded had been removed. I considered the ham I'd eaten the night before.

No, don't think about that, Christopher. You're alive, so shut up.

Onto sand. The sea. The Viking longboats were charred, smoking hulks. Charcoal boats. The Aztecs had burned them. Everything stank of drowned fires.

David cursed. "That's a crime."

"That's a crime? They burn some boats, that's what you object to in their behavior?"

"What it is is stupid," Jalil said. "All that wood. Even if they didn't know how to sail the boats, they could have salvaged the wood,"

"Let's keep moving," April pressed.

We kept moving along the beach, down the longboat graveyard.

"Nice robe," I said.

April gave me a weary smile. "What, this old thing? Just something I threw on. And now I think I'll just throw it off."

She whipped the robe off, twirled it into a ball, and threw it into a smoking hull. It began to smolder.

April still had her backpack with most of our worldly possessions. A CD player and some mostly bad music; a bottle of Advil; a book or two.

"So, what's your story?" David asked her.

"Well, I was in the boat. Saw the Vikings all come running when Huitzilopoctli showed up. I hid, but it didn't work. They found me. I thought they were going to kill me."

"Kind of was afraid they had," I admitted. "Or else . . . never mind."

"Yeah, or else," April said darkly. "I think that was the plan. Only this priest showed up. He asked me if I was a virgin."

"So naturally you lied?" I suggested.

"I said, 'Absolutely. I'm even a vegetarian.'"

I laughed. The first laugh in what felt like a million years. David and Jalil smiled.

"Anyway." April shrugged. "The priest decided I'd look good in the temple. They don't get many green-eyed redheads. So I was an official temple virgin."

"Good gig."

"Uh-huh. Till the ceremony's over. Then I think the virgins become property of the priests, who have their fun and kill the girls in another sacrifice. That's what I understood, anyway."

"Sick, messed-up people," David said. "Nazis without the tanks."

Jalil was walking backward. "I don't see anyone following us."

"They're busy," David said. "The Vikings finally got it together. I guess the hammer did it."

"Where are we going?" I wondered.

"Away from that place back there," April spat. "I just hope she makes it out of there."

We all stopped dead. "She? Who?" Jalil snapped.

April looked surprised. "Senna." She must have noticed our spooked expressions. "Yeah, I saw her. She showed me where to find the weapons I smuggled to you."

"Ha!" David yelled. "She was trying to help us."

I wasn't convinced. I knew what I'd seen. Or at least, I thought I did. But I kept my mouth shut.

"We can't leave her back there," David said flatly.

"We have no choice," Jalil said.

April said nothing. She was not rushing to the rescue of her half sister.

"We can wait till it's calmed down a little, till the heat is off us. We can go back. Find her." David nodded vigorously, trying to convince himself.

"You know what, David? On my big list of things that ain't happening, going back into New Whatever is number one. It's higher than 'sticking needles in my own eyes.' Not happening."

"She saved our lives," David argued. He stepped closer, bristling, playing the tough guy. "You're going to leave one of our own behind?"

I laughed. "David, I've just thrown down with Huitzilopoctli. You think you scare me?"

"You're just scared, period."

"Just scared? No. I'm not just scared. See, that makes it sound like some plain old everyday emotion. I'm terrified. Horrified. Overwhelmed with dread. I feel like my brain has been filled full of sewage and I'll never, ever be able to get it clean, like this stuff will eat me alive in my dreams, like I'll never see the world the same again. Scared? They want to eat us, you moron! They want to cut out our hearts and they almost did, you fool! You want to save Senna, go for it, Batman. See you later."

He didn't start walking toward the city. And I didn't start walking away down the beach.

"Look, Testosterone Twins?" April said. "Go

back, don't go back, either way, right now we need to get somewhere where we can rest and sleep and eat and be away from those freaks. We are beat-up, exhausted, worn down. David, you'd be lucky to walk back before you fell asleep in your tracks. So let's compromise, all right? Let's find a safe place."

"I know a safe place," Jalil said. "The real world. Didn't used to think it was safe. Gangs and drugs and racist cops and one thing or another, but I have changed that opinion. Nothing that exists in the greater Chicago metropolitan area is half as bad as what goes on back in that lunatic asylum. If I believed in hell it would be approximately like that city."

"All of Everworld can't be like that," David said.

It began to occur to us that we were moving farther from the ocean, now following the line of the riverbank toward the interior. The river even looked like it might curve back closer to New Tenochtitlan. No one was enthusiastic about that.

The river wasn't impossible to swim, but no one was ready to hand out any guarantees as to the animal life out in that increasingly brown, almost chocolate water. You see jungle, you see water, you think piranha.

Then we came around a spit of land, the last of the dwindling sand, and saw a bridge.

We crouched behind a tree that was far, far too small to hide us. Like four big Sylvesters trying to surprise Tweety Bird.

"Bridge," David said.

"Oh, is that what it is? You know, because I wasn't sure, what with it being this big stone walkway going from one side of a river to the other."

David blushed, embarrassed. "No guards. Not that I can see, anyway."

"Not even with your superpowers?"

This time he just ignored me. "We better move fast. No guards now, but there might be real soon. If they want to cut us off, this is the place."

He was right. He was also annoying. I considered telling him so, but now was not the time for a battle over who was in charge.

We started walking toward the bridge. Then faster. Faster, as the sense of urgency grew, faster, and then we were running, panting with the escape-panic chasing us.

Up onto the bridge, racing one another like all the bogeymen who ever hid in a dark basement were after us.

We reached the far side of the river. Stopped. Looked at one another and laughed sheepishly.

We started walking again. Down the far bank. Toward the ocean. Jungle to our right. Away from the city. Away from Senna.

Away from that city of blood and horror. And as far as I was concerned, I was never going back.

I was cured of the desire to learn what Senna had in store for me. Cured of that witch.

"Yogurt."

I started at the list in my hand. White, college-ruled notebook paper, folded in four.

Yogurt. Coffee filters. Double-A batteries. Toilet paper. Cookies. Liquid hand soap. Ground turkey.

The list was in my left hand. My right hand was on the push bar of a shopping cart. I was standing by the dairy case of the Jewel.

A woman in a long coat stared at me.

"Yogurt," I said.

She looked at me like I might be dangerous. I stared down at the yogurts. So many kinds. So many styles.

"So," I muttered under my breath. "The real world."

I was shopping for my mom. I remembered

her asking me. I remembered that the Real World Christopher hadn't slept much last night because the Real World Christopher knew that Everworld Christopher was getting ready to take a one-way trip to the human butcher shop.

Now RW and EW Christophers became one. I was me, and him. And who was me, and who was him, was impossible to say.

"So. He did fall asleep," I said, referring to EW Christopher. But it felt wrong calling him "he." Like he wasn't me.

It was evening here. My dad had forgotten to pick up the groceries, my mom was working late and wouldn't have time, so, restless, I'd volunteered.

Now here I was in the bright, overlit, too-busy, too-colorful, too-much-going-on-all-around-me grocery store and yet, I knew I was also asleep in the jungle at the edge of an empty beach.

"Excuse me," a middle-aged guy said and made a polite smile.

I pushed my basket out of the way. I needed ground turkey. I moved on to the meat counter and ordered a pound. Big slabs of red and pink and pale meat lay in rows, in mounds, in stacks.

I remembered the ham I'd eaten. I remembered the fact that all the bodies were quickly taken off the battlefield.

Had to be ham. The Aztecs must have pigs, right?

"Pound of ground turkey," I said to the butcher. I was sweating. This body was tired. Not as tired as my other self, but tired. It had been a rough couple of days. Two days here to one over there. The ratio seemed to change. The two universes were not in sync. The cog wheels of time moved in jerks, slips, forward, far forward. Fast, slow.

Two days here since I'd last slept, so briefly, over there. Two days of knowing that I was destined to be a human sacrifice. Two days of wondering, fearing, waiting to suddenly pop out of existence altogether, victim of a murder I'd never see or feel.

"Here you go. Anything else?"

I shook my head. Don't throw up. Don't throw up in the Jewel, Christopher.

I pushed the basket toward the checkout. Long lines. Forget it! Who cared about yogurt and coffee filters and . . . No. No. Don't lose it, Chrisman. Hang in there, Hitchcock. This is the real world. This is where you want to be.

I waited. I glanced at the *National Enquirer* and the *Globe* and the *Sun*. I considered picking up a *TV Guide*.

I had stopped sweating. My heart was calmer. My stomach . . . as long as I didn't think about it.

"Paper or plastic?"

"Plastic," I said. The big choice in the real world: paper or plastic bags.

I paid and pushed the basket out into rain that had made the night fall sooner. Not bad rain. Just enough, and cold enough, to make you want to run.

Over there, the other me was thirsty. We hadn't found water. Or food. Over there my head wound was throbbing. Over there we'd finally just fallen down where we were, dropped to the ground in a small clearing between towering trees.

I was standing watch. Only I wasn't, was I? I was here, which meant I was asleep. The jungle animals could creep up on us anytime. And worse than animals.

I piled the stuff in the back of my Cherokee. I drove home down tree-lined streets.

Home. My house. With the decrepit tree house out back that had been taken over by my little brother. My house, my lawn, the lawn I would have to mow on Saturday. Assuming I was alive and the rain stopped.

I loaded up the groceries, wrapped the handles

of the plastic bags around my wrists, wanting to make it all in one trip. Through the garage, up the deck, through the back door.

"You get the coffee filters?" my dad asked.

I nodded. "Uh-huh."

He was standing by the kitchen island, turning the salad spinner, TV on with the news. He's shorter than me by a couple of inches. The tall genes come from my mom.

"Is Mom home?"

He shook his head. "Not yet. Man, I should have had you pick up some new lettuce; this lettuce is going limp."

"Kind of like you, huh?" I said.

He nodded, accepting the hit. "A) Don't make crude jokes; B) don't make crude jokes about me; and C) come over here and put your hand in the Cuisinart."

My dad and I share a sense of humor. He has a medical supply business. You know, sells stuff to hospitals. I guess he doesn't get a lot of opportunity to be funny at work.

My mom is different. It's not that we're not close. But she works hard. She's a lawyer. Put herself through law school while she was pregnant with my little brother and my dad was being a dog, getting down with his secretary at the Holiday Inn. It all made her a little hard, carrying all that weight, me, my brother, my dad.

She's more serious than me or my dad. Has more of a temper, not that it's her fault. Her job is stressful and sometimes she'll blow up and then, look out. Ten minutes later she's apologizing and rubbing your shoulders and asking if you want a cookie or whatever, but that doesn't change the fact that we all take a step back when she gets that way.

"Is it a major tragedy if I bail on dinner?" I asked.

He gave me the fish eye. "You see that I'm cooking so you run away?"

I shrugged. "Well, there's that. Plus I wanted to hook up with some friends."

He didn't answer right away. "How are you doing, Christopher?"

"What do you mean?"

"I mean the last couple days you've been wandering around here like someone ran over your dog."

"I don't have a dog."

"A figurative dog, not a literal dog."

"I'm fine. It's just this whole heroin addiction thing," I said.

My dad rolled his eyes. "Go. Go chase some

girl and leave your mom and me and Mark to enjoy my world-famous limp salad and grilled chicken."

I laughed. I started to go. But then I didn't. I don't know why. The kitchen just seemed warm and, you know, like my kitchen. My house. Normal.

My dad looked up, saw I was still there. He shot me a questioning look.

"The ladies will just have to wait. I'm not going to let all of you get salmonella and leave me out."

I should find David and April and Jalil. I should check in. Plan. Work something out. Find an escape from our nightmare.

But I didn't want to think about Loki or Huitzilopoctli, trolls or blood-caked priests, Vikings or Aztecs.

I wanted a normal dinner in a normal world. I wanted my dad and my brother and, yeah, I wanted my mommy.

CHAPTER
XIX

Sitting on the couch watching sitcoms on TV. The definition of normal. When life goes weird on me I touch base with sitcoms. The familiar sets. The familiar sound of laugh track or live audience. The entrances and exits. The pauses as the actors wait for the laugh to build and fade. The familiar setups and payoffs to the jokes.

All that stuff is like part of my DNA. The new and the fairly recent: *Frasier* and *Seinfeld* and *Friends*. The older stuff, *M*A*S*H* and *Mary Tyler Moore* and especially the great, the incomparable *Dick Van Dyke Show*. The stuff is the map to my brain. The foundation of my thinking.

When life becomes surreal, unrecognizable, strange, I go back to the source. Talk to me, Niles; toss off that snobbish line and Frasier will take that Jack Benny reaction shot that milks laughs

out of thin air. Talk to me, Tim and the Tool Man;
show me that tired, satisfying formula, hah-hah,
too much power, better talk to Wilson about it.
Phoebe! Monica! Chandler, could you BE more
funny? Talk to me, Rob and Laura; make me
laugh, make me laugh at all the jokes I've heard
and seen a million times before.

Master of your domain. I hate spunk. Rucy,
wha are you ap to now? Ohhhh, Rooooob! So no
one told you life was gonna be this way, *clapclap-
clapclapclap*.

You're the guys I can count on. You're the guys
who stay the same, day in, day out.

I clicked back and forth, thumb on the "last
channel" button between an old *Mary* and a not-
quite-so-old *Friends*. A definite resemblance between Mary Tyler Moore and Courtney Cox.
Huh. Never noticed that before.

Stay focused on that, Christopher. Not Loki's
son the gigantic wolf, or Huitzilopoctli's priest-
killers, or the thousand terrors that even now
may be crowding around your sleeping body in a
jungle that may be a trillion miles away or right
here, in this very room.

The phone rang. I jumped. I tried to ignore it,
but it felt bad. Then my mom's voice.

"Christopher! It's for you."

"I'm not home," I yelled.

"It's someone named April, and I'm not paid to lie for you."

"No, you're paid to lie for your clients," I muttered so that she could hear me muttering without hearing what I'd said. I clicked the TV off. "Sorry, Mary, sorry, Monica, gotta go."

I got up and went to the phone in the hallway. "What?" I snapped.

"You fell asleep while you were supposed to be on watch," she accused.

"Sorry. I was tired. Arrest me for dereliction of duty. Are you here or there?"

"I'm here. Jalil took over guard duty, so he's over there and I went back to sleep. David says we should get together. We need to talk. He's at his job at Starbucks. He gets off in an hour."

"I'm busy," I said.

"Busy? Doing what?"

"Watching TV, April. Is that okay? I'm very busy watching TV. So why don't you and David go have your little conference without me?"

Silence. No answer.

"Well, bye, April," I said.

"Christopher, we need to figure a way out of this."

I laughed. "You don't get it, do you? We have no control over the situation. None. We didn't ask to be in this. We had no control. And what do you think we're going to do now? Did you happen to notice an escape hatch when you were playing vestal virgin? Something you didn't tell us about? Because if there's an escape hatch, I'd love to hear about it, but right now, April, I'm going to go back and figure out the mystic connection between Mary and Monica. Good luck, say hi to David for me, that's all."

I slammed down the phone.

My little brother, Mark, was standing on the stairs above me, pretending like he was about to come down but actually spying.

He resumed his descent once he heard me hang up.

"What, are you with the CIA now?" I asked him.

"Don't need to spy, homes, I could have heard you outside."

"'Homes'? 'Homes'? Well, listen up, homey. A) you're a lily-white kid from the upper middle class whose mommy and daddy drive minivans that would match except that one is blue and the other is green, so you are not, repeat, not a streetwise black kid. And B) don't listen to my phone calls."

Mark sneered. "You need to get over this attitude toward black people."

"I don't have an attitude toward black people, I have an attitude toward punks. Punk."

"Yeah, right. Just so happens all your friends are white."

"Hey! It so happens I'm trapped in hell with a black guy, I spent last night with a black guy! I'm sleeping with him right now in —"

I stopped. About two-dozen words too late.

"No way!" Mark yelled, his face a mixture of shock, amazement, gloating, and unease. "Oh, man. Oh, man."

"That came out wrong," I said.

"Oh, man. No, no, that's cool. I'm down with that. That's cool. Each his own, man. I support you. You know, you gotta be what you gotta be, Tinky Winky."

I started to explain. Started to correct. But he was gone, out the door, no doubt to spread the word.

"Not that there's anything wrong with that," I said to his back. A classic *Seinfeld* line.

I had just had a perfect sitcom moment. A classic sitcom setup. Sitcomworld had just intruded into the real world. Surreal. It made me a little uncomfortable. Not as uncomfortable as Fenrir, Loki's bus-sized wolf-son popping into my world had made me, but uncomfortable.

Then I laughed. Sitcom reality was my friend, trying to save me. It had opened its arms to me and wrapped me up in safety. I was good till the next commercial. Good till another me, a faraway me, a me I didn't want to be anymore, woke up.

"Not a sitcom over there, my man," I said to myself, flicking the remote again. "Action-adventure? Horror? Fantasy? Not my fantasy."

I hit the remote. The credits were rolling beside a promo for a lame Steven Seagall movie.

I was part of the cast of a movie directed by lunatic immortals. I was one of the actors. Question was, was I the hero? Or was I the guy they kill off early to give the audience a good fear-rush?

"No, that's not the question, either. The question is, 'How the hell do I get out of this movie?'"

Chapter
XX

I was asleep in my bed when I awoke in Ever-world.

I lay there confused. Lost. Looked for the numbers on my clock. Looked for the faint outline of my window. For the line of light under my door cast by the night-light in the hallway. None of the above.

I felt like crying. I didn't want to be here.

Suddenly a hand clamped over my mouth. Soft hand. April's luminous eyes just inches above mine. A finger over her mouth. A silent, voiceless, "Shhh."

I nodded. She took her hand away.

Jalil lay nearby, on his stomach, awake, alert. I was on my back. Not the best way to deal with an attack.

I strained to hear what was happening. The

sounds of the nocturnal forest. The breeze rustling tall branches, the unsettling sounds of tiny things creeping and crawling beneath the fallen leaves. And something more purposeful.

Whatever it was, it wasn't afraid. It wasn't creeping. Wasn't stopping to listen. It moved confidently, swiftly, quietly.

Toward us.

I saw David off to my right, gripping his sword, kneeling, poised, tensed. I rolled over, ever so quietly. Fumbled in the darkness, feeling for my ax. I couldn't find it, fought down the panic, felt around more methodically, grabbed April's ankle instead, didn't want her ankle, wanted my ax, wanted something I could use, man, something I could use to kill, stay alive.

Welcome back to Everworld, Christopher Hitchcock.

"Sounds like more than one," Jalil whispered.

"More than one what?" I muttered.

Whoever was moving stopped. I froze. All but my fingers, which kept up their blind search for the ax. Got it! Fingers tightened around it, security, God knows not much, but some. I never wanted to be without a weapon in Everworld again.

And then, a chill that shivered my back. I felt

something land on my shoulder. Not heavy. Small. Alive. Something definitely alive.

A needle-sharp point pressed against the side of my neck. A poke, a threat, a warning. Something sharp pressed against an artery.

"If friends, no fear," a flutey voice said from the darkness. Not from whatever was on my shoulder. "If foe, fear."

"Friends," I said, ordering myself not to move, not to move a millimeter.

"Show," the odd voice said.

I stayed very still. I didn't know what was sticking me in the neck. Didn't know if it was dangerous, deadly, or just painful, but there is something about a dagger's point against your flesh, against the prickling, goose-bumped flesh that stretches so ineffectually over the pulsing jugular vein that concentrates all your attention.

"They want us to show ourselves," Jalil said.

"Something . . . is poking . . . my neck," I said.

"Stay ready," David warned. "Stand up slowly."

I stood up slowly. The needle point stayed with me. I didn't let go of my ax. Didn't try to use it, either. You don't want to use an ax to swat something on your neck.

"We're friends," April said in her gentlest, talking-to-rabid-dogs voice.

"Whose?" the voice asked. Amused.

"Whose friends? Um . . . we're one another's friends. We'll be your friends if you don't mean us any harm."

"Light," the voice said, and instantly the woods around us were illuminated by a dozen wobbly, wavering lights, each perhaps as bright as a candle. In the pitch-black it seemed pretty bright.

Bright enough to show me that we were a lot worse off than we thought. They were all around us. What I had taken to be one or maybe a few creatures moving quietly was in fact twenty or twenty-five creatures, each the size of a man.

The size of a man. And that was it for resemblance to anything I'd ever seen before. They were dark gray as well as I could tell in the shadows. Maybe six feet tall, but closer to twelve feet long from nose to toes. Or from nose to tail.

The face was a long, very long, maybe three-foot-long point, a hard cone, a needle, like an anteater who'd evolved to hunt for ants inside of concrete. Resting above, at the back of the needle were two eyes, enormous, blue-irised within dark red.

The rest of the body was a sort of a cramped letter *C*. The body arched from nose down to claw feet, so that the sharp talon toes were almost directly beneath the point of the snout. It had a sort of short tail or long fin halfway around the arc to provide some kind of balance.

Two legs thrust forward, two brawny arms at mid-arc, two smaller, delicate arms jutting out just below the eyes.

That was most of them, the big ones. But there were the others. Smaller, miniature versions, but with gossamer wings. One of these was resting comfortably on my shoulder, with its six-inch version of the needle mouth pressed against my neck.

The candle lights were coming from the bellies of the little ones. Fireflies the size of pigeons.

The nearest of the big ones walked toward us. It was an impossible movement. A balancing act with each step. A leg stretched out, almost telescoping out, with loose-fitting gray flesh unwrinkling. The foot would touch down, balance would be reestablished, then the other foot would come forward, very slowly.

We could run and there was no way these things were going to catch us. Then, as if reading my mind, one of the lights, the little ones, jerked toward David. David had twitched. The little one had covered twenty feet before David could go from start of twitch to end of twitch.

I did a quick, desperate brain-search. What

were these things? What dark myth had these monsters crawled out of?

But I knew: There was nothing human here. Man's gods and demons and monsters are always mostly human. Distorted in form or power, but mostly human.

I sucked in a deep breath. "Who are you people?"

CHAPTER XXI

"We are Coo-Hatch of the Third Forge. You?"

"Um . . . humans," I said.

The main Coo-Hatch blinked slowly. "Two legs, two arms, small eyes, fur on head, clothed. Human," he said, adding an unspoken but implied 'duh.' "Which humans?"

"We're minstrels," David said. "Traveling entertainers. I'm David. That's April, Jalil, and Christopher."

I couldn't believe David remembered our cover story. Minstrels. Yeah. It worked with the Vikings. But the Vikings were party animals by nature. These guys didn't look like they'd really care for any drinking songs.

The Coo-Hatch used one of his tiny uppermost hands to point at my ax, at David's sword. "Viking weapons. Poor steel. I am Estett."

Jalil said, "The Coo-Hatch. I remember the Vikings, when they were asking us about the Hetwan and Loki? They mentioned the Coo-Hatch."

"Sven Swordeater said they trade with the Coo-Hatch for steel," David recalled.

"Not Coo-Hatch steel," the weird thing named Estett said, eyeing our weapons again with unmistakable distaste. "Lend."

He held out his hand for my ax. It had been mere moments since I swore never to give up my weapon. I handed it to him anyway.

Estett used one of his medium arms to test the balance of my ax, then threw it, twirling, end over end. It thunked into a tree and quivered there.

"Viking steel," he said with no effort to hide his condescension.

Then he opened a slit in the skin of his flank, and I realized for the first time that it was some kind of clothing. With one of his middle arms he drew out what looked like a small airplane propeller, a foot in diameter, with the blades bent back and a round hole in the center. The steel shone in the dim light. Glittered. Like it was radioactive. Maybe it was.

With feline speed, the Coo-Hatch threw the weapon. It flew through the air, twirling, level, sliced into a tree, through a tree, so fast, so easily that the tree stood still, poised, needing a fresh breeze before it began to fall.

The tree fell straight toward us, fifty feet of bare trunk before it spread into branches. Right toward us.

"Run!" David yelled. But before we could react, before we could do more than flash on some red-plaid lumberjack yelling, "Timber!" the rest of the Coo-Hatch struck.

With no word spoken, no evidence of haste, no sign of concern, but with easy, liquid grace, the other Coo-Hatch all drew similar weapons and sent them flying.

The tree's trunk, already at a sharp angle and accelerating down toward my head, was sliced into two dozen separate logs.

The logs fell. The Coo-Hatch didn't move. And some subconscious instinct for survival kept us all rooted, too.

Like mortar shells, the logs fell around us. Each log was a neat two or three feet long. Each impact made the ground jump. Bruised my soles and rattled my knees. The branches fell far behind us.

The spinning propellers all arced back toward their owners, who caught them on their needle noses or mouths or whatever they were. It was a disconcertingly comical thing to see.

I decided not to laugh.

"Coo-Hatch steel," Estett said with evident satisfaction.

It could have been a threat. As a threat it was a pretty good one. The message was so, so clear: We can make you into salami.

But I had a feeling maybe scaring us wasn't the point. My dad's a salesman. I know salesmen.

"Pretty good," I said. "So how much do they cost?"

CHAPTER
XXII

The Coo-Hatch led us through the darkness before dawn. We followed. Quiet. Not terrified, but nervous. I wondered if there was ever going to be a moment in Everworld when I wasn't at least nervous.

They were strange creatures, that's for sure. But strange as they were, dangerous as they could clearly be, they didn't give me the sick pit-of-the-stomach dread I felt when facing a simple, dirty Aztec priest. For one thing, they'd chopped up a tree. Not one of us.

For another thing, it was hard to take that bizarre walk of theirs without wanting to giggle. Sort of like an exaggerated Groucho walk. Funny. There was no avoiding it, it was funny.

I guess Jalil saw me grinning. "Here's a suggestion: Don't laugh at them. Or if you do, go stand far away from me."

"They seem nice enough."

"You're not even nice enough," Jalil said darkly.

They led us to a stream, barely visible in the light cast by the hovering bird-creatures. We could hear it gurgling and chuckling like any stream in the real world. But it was concealed by high-grown ferns and palms and weeds.

The Coo-Hatch made a clearing. They used their throwing blades. It took about three seconds. They turned the overgrown weeds into a lawn. We could have played a game of croquet.

They made a fire by striking sparks from a chunk of rock and a small triangle of steel.

"Not Coo-Hatch steel," Estett explained, indicating the triangle. "Coo-Hatch steel cuts rock."

Then all of us, Coo-Hatch and human, sat down around a modest fire and crossed our legs.

It felt okay, weirdly enough. Sitting with a bunch of aliens in the middle of a jungle in the night. Odd to be more at ease with a bunch of aliens, a bunch of off-world freaks than the Aztecs, or, for that matter, some of the Vikings. But "odd" was the synonym for "normal" in Everworld.

I almost wished the Aztecs would come after us

and have these boys demonstrate their blades on them. I wished that a lot.

"What now? We sing 'Kumbaya'?" David whispered.

"Now we do business," I said.

"Why?'

"Because that's what these guys want to do," I said. "They're salesmen, can't you tell?"

David nodded. "Fair enough. I don't need to be sliced and diced. We do what they want."

"What do we have to trade?" April asked. "And what are we buying?"

"I wouldn't mind having one of those throwing knives," Jalil said.

"I still have the stuff in my backpack," April said. She swung if off her shoulder and onto her lap. "Advil? I have Advil. The CD player. Maybe they'd be interested in that."

She was pulling things out one by one. The rest of us were reaching under our various Viking-issue animal skins to dig in our jeans pockets.

The Coo-Hatch were staring. I watched the royal-blue irises within the bulbous red eyes. The blue expanded and contracted. But mostly there was no response. The expressions seemed easy enough to understand. Mostly indifference. No reaction to a bottle of Advil.

"Let's see if they'll sell us Manhattan for twenty-four dollars' worth of beads," I said.

Item after item. April emptied her bag, then we started emptying our pockets. We still had a lot of keys. Useless. I'd had to get myself a spare for use on the other side, back in the real world. The Coo-Hatch looked at the keys, tested the metal, shrugged, handed them back.

They were marginally more interested in Jalil's thin Swiss Army knife. They sneered at the steel, of course. Not impolite, just like, "Yeah, big deal." But they liked the idea, the mechanism. They opened the tiny blade and the tiny screwdriver.

"They come bigger sometimes," Jalil explained. "Several blades, Phillips, corkscrews, scissors, saw, so on."

Estett nodded, a very human gesture. "Poor steel, but interesting." He shot a sidelong look at some of his people. I had a feeling that if we ran into the Coo-Hatch a few months down the road they'd be offering little Coo-Hatch Army knives for sale.

A slight glimmer of reaction to the CD player. The Coo-Hatch touched it. Then pushed it away contemptuously.

More keys. A felt-tip pen. No reaction.

Two books.

No reaction.

"Wait," April said. She reached across me to grab the top book. *Chemistry: Principles and Application.*

She flipped through the pages. Then went to the index. Then went to a particular page. She opened the book and held it out for Estett.

Red eyes stared. Then . . .

"Ah!"

The Coo-Hatch almost snatched for the book, then caught himself. "Lend? Examine?"

"Sure," April said. She handed the book to the alien.

Estett turned the pages reverently. He held it with his middle arms and turned the pages with his upper, delicate arms. He kept turning. Then, looking embarrassed, he closed the book reluctantly and handed it back.

"What did you show him?" I asked April.

"A description of the steel-making process."

"Trade?" Estett asked.

"What do you have on the table, dude?" I asked him.

He considered. "Fix small red knife."

"It's not broken." Jalil said.

"Weapons," David interrupted greedily. "We want the throwing blades."

Estett may have laughed. Sounded like a laugh. It shouldn't have, though. Not with that mouth, that throat. Then again, he was speaking English, and reading English, so who was I to object to the fact that his laugh sounded almost human?

"Three years' training to master the throwing blade," Estett said. "Handle wrong way, no fingers, no arm. Drop, no foot. Throw badly, no house, many die. Coo-Hatch do not sell weapons. Sell tools. Humans do not need more weapons."

"Hey, I need more weapons," I said. "This human sure needs some serious heat. You want to know where I've been lately? I could use artillery, let alone a knife."

David's eyes glinted angrily. "Estett, what we want is the —"

April interrupted, putting a hand on his arm. "He's right, David. You've never used a weapon like that. It'd be like giving a machine gun to a little kid."

"Ouch."

"I never used a sword, either, but I figured it out," David argued.

"Swords don't cut through trees, David. You think you're going to grab one of those blades and go back after Senna? You'd kill yourself or me. Or her. Or a bunch of innocent people."

"There are no innocent people in that city," Jalil muttered. "But April's right. So is Estett," he added, with a nod to the alien. "A weapon that wild and dangerous, you'd need to know exactly what you're doing. Takes these guys three years to learn how to throw one? Let it go, David."

"Well, what are they going to trade us, then?" David demanded.

"How about we ask them?" April said, obviously annoyed at David's continuing display of attitude.

"Okay, if they won't give us the throwing knives, how about a ticket to the Bahamas and three weeks at a fabulous resort with hot and hotter running bikini babes?" I suggested.

"Steel secrets very old. Good steel would be made from book, but not Coo-Hatch steel," Estett said, pointing at the book.

"He's dissing the merchandise. Ah, so we bargain, eh?" I said.

April shook her head. "He's just pointing out the obvious. What, you think that book has some formula for making better steel than these guys can make? Get real. It's something else he saw in there. Or maybe it's all of it. Either way, I wouldn't mind getting rid of that book — it weighs a ton."

"What do you offer?" Jalil asked the Coo-Hatch.

"Coo-Hatch steel."

"Are we going in circles here?"

The Coo-Hatch don't smile. Couldn't, probably. I never did see its mouth. Not for sure. "Show knife. Small red knife."

Jalil fished for his knife again and handed it to Estett.

Estett opened the blade. "Poor steel. Coo-Hatch steel better."

CHAPTER
XXIII

"Oh, this is good," I said. "What was that sword in King Arthur? You know, his magic sword or whatever?"

"Excalibur," Jalil supplied.

"Yeah. That's it. So our Excalibur is going to be some two-inch-blade Swiss Army knife? Great. Hold up there, Big H, while I unsnap my teeny-tiny knife and trim your evil toenails. Yo, Loki, call your monster wolf-son back or I swear I'll shave off some of his fur!"

"It's more than we have right now," David said. He was pissed, obviously. He wanted some big, nasty firepower, same as me. In the land of the sword, the man with the Glock is king.

"Should we really be giving them all the information that may be in that book?" Jalil wondered.

"What, you don't want to violate the Prime Directive, Spock?" I said. "So they learn how to make cleaning solution. Who cares?"

"There are explosives in that book," Jalil whispered. "Or at least that can be extrapolated."

"Don't use words like 'extrapolated,' Jalil; it's not necessary, we all know you're smarter than we are. And who cares? So they make plastique and go around blowing up buildings. I don't care about this place! This place isn't my home, all right?"

Jalil gave me one of his sideways looks. "You're not finding Everworld scary enough? You want to spread around some new weapons information? I'm not talking 'Save the Aztecs' here, I'm looking at me walking down some street somewhere in this little universe and getting blown away because I wanted a cool knife."

April smiled at Estett. "We need to consider this for just a few seconds." She turned to us and in a low voice said, "Look, I'm sick of carrying the book, anyway; it weighs a ton. Besides, have any of you considered what they might do if we just refuse to trade? I mean, maybe that's like a mortal insult to the Coo-Hatch."

This put a new light on things. I saw a mental picture of a Coo-Hatch blade bisecting me so neatly, so smoothly that the two halves of me would continue alive for a while, blood pumping through arteries, nerves communicating across the minuscule gap, me realizing I'd been chopped in two, trying to use my hands to hold onto my stomach and keep my bottom half attached.

Too easy to picture, that was. I'd seen it in living color, or something close, when Huitzilopoctli's mirror made one Sven Swordeater into two.

"I'm thinking, let's not make anyone mad," I said.

"We do the deal," David said.

"Hey, hey, back up there, Saddam. You don't give the orders here."

He looked surprised. "I'm agreeing with you."

"Fine, then say, 'I agree with Christopher,' not 'We do it,' General Jerkwad."

"What's climbed up your butt now?"

I jabbed a finger at David's face. "You're not the hero of this story and the rest of us your faithful followers. The hero lives, the best friend gets killed. The rules of the form, man. You're not the hero of this movie, so back up."

David rolled his eyes. "He's having a breakdown. What is it they call it? Post-traumatic stress something syndrome? You having flashbacks about the pyramid, Christopher? You seeing obsidian knives?"

"Ignore them." April smiled at Estett. She took the knife from Jalil's hands, lifted the book up off her lap, and handed both to the Coo-Hatch. "Deal," she said.

It took the Coo-Hatch an hour. They took our little campfire and began blowing into it with their needle mouths. Out of rucksacks and their pouches came various bits of lumpy-looking material, stuff that could be dirt clods for all I knew. They worked. Banged. Blew. Collected water in a little trench they dug from the stream.

April found what may have been, could have been a Coo-Hatch female. She went off and had some girl-talk time. David and Jalil and I just moped and watched the Coo-Hatch and wondered how our lives had brought us here.

After a while, and with gray light beginning to outline the treetops above us, the Coo-Hatch handed the knife to Jalil, still warm to the touch, along with a lot of warnings like, "Don't test it on your finger or you'll be counting in base nine, you idiot human." Or words to that effect.

Then they took off, the big Grouchos, the little Tinkerbells; they just walked into the woods carrying a high-school chemistry textbook and reading it by the light of the gray dawn.

We were alone.

April looked grim.

"What's up?" I asked her.

She shook her head. "I was talking to the Coo-Hatch. They're here like us. I mean, they didn't ask to be here, they were carried here by some god of the fire and goddess of the ore or whatever, it was hard to make sense of. Anyway, it was a century ago. They've been trying to find their way back to their own universe ever since. Talking about their families and all, their villages, their forges and mines and so on. They're lonely."

"Trying to get out of here for a hundred years?" Jalil asked.

April shrugged. "That's what they say. There are seven groups of Coo-Hatch wandering around Everworld. A hundred years. They can't get back. Stuck here."

She was acting tough, but there were tears in her eyes and she was swallowing too much. April wanted to go home. So did I. In about ten seconds I was going to bust out crying, too.

"That doesn't mean we're stuck here," I said, doing my best heroic, "never say die," "on to the summit!" voice.

I looked to David for support on that, but David's face was carefully neutral.

Of course, I thought. That's good news for the glory dog. David never wanted to go home.

"A hundred years," April said.

"Yeah."

Jalil opened the knife very, very carefully, as we'd been warned. He found a sapling maybe two inches thick. He cut it once, with an effortless movement, almost a flick of the wrist. With a second reach-around cut, the sapling fell.

"Well," I said. "We have the Magic Toenail Clipper of Power! We have Ex-freaking-calibur. Let us go forth and conquer."

CHAPTER
XXIV

"I'm starving. I'm thirsty," I said.

"Yeah, well, talking about it every five minutes, that'll make it better," Jalil said.

We were on the beach again. Out of the jungle. Standing there. Just standing. Lost. Confused. Depressed. Mad. Mostly mad.

The Coo-Hatch story hung over us. A hundred years they'd been trying to find a way out of this universe, this bubble in a bubble, this pocket of madness.

If they couldn't get out, how were we going to get out?

The reality was setting in. There might be no way out. This might be it. This could be our lives now. A few hours in the real world and a lifetime here.

From the start of it all we'd kept going on adrenaline, and then relief at having escaped the obsidian knife. But we were tired. Past tired, all of us. And more lost than any four humans have ever been before.

The sun was up and with it the heat and humidity. If we stayed on the beach, our unprotected faces would blister. If we went back into the shade of the jungle, the bugs would eat us alive.

Fear, hunger, thirst, heat, hopelessness, and a simmering, undirected anger that was all the hotter for having no clear target. I was ripe for a fight. David had worn out my last remaining nerve.

An explosion had to come. Sooner or later. We were up against the decision of what to do, and I knew, knew, knew what David wanted. Knew it and was determined to stop him, and, while I was at it, to haul him down off his throne for good. The jumped-up junior general, I wasn't taking that anymore.

If I were a more mature person, a better person, I'd have tried hard to avoid a fight. But that's not me. I was OD'ing on the rage that grows out of fear. I wanted to hit, to hurt, to scream and threaten and flail around like a toddler having a temper tantrum. I was trapped and powerless. Helpless.

"I am starving," I complained. "It's a toss-up as to which I want more: a drink or a meal. Both would be nice. Isn't there supposed to be fruit on the trees in the jungle? Palm trees with coconuts or bananas or whatever?"

"We're well within foraging range for the Aztecs in the city back there," Jalil pointed out. "They were thin, as you might have noticed. Hungry. If there were fruit on the trees, they'd have picked it, probably did pick it already. You'd probably have figured that out yourself, Christopher, if you'd quit whining long enough to process a thought."

In a millisecond I switched gears from being ready to kill David to being ready to kill Jalil.

"Don't piss me off, Jalil, just don't, okay? Because I am plenty pissed off. You aren't going to like what happens next if you keep it up. Fair warning."

Jalil glared at me, his mouth twisted with bitter anger. "You know, I'm here in the nuthouse with crazy killer gods and alien steel salesmen and alcoholic Vikings and cannibal Aztecs, and despite all that, the biggest pain in my butt is some big, dumb cracker. Now, why is that?"

"Cracker? Now it's racial stuff? You want to start throwing words around, Jalil? Jalil, what's that, Muslim for —"

"That's it, all over," David said, stepping in between us. "You shut up." He pointed a finger in my face.

That was it. The fuse had burned all the way down.

"Hey, maybe you need to figure out which side you're on, David!" I yelled. "You want to throw down with me to save the 'brutha'?"

At the same time Jalil was yelling, "Back off, David, I don't need the Hebrew army to help me deal with this racist piece of —"

David emitted a short, harsh laugh, put up his hands, and backed up. "Forget both of you."

After that it was just me and Jalil yelling, shouting, chest-pushing, shoving.

"You want to do this? Let's do it!" I yelled, my face an inch from Jalil's.

My hand went to my ax. Jalil's was on his long dagger. Face-to-face, the two of us. Sweat popping out of tight skin, eyes bulging, lips stretched over bared teeth, chests out.

"You know what?" April said to David. "Let them fight. The three of you, it's all you know how to do. So here's the thing, you two fight, then David fights the winner."

I barely heard her. All I saw was Jalil, all I heard was his ragged breathing, poised, ready to explode with violence on his first move.

Stupid. I did know that. It was David I was mad at, not Jalil. But at the moment logic was a tiny, faraway voice way, way back in my head. Up front, filling all of the rest of my skull was panic — fear and fury.

April came over and pushed her way between us. Ludicrous, of course, I noted that way back somewhere in my head. I did know it was an absurd picture, me and Jalil making a sandwich of April.

"Okay, look," April said. "I'm tired of trying to get the three of you *boys* to behave like adults. I don't know, maybe males aren't capable of ever really being adults. Maybe you're crippled by your hormones or something."

I turned on April. "You know what, I'm sick of your 'better-than-everyone, my crap doesn't stink' attitude. In case you missed it, this isn't Political Correctness World, okay? So why don't you go sit over there, out of danger, like you sat on your butt on the ship while the men were taking care of business back, back . . . then. Day before yesterday. The battle and all."

I was babbling. I knew I was babbling. Didn't care. I wanted to hurt someone. I wanted to hurt someone so badly. But April was looking up at me from an inch away, and mad as she was, there was this mocking thing going on. She was laughing at me. At both of us.

"Not worth the bruised fists," Jalil sneered at me and stepped back suddenly.

I stepped back at the same moment. April took a deep breath, ran a hand back through her hair, and straightened her top.

Jalil was pressing his hands against the side of his head like maybe the left half and right half had come unglued. "Look what's happened to me, man. What I said, David, that was uncalled for. I'd take that moment back if I could."

"It's been a slightly tense week," David said. "Forget about it."

"Look what's happened to me," Jalil repeated, oblivious to David's answer. He wiped sweat from his forehead with the back of his hand and stared at his wet hand like he'd just noticed the early signs of leprosy.

"Yeah, well, I'm not some kind of racist, either," I said, huffy, still trying to sound mad and tough. "That's bull."

"Okay, line up," April said.

"What?"

"Line up. The three of you. You, too, David. Shoulder to shoulder, right there, line up, just do it!" Her voice rose to a yell on the last three words.

We lined up.

April stood in front of us, hands on hips. "Look, you need each other. I need you, all of you. And, since I did happen to save your worthless, pathetic lives, all three of you, I think it's fair to say you need me. So I don't care what stupidity you have hidden away inside your heads, that has to be it for this kind of thing. The four of us are all any of us has. We are in it deep here. We're in it so deep we may never get out. So basically, and I say this with respect and affection: behave. Behave like civilized human beings, and if you *boys* can't figure out what that means, ask me and I'll tell you. From now on, if we have disagreements, we have a vote, majority rule, and if it's a tie we do what I say."

She said the word "boy" in a way that made it sound belittling and yet was somehow sexy.

"Will you spank me if I'm bad?" I asked, batting my eyes.

"No," she shot back. "But if any of you want to fight again, I'm going to let you fight. No weapons. Bare fists. And bare bodies, too, like the ancient Greeks."

"Say what?" David said.

She flashed her provocative April grin. "I

mean, I have to get some entertainment out of this."

We all laughed. Moment passed. Rage burned out. We were still lost and scared, but not quite homicidal anymore.

Still, it took me twenty minutes or so before I got around to saying anything to Jalil. And when I did it was to ask if he thought we should go deeper into the jungle to find food.

Not exactly an apology. Neither of us ever did that.

Chapter XXV

We trekked into the jungle again and found the stream where we'd met the Coo-Hatch. We drank. Wasted time. Back where we'd started. Nothing accomplished but a stupid fight.

We hadn't even gotten to the main issue: Where were we going? We all knew that would be a fight and our peace was still pretty tenuous. But in the end, there was no avoiding it. We stayed or we moved. If we moved, we needed a direction.

"Okay," I said, after taking a moment to enjoy the sight of April leaning far over into the stream, "unless we're planning to set up house-keeping here we'd better figure out where we're going. What we're doing."

April stood up and wiped her mouth. "Where's David?"

Jalil shrugged. "Saw him heading back toward the beach. Figured he wanted a P.M."

P.M. Private Moment. That's what we'd started calling the need to disappear behind the bushes for some basic biological functioning.

"David!" April yelled.

I had a sudden sinking sensation. The feeling you get when you've guessed something you really hope isn't true.

I jumped up and started plowing through foliage toward the beach.

"What are you doing?" Jalil yelled after me.

"David, man, he's taken off."

"What do you mean? Where would he . . . Oh, man!"

We found fresh footprints on the beach. Running-shoe tread. And there, in the damp sand near the shore, he'd written with the tip of his sword.

We stood there staring at the four words outlined in foot-tall sand letters: *Going back for her.*

The three of us spent about thirty seconds running through our vocabularies of curses, insults, and threats.

"Now what?" I demanded.

"Now we deal with the choice David has left us: Go after him or go on alone," Jalil said.

I shook my head. "This sucks. Maybe he is the

hero of this story. But that can't be, man. We have to walk away, let him go off on his own. Otherwise, what are we? We're supporting actors, that's what. We're dead."

Jalil favored me with his sideways look, a look I now saw had a strange similarity to that of Huitzilopoctli. "What are you babbling about, and I ask that as a friend?"

"Any movie you ever see, man, the hero survives. He's got a best friend, a babe, and a black guy. Sometimes the best friend is the black guy. Don't you ever go to the movies? The best friend and the black guy? Dead meat. Dead freaking meat. Even the babe if there's going to be a sequel. Like a Bond movie or whatever. That bear movie? That Baldwin brother and that other guy, the old one, and they're all alone except for, ta-da, the black guy, and who does the bear eat? Not the Baldwin brother."

Jalil nodded. "Uh-huh. Again, I want to say this as a friend, and with no racial animosity, because it's not about you being a redneck, all right? But you, Christopher, you are an idiot."

"You ever see Schwarzenegger get killed?" I shrilled.

"Yeah, *Terminator Two. Terminator One,* too."

"He was a robot!"

"Okay, let me waste some more minutes of my

life to figure out what your malfunction is. You think life runs according to the way it does in action movies? The hero lives, everyone else is expendable."

"I'm just saying, David's off playing tough guy. He's Clint, we're standing around here with our fingers in our noses."

"Clint Eastwood didn't go off after some psycho chick," Jalil argued. "The hero doesn't do that stuff unless it's like some kid's fairy tale."

"Prince Charming," I spat bitterly.

"Jalil's right," April said. "Face it, David's not heroic. He's just obsessed." She bit her lip, thoughtful. "Or not obsessed. Not obsessed — under a spell."

It came out sounding so natural. Like nothing important had been said. But I knew it was important. It was the first time any of us had ever talked like maybe, maybe it was true. Maybe Senna wasn't the girl we all thought we knew. Maybe she really was something inexplicable. Something magic.

Jalil threw up his hands. "Am I the only rational human being here? Hey, hey, it's the twenty-first century; this is not the Dark Ages. It's not even the sixties. One of you thinks life works like the plots of the crap you find in the action-adventure aisle at Blockbuster, and the other thinks what? Magic spells and potions?"

He rounded on April. "What happened? Senna put the whammy on David? Cast a voodoo spell? Now he's drawn to her because she has some magical power over him?"

Jalil threw up his hands. Literally. Then looked up at the sky and muttered something about inventing his own universe so he could crawl inside.

A spell? Crazy. Of course it was. But in my mind I was back at that pool party. Feeling like I'd never noticed Senna before. Feeling like suddenly I couldn't notice anyone else.

I felt a shiver. How did you know when you were under a spell? My gaze refocused. Refocused on April's green eyes. Her expression was angry. Suspicious.

"Why were we all there?" April asked me. "Why were we all down at the lake, standing around there, drawn there, waiting, watching Senna? Why? How did that happen? How about you, Jalil? Why were you there? You have some rational explanation for why you were there?"

Jalil took a step back. His face blanked.

"Yeah, what were you doing there, Jalil?" I asked. "Me, I was going out with Senna. Then

David was with her. April's her half sister. What about you, man? What did you and the witch have going on?"

"I don't know why I was there that morning," Jalil admitted. But that must have been too much like he was agreeing with us because then he said, "Maybe I just woke up early and was restless. Felt like going for a drive."

"You ever do that before? Get up that early and suddenly decide to take a drive down to the lake?" April pressed.

Jalil didn't answer. He sidestepped the question and pushed back at us with sarcasm. "It's not exactly bizarre behavior, you know. People do drive down to the lake. That's why they have parking, so people can drive down there."

I felt the cold creeps crawling across my flesh. We'd been in one crap storm after another since showing up in Everworld. There hadn't been time to think. No time to really ask the basic questions.

Why were we here? Why had we been drawn to Senna at the very moment when she could pull us into this madness?

April laughed without humor. "David's not the hero. He's just a fool. A puppet. Like all of us. This is all Senna. It's all her. This is her game we're playing. We're all fools."

We stood there, the three of us, each hiding his own little secrets, each nursing his own little grudge. Each with his own superstitions, even Jalil. Maybe especially Jalil, holding on with a death grip to a philosophy that belonged to a whole different universe.

Although, I had to admit, it was hard to be much crazier than believing the world ran according to the neat, predictable rules of sitcoms and action movies.

April whispered something. I couldn't hear it. I don't think I was supposed to. Then she started walking.

"Where are you going?" Jalil demanded. "Are you going after David?"

"No. I'm going after Senna."

Chapter XXVI

New Tenochtitlan. Not a place I'd ever thought I'd see again. Not a place I wanted to see again.

We knew the way back. Easy to find. All we had to do was follow the beach. Over the bridge, then follow the beach to the burned-out Viking ships, hang a left across the battlefield where Olaf and Sven had died. We knew the way.

And even if memory had not shown us the way, the neat imprints of running shoes on sand would have been roadmap enough.

We walked till we could see the river's mouth turning the beach inward toward the bridge. But then the trail of running-shoe waves cut left, inland. Into the jungle. The trees were smaller, more stunted here, closer to the city. The forest seemed dead. Scarcely a bird to cry at our approach. Nothing but bugs the size of rats and rats the size of spaniels.

It was harder following David's track through the jungle, looking for the crushed weeds, the occasional clear footprint in mud.

Thirst was back. Hunger, too. We were pampered products of a well-ordered world, after all. Three meals and between-meal snacks and a faucet or a bottle of Dannon spring water there for the taking.

I was sweaty and slashed by thorns and whipped by weeds and muddy and the gash on my head was itching and I kept having to touch it to be sure something wasn't crawling into it.

It was a toss-up who I hated more right then: David for being a weak-willed fool, Jalil for being a tiresome know-it-all with a chip on his shoulder, April for so clearly not having the least little interest in me. Or Senna for seducing me, enthralling me, trapping me in this schizophrenic's vision.

Putting a spell on me.

Or maybe I was just mad at good old Christopher. I was whiny, bitchy, snide, resentful, childish. Picking stupid fights. Acting like the kind of person I couldn't stand.

That's not the way it was supposed to be. That wasn't the movie in my head. That wasn't the fantasy. I was on an adventure, wasn't I? I was supposed to stand tall and keep my jaw clenched and my eyes steely, and laugh at danger and laugh at difficulty and never show a flicker of emotion, and triumph and get the girl — that was the picture, that was the script.

Instead I was wandering around, waiting for the next nightmare to come popping up out of nowhere and do to me what Huitzilopoctli had done to King Olaf.

Then again, I was alive. Olaf was dead. Maybe Olaf should have complained more and spent less time being bold and brave.

We were walking uphill now, which was just great because if there's anything more obnoxious than walking through untracked jungle with your dirty clothes glued to your body by a combination of heat and humidity so high you could cook a lobster, it's doing it while struggling against gravity.

"Loki and Huitzilopoctli and the rest of these stupid gods create this universe and can't dial the gravity down a few notches, make it easier for people?" I muttered.

Suddenly we emerged into a clearing. A clearing atop a hill maybe three hundred feet tall. Not exactly Mount Everest, but taller than the surrounding countryside.

David was standing with his back to us, on top of a mossy rock.

"Oh, look, it's Lewis and/or Clark," I said. I shouted, "Hey! Hey! We've been looking for you."

David glanced back over his shoulder. Then turned away again. "I heard you coming."

April and Jalil walked over and climbed up on the rock. So what was I supposed to do? I went and climbed up. Four of us on a big rock.

I could see quite a bit from up there. The city, mostly, the pyramid, like I needed a refresher on that. But I could also see the beach and the jungle beyond the city, too. A volcano far off, inland. A hint of a distant river. And on my right, the ocean or sea, or really big lake, whatever it was.

I cringed at the sight of the city. If I could see it, maybe Huitzilopoctli could see me. I guess we were a mile from the pyramid. Not one percent of the minimum distance I wanted between me and Big H.

My eyes slid away, then back. Tried to look away, but how could I when he might even now be looking at me?

There was smoke rising from the city. Cooking fires, I assumed. Then I saw the mass of people moving away from the city. They were leaving by a far gate, heading away from us into the jungle.

"'Fugees," April said.

At least that's what I heard. It took me a minute to track. 'Fugees. Refugees.

"Yeah," David agreed. "The city is emptying out. I've been trying to count, or at least make a guess. Thousands of them. Maybe everyone in the city."

"Maybe everyone," he said again.

CHAPTER
XXVII

It took us two hours to reach the city, the gate we'd arrived through as prisoners. Might have gone quicker but my feet were dragging. My brain may have been dumb enough to go there, but my body was doing everything it could to hold me back.

Not much had changed in the city. Except there was no one home. The streets were empty. Not a man, woman, or child. Not a soldier or priest.

Here and there, a smashed pot or out-of-place chair in the middle of the street. Simple things made eerie by where they shouldn't be. An Aztec robe ruffled by the slight breeze. A shattered Aztec sword. A primitive doll or statuette, head crushed.

Smoke drifted from windows. Old fires, mostly burned down now.

There were no bodies. None. Aztec, Viking, someone, lots of someones had died but there were no bodies. Just blood. Smeared against walls. Puddled on pavement. Dried stains marking windows where life-and-death struggles had taken place.

A war had happened here. Brief, violent, final. A massacre while we'd hidden in the jungle and on the beach, trading with Coo-Hatch and arguing amongst ourselves.

"Ghost town," I whispered. It did that to you. It made you whisper.

"It is quiet," Jalil agreed.

We walked, our sneaks almost noiseless. Hands on our weapons, ready, ready to be jumped by ghosts if nothing else. Ready, scared, relieved. Guilty to be feeling relieved because this was a disaster, this was a horror, a battle involving civilians, not right, but I didn't care what had happened, didn't care what the Vikings had done.

The man-eaters, the heart-thieves, the hungry, ruthless, desperate children of Huitzilopoctli were gone.

We were silent. Our footsteps seemed too loud, advertisements to any that still lived and might attack, a desecration of the many who had surely died.

I don't know if it was deliberate or not, but we were making for the pyramid. I guess it was inevitable. I guess it was what we had to see, to be sure. When we'd seen her, Senna, she'd been near the pyramid.

The pyramid was the heart of this city. If anything still lived and had not run away, it would be there.

And if we found her, what then? "Hey, Senna, what's happening?" What do you say to a witch?

The pyramid was still as it had been. I'd already seen way too much of that foul pile of rocks. I'd see more of it in my nightmares, of that I was sure. I could feel the thing sitting down deep inside my brain, curled up like a rattlesnake in my unconscious mind, ready to strike when I was vulnerable. I knew, knew absolutely that I would climb those steps and watch the bodies slump and the blood trickle, and feel my own heart beating behind my ribs, beating so hard because it wanted to stay alive, didn't want to be torn out, didn't . . .

I stopped and took a couple of deep breaths. Only then did I realize we'd all stopped walking. It was like some invisible force field had frozen us. We stood, a disorderly gaggle of kids from a different universe, looking up through fear-dark eyes at the home office of evil.

"She'll be in the temple," David said.

"If she's here at all," April said.

"How do we know that?" Jalil asked.

"Where else?" April sneered. "Where else but at the middle of it all? Where she's been from the start. Where else, hiding in some burned-out house? No. If anything's alive in this place, it's up there."

"I guess I don't need to point out that something else might be alive up there," I said.

David shook his head "No. Big H is gone. I'd bet on that."

I felt it, too. The sense of emptiness. Abandonment. The sense that people had just gotten up and left at a run, left the blood baking dry on the pyramid steps.

Could Huitzilopoctli's people be gone and Huitzilopoctli remain? It was almost a philosophical question. Maybe someday I'd lay it on Jalil. Show him I did occasionally think beyond the next meal, the next girl, the next joke.

"You know what?" I said. "We climb that stupid pyramid or we never get past this."

"She's up there, waiting, thinking maybe we'll come back and get her. Rescue her. Or she moved out with the others." David squinted up into the sun that seemed to be resting on the temple roof. He started to climb.

"Careful," I muttered. "Don't slip on the blood."

We climbed. I won't say I was as scared as I'd been the first time I went up that pyramid. I don't think I'll ever be that scared again. Lord, I hope not.

But I was scared. Scared enough.

Up we went. Quiet, mostly. An occasional word or remark that died instantly, swallowed up, muffled by the crushing silence.

We topped the platform. The temple now loomed above us. The altar, the black stone operating table, blood-caked six, eight inches thick all around it, years of sun-cooked blood encrusted on it. I wanted dynamite. I wanted to blow it up. Make gravel out of it.

"Look," Jalil said. He pointed. There was a hole through the back of the temple. A hole big enough for a man to jump through. Sunlight blazed through the hole. "I'm guessing Mjolnir."

The inside of the temple was still shadowed but now, with the Viking remodeling job, it was a bit less of a pit.

A noise.

"What was that?" April whispered urgently.

The four of us crouched. I don't know what

kept me from pelting back down that pyramid. We crouched. I gripped my ax. The ax would be useful if Huitzilopoctli came out of that temple. Yeah. About as useful as a feather would be for stopping a Doberman.

Another noise. Like someone had accidentally kicked a can. Not a frightening noise. Except for the fact that no noise is innocent when every nerve in your body is stretched as tight as a guitar string.

"Probably a rat," Jalil said.

"Come on," David said. But he didn't move.

"Oh, after you, General. I insist."

David took a deep breath and started walking like a burglar hoping to fake out the motion sensors. The three of us were right behind him.

From brilliant sunlight into shadow. My eyes took a moment to adjust.

Nothing to see. Mostly emptiness. Some humongous stone platforms, tall and massive as marble mausoleums. Maybe Huitzilopoctli's bed or whatever, who could tell? Some pots. A table.

A man.

CHAPTER
XXVIII

He was rummaging through a sort of shelf inset in one wall. There were earthen jars arrayed neatly, unbroken.

He was tall. Thin, as well as I could tell, given that he was wearing a sort of blue robe or cape.

He spun, surprised. He flicked aside his robe. His hand went instantly to the hilt of a sword hanging in a scabbard. His eyes darted to our weapons, then back to us. He took a quick survey. Then he relaxed.

First impression: He reminded me of my uncle George, an English professor at U of I.

He had blond hair, scruffy, long, dry. The man needed conditioner. His beard and mustache were going gray, giving him overall a sort of greasy, seen-better-times look.

The eyes were intelligent: blue, quick, sunken deep beneath a heavy, lined brow.

He nodded, surprised we were there but not surprised by us. Like he was expecting us, only not here, not now. Like maybe we'd been supposed to meet him later at a coffee shop, and here we were on his front porch.

"Can I help you?" he asked.

I stifled a laugh. Then I stifled an urge to say, "Yeah, party of four and we'd like a booth."

"We're um . . ." David looked at me for guidance. I shrugged.

"We're looking for a friend," April said.

"Indeed?"

"Yes. Yes, indeed."

"I doubt your friend is here. And I doubt that anyone here is your friend," the man said. He shook his head regretfully.

He was blowing us off. Sorry, no one here, maybe you could try back later, now take off because I have things to do. No need for us to waste each other's time any longer, ta-ta.

April was no more interested in being blown off than I was. "We're looking for someone named Senna. Senna Wales."

The man's shrewd eyes were just a bit too indifferent.

"Yes, well, as I said, there's no one here."

"Senna Wales," David pressed. "Our age. Blond hair. Pale eyes."

"A witch," I added dryly.

"For the third, and one can only hope last time, there is no one else here but me, and him."

"Him?"

I looked left. Right. Nothing. Then, slowly, like some horror-movie extra doing a slow take, I looked up. Up to the central mass, the mausoleum-sized table.

My eyes had adjusted to the dark now. And now I could see him.

My knees just gave way. I fell. Kneeling. My heart stopped. Couldn't breathe. No. No. Couldn't be.

He was there. Sitting cross-legged, gigantic, leaning back against the wall of the temple, eyes dark and dull.

Huitzilopoctli.

No one moved. No one breathed. No heart beat.

Then the man in the blue robe laughed. "Don't worry. He's harmless enough at the moment. Well-fed. Overfed."

The man half-twisted to take a critical look upward. "A very stupid god, really. A war god, of course. The gods of war usually are rather dull."

"Is he dead?" April asked.

"No, no. Sadly, no. But injured. And sated. He's a predator, of course. It's all hunger with him. Once he's fed he isn't capable of much beyond sitting and digesting and waiting till the hunger sends him out once more to demand slaughter."

"The people all left," I said.

"Yes, of course. The Norsemen made the city uncomfortable, didn't they? And the people here are starving, so off they've gone to make war on Quetzalcoatl. They need captives, don't they? Prisoners? Fresh hearts for this foul beast of theirs."

His tone had been tolerant, even amused, till the last few words. Then some dark anger had risen to the surface.

"Can he be killed?" Jalil asked.

The man's bemused tone was back. "Oh, Ka Anor will kill him eventually." He turned back to us, smiling. "But then, Ka Anor will kill us all, won't he?"

I shook my head. "Don't ask me, man, I'm just passing through."

The man did not find me amusing. The look he gave me was disappointed. Again he reminded me of my uncle. And most of my teachers.

"We're looking for Senna," David said.

"I wish you well."

"Do you know where she is, yes or no?" Jalil snapped impatiently.

The man laughed. "Do you always show such disrespect for your elders?"

"He asked you a question," David said.

"I have suffered indignities in my long life," the man said. "But I have never before suffered the indignity of being cross-examined by ignorant youths. Youths with no more sense than to come wandering into the temple of Huitzilopoctli."

I laughed. "You know, the thing is, old man, we met Huitzilopoctli earlier, when he was still hungry. Scared the hell out of us." I shot a nervous glance at the dozing blue monster. "Still scares the hell out of me. But you? You're not him, and we've been scared by the best in the business, so you'll have to do better than wiggle the big eyebrows at us if you expect us to run off with our tails between our legs."

Then he laughed. A big, hearty haw-haw-haw laugh. His eyes squinched up small and blue. And nothing about that laugh reached into those cool, calculating eyes.

"Well spoken," he said. "Well spoken, youngster."

He stopped laughing as suddenly as he'd begun. "You may do. You may well do. But for whose purpose, and to what end? Perhaps the witch chose well. And then again, perhaps the witch has outsmarted herself, eh?"

He took a last look at us, turned, and walked away. Jalil was between him and the stairs.

"Hey! Uh-uh, you don't walk away," Jalil protested. He stepped up to grab the old man, but Jalil stopped moving very suddenly.

The rock of the temple floor had grown up and over Jalil's feet. It flowed like lava, then hardened instantly. He was locked, unable to move. A man who'd stood too long in wet cement.

"Son of a —" Jalil yelled.

David ran, sword high, trying to block the old man's way. Suddenly the animal-skin cape David had worn since we escaped from Loki came alive. The fur wrapped around his front and squeezed. David's sword arm was drawn down. He twisted, trying to free himself, fell, rolled. He was no longer a threat to the old man.

I could see the way this was going. I didn't move. April and I exchanged a wary look. This guy, this answer-a-question-with-a-question character in front of us, Huitzilopoctli behind us.

David's clothes became clothes again but he didn't renew his attack.

Jalil whipped out his Coo-Hatch Army knife and sliced at the rock.

The old man saw this and nodded approvingly. "Coo-Hatch steel. It's quite wonderful. I believe they could turn base metal into gold, given the motivation."

"Excuse me, listen, please," April said. "No one wants to annoy you, no one wants you mad at them, we seem to have enough people trying to hurt us, one way or another, but please, please."

He stopped. Smiled. "Please what? Do you have a question?"

April spread her hands placatingly. "Sir, whoever you are, we want to know where we can find Senna. And even more we want to find the way home, back to our universe."

The man considered. Looked at each of us in turn. He was weighing something. Wondering. Concerned. "Never use another man's tools," he muttered under his breath. "Or woman's."

"Will you help us?" April pleaded.

He smiled again, charmed I would almost have thought. "Three questions. Will I help? Perhaps. Where is the witch? Gone. To what place, I do not know. How do you find your home? Home is not found, it is made."

"Great. Runaround." I jerked a thumb at the

man. "Who is this guy? Hey, dude, if you won't help us, at least tell us: Who are you?"

"I've had many names down across the ages, and none of them are any of your business. But I would not be terribly surprised if we were to meet again, so for the sake of polite discourse in the future I'll overlook your present impertinence."

"What'd he say?" I whispered.

The man turned his back on us and stepped off the edge of the platform, down the steps, and out of sight.

"Call me Merlin," a voice said.

A voice only, because by the time we had run to the edge of the platform, the old man was gone from sight.

We followed him soon. We waited for only one reason. The big blue deity of death. It seemed wrong to leave him there. Alive. Alive to enslave his people and murder everyone else.

But there are limits to what a mere mortal can do. Lesson Number One in Everworld: There's them, and there's us. And any day we can keep them from destroying us, that's a victory.

"Merlin," I said. "Of course. Why not Merlin, that's the question? Why not the Keebler elves? Why not the Lucky Charms guy, Magically Delicious."

April squinted at me. "That's not his name. You know that, right? His name is not Magically Delicious."

"Hey, wait ten minutes and he'll show up and tell us his name himself," I ranted.

We were on the road, heading out of New Tenochtitlan, following the path the Aztecs had taken, marching through the heat and humidity, along a jungle-crowded trail. Why? Because we were looking for Senna, that's why.

And why were we looking for Senna? Because no one had any better plan.

Or as David put it, "What's the alternative? Go looking for the nearest House of Pancakes?"

"No, we make our own little twenty-first century, U.S. of A. enclave. We wander from place to place like the Coo-Hatch, only we don't obsess over steel, we obsess over the Internet and the economy and the music industry. We go from town to town babbling about our favorite web sites."

"We're going to starve, you realize that," Jalil said. "We're following behind an entire city's worth of hungry people. They'll strip everything, like army ants. There's not going to be a banana peel or a mango seed within a mile either side of this path. Let alone a pig or a . . . a whatever else"

"I guess that means the Aztecs will starve, too," April pointed out.

David sent her a strange look. "They brought their food."

"What? What food? I thought everyone was saying how hungry they were."

I took a certain ghoulish pleasure in filling her in. "The bodies, April. All the dead Aztecs and Vikings? They're just so much jerky now."

We were all quiet for a while after that. Quiet but for the rumbling in our stomachs. Water wasn't so bad a problem. The path seemed to have been cut close to a stream. We could see crushed vegetation where the Aztecs had left the path to grab a drink.

But hunger will get to you pretty quickly. It nags at you. And when nagging doesn't work, it starts yelling. Demanding. Hectoring. Screaming, "Feed me, you moron, I'm starving here!"

"Hey," I said. "What if we go to sleep? Maybe we can eat on the other side and feel full here."

Jalil cocked an eyebrow. He thought it over. Then shook his head in disgust. "That's how hungry I am. I'm starting to actually consider ideas like that."

"At least we'd have the sensation of eating. The memory," I said.

Quiet. Feet on dirt, tripping on rocks and roots. The sound of our own panting breath.

Then April said, "Bibim Bop at the Blind Faith. Carrot cake for dessert."

I made a face. "Bibim Bop? What is that, some vegetarian rabbit food? Keep it basic. Pair of Gold Coast dogs with the works: mustard, onion, chopped tomato, big fat slice of dill pickle, hot peppers, celery salt."

"No ketchup?" David asked.

"Heathen. No. No ketchup on a dog. Mustard, man. Ketchup is for fries. Jeez, how long have you been in Chicagoland, anyway? There's guys at Wrigley Field who'll hurt you over that."

"This is so not helpful," Jalil said angrily. "Talking about food does not help hunger go away. Besides, dogs? That's what you come up with? We're starving, so April wants some vegetarian mush and you want a tube filled with ground-up pig snouts or whatever? That's just sad."

"Okay, Jalil. Let's hear yours," April said tolerantly.

"Best meal I ever had. Best meal anyone ever had. My dad gets promoted, right, big raise and all, so he's feeling like Bill Gates. So he says, 'Hey, let's all get a great meal. Let's get the best meal. The ultimate meal. Charlie Trotter's.'"

"What's a Charlie Trotter? That some kind of horse meat?" David asked.

"Charlie Trotter's, man, it's this restaurant down in Lincoln Park. You don't even order, okay? They bring you everything they have that night. Scallops and chicken and veal and —"

"You shouldn't eat veal," April interrupted.

"— goose liver —"

"You shouldn't eat goose liver, either."

"— just one dish after another, till you can't believe it, man. Just more and more, better and better."

"I'd eat a goose head right now, let alone a goose liver," David said. "I would eat some Aztec jerky about now. Although, what I really want?

Breakfast. I'll eat breakfast any time of the day. Eggs. Over medium. Bacon. Home fries."

"You like the onion in the home fries or not?" April asked.

He shook his head. "No. Just potatoes. Rye toast. Can't always get it, but I like rye toast with just the butter. No jelly. Yeah. Mop up the eggs with that."

He sighed. We all sighed. And the sun slid down toward the horizon.

"What do we do when it gets dark?" I asked.

"We talk about dessert," April said.

CHAPTER

XXX

Night seemed to take forever to come, but when it came at last, it dropped like a midnight-blue curtain. The sky filled with stars. Fewer stars than we'd have seen in the wilderness back in our world, but brighter, larger, nearer. Not like far-off suns burning atomic fires. More like the sky was a big, black bowl slammed down over us, shutting out the light of day except for here and there where someone had bored holes in the bowl. You felt like you were looking at buttery, warm sunlight peeking through a thousand tiny ratholes.

Who knows? In this place, maybe that was true.

The hungry walk had been depressing enough. Night didn't turn it into a party.

"Better find a place to pull off and catch some

Z's," David said, when at last we could no longer clearly see our feet on the trail.

"Not yet," April said.

"Why not? You in a hurry to get somewhere?"

She took David's head from behind with both her hands and pointed it. "There. You see something?"

"What?" Jalil demanded.

"A light."

"Campfire?" David speculated.

Jalil said, "Group of Aztecs most likely. Or else thieves."

"Or else trolls or goblins or leprechauns or fairies or magic flying pigs," I muttered.

"Maybe they have food," David said.

"Maybe the food they have isn't exactly something we want to eat," April said pointedly.

"Never eat anything with a face?" I joked.

"At least not a human face."

"Ouch."

"It's a simple question," David said. "Either we go in or we hide. I —" He started to add something else, then stopped himself. "What do you guys think?"

"What do you know? General Patton pauses to consult the privates," I said. "Okay, we go in. IMHO. Because if we don't find some food, we are gonna be food. And if we starve we can't sleep and we can't even go home and eat back in the real world."

"Approach with caution, I'd say." That was Jalil.

"I need a weapon, I don't have one," April said. Then, to David, mocking, "See? Was that so hard? Ask people."

"Give the woman Excalibur, Jalil," I suggested.

He handed her the tiny knife. She gave it a skeptical look. "Hey, I bet I could shave my legs with this."

"Yeah, down to the bone. Be careful with it."

"Okay. We move in, surround the fire," David said, Patton once more. "One goes in all innocent, the other three spread wide, come in from three separate angles. The one who walks in is on the spot."

"Let's have four coins," April said. "We flip till we get three of one, odd-person-out walks in with a big smile."

"I knew there'd be some use for this money," I said.

We flipped. First time, it was me with tails. Three heads and my tails.

"Best two out of three?" I joked.

David looked hard at me, like he was sizing me up for the mission. Man, I was getting to really dislike him.

"Give us twenty minutes to get into position," he said.

"Yeah, no problem. I'll just sit here and play a few rounds of solitaire."

"First sign of trouble, yell. We'll be all over the place. If it's obviously trouble, you know, a bunch of guys, something we can't take down, back off fast. Yell if they come after you, we'll give you cover."

I laughed. "David, do you understand it's just you, Jalil, and April? You understand there's no artillery to call in for cover, right? I mean, unless you've been holding out on us and you secretly have a troop of cavalry back in the jungle over there, it's just the three of you."

He grinned. I could see his teeth and the whites of his eyes. "We escaped from Loki, we rocked with the Vikings, we beat Huitzilopoctli. Who's up there by that fire that we can't handle?"

"I guess we'll find out in about twenty minutes," I said.

They left. David to the left of the trail, Jalil and April to the right. I could hear them thrashing around. Then, gradually, silence.

I stared hard through the darkness, stared at the faint fire, if that's what it was. Pictured some old black-and-white movie — maybe they were hobos, that's what they called them back in the old days. Hobos. Bums. Sitting around a campfire warming a can of beans.

Or maybe it was Girl Scouts. I forced a smile for my own benefit. What did they call the older Girl Scouts? Explorers? Was that it? A troop of high-school-aged Girl Scouts, that was it, working on their merit badges in Hospitality to Strange Men.

Maybe they'd have cookies. Thin Mints. I'd take the beans or the cookies, I could go either way.

Hard to hold on to those pleasant fantasies, though. Those images were made out of air. The other fantasies were flesh and blood. Renegade Aztec warriors. Loki's trolls. Some other bunch of aliens.

Hey! Maybe it was the Coo-Hatch. Yeah, that was it. Coo-Hatch. They were okay, they were cool. Weird but not violent, at least not so far.

Or maybe it was the guy who called himself Merlin. You could talk to him at least. Probably wouldn't eat us. Probably wouldn't kill us; he could have done that if he'd wanted.

Twenty minutes? Was the time up yet? How was I supposed to know?

"Close enough," I muttered. "No point hanging around wondering. Come on, old son, march."

I started toward the fire. Not a happy walk.

It's never a party when you're walking through darkness, utter darkness, when every weed that brushes your arm is the reaching hand of a monster.

"Man, this so chews," I said, talking to keep myself from running. "Like I could run. Where would I run?"

You'd think it would be easier to be brave when you know you don't have an alternative. But I wasn't finding that to be true.

Closer. Walking. Then creeping. Tiptoeing. Holding my breath, cursing the noise of my rumbling stomach. I was gonna get killed for being hungry. Maybe they had food. Cookies. Beans. A nice leg o' human.

The fire was definitely fire. Small. That was good. It was a fire built for one or two, maybe three. Not a whole army.

Closer. Pushing the leaves aside, trying to see what there was to see. A hint of something near the fire. Couldn't see. Eyes straining, aching from the squint, head pounding now with the tension.

I was lower, hunched over. *Don't see me, don't see me. Let me see you, but don't see me.*

No! This was wrong. Whatever was out here in the middle of nowhere might be scared, too. Jumpy and armed, a bad combination. If I crept up, snuck, seemed to be attacking, it was all over.

No, David was right: big smile, innocent look, arms wide.

I sucked in wet air. I stood up. I walked on wobbly legs.

I stepped into a clearing. A neat, circular space, walled by close-packed bushes and saplings and weeds.

In the center, a small fire.

Sitting by the fire, legs crossed, arms resting palms up, face worried, eyes staring into the fire, was Senna Wales.

CHAPTER
XXXI

"You!" I snapped.

"Christopher?" she said, sounding for all the world like I was exactly, precisely the person she'd been waiting for, hoping for.

I didn't have anything brilliant to say after "you." I didn't have anything to say at all. We'd been looking for Senna, but now that she was sitting, apparently calmly, by a cheerful little fire, none of it seemed real.

I'd been ready for trolls or elves or Loki's big nasty son, Fenrir, the gigantic wolf. I'd been ready for Coo-Hatch or Merlin or one of Ka Anor's strange, half-insect people. I'd been ready for monsters. Not for her.

She waited expectantly, ready to listen to what I had to say.

"You have any food?" I asked. "I'd trade my left arm for a bag of Doritos and some salsa."

She nodded thoughtfully. "Yes. I have food. Not Doritos. But I have some little cakes."

Once again, the conversation died. She said nothing else. Just waited. Like this whole thing was my idea and she was my guest, waiting to see if I had any new activities planned.

I couldn't see her as Senna. Not the Senna I'd known. Too much had happened. I knew too much, and suspected more.

"You know, I really want to thank you for bringing me to this party," I said. "So far I've been hung from Loki's castle walls, chased, half-drowned, had to sing the "Battle Hymn of the Republic" to keep from being killed by drunken Vikings, hunted by crazy Aztecs, and almost had my heart cut out and fed to a big blue god. So, as vacations go, this one is great."

Senna said nothing in direct response. I'm pretty sure she detected the note of sarcasm in my voice. She'd have had to be deaf not to detect the note of sarcasm.

She leaned to one side and opened a sort of shoulder bag I hadn't noticed before. She withdrew a parcel wrapped in green leaves. Within the leaf wrapping, a small round cake.

She handed it over, I took it, our fingers touched accidentally. I felt a charge. Excitement. A rush.

I stuffed the cake in my mouth. It tasted like corn bread.

Then I yelled, "Okay, you guys, it's okay."

"The others are alive?" Senna asked. A polite question. Sort of like, "And how is your grand-mother doing after the surgery?"

"Oh, yeah, we're all fine. Time of our lives, Senna. We all love it here at the Everworld Club Med. It'll be a shame when we have to go home."

I swear I wanted to slap her. Not a glimmer of guilt. Nothing.

"You don't happen to know how we do that, I guess? Go home, I mean. North? South? Take a left at the first lunatic god and go past three elves? Do we take the troll road?"

That brought a faint smile.

Then David stepped into the firelight. He stopped and stared at her. Not a happy stare. It was too complex for that. I swear the first expression that crossed his face was disappointment.

I don't know what I expected from David. I wouldn't have been surprised if he'd yelled, "Oh, baby!" and run to her arms. Disappointment? Why? Didn't like her outfit?

Ah, no, no, of course. David was worried that maybe the big adventure was all over. Me, I was worried it wasn't.

Neither of them said anything. But I could tell Senna was disappointed in her own way. I had a feeling maybe she was looking for the big Hallmark moment, too. Expecting her little love puppy to come bounding over and lay his head down on her lap to have his ears scratched.

"Hello, David."

He nodded. Said nothing.

Then Jalil and April emerged into the light. Jalil went into cautious mode. He knew, just like I did, that the Big Show, the Main Event, was between David and Senna. He was hanging back, waiting to listen and understand.

April didn't hang back. She walked straight to Senna, stopped, leaned down, drew back her right hand, and nailed Senna with a slap that echoed against the trees.

The two girls stared at each other. Fury from April. And what from Senna? Not rage. Not guilt or remorse. Not fear, certainly.

Arrogance. That was it. The calm, superior, sneering look of the two-hundred-and-fifty-pound linebacker who's just been punched by the ninety-five-pound gymnast. The look said, "Go ahead, slap me again. I'll crush you in my own good time."

I guess April saw the look the same why I did. She didn't repeat the slap.

"You were happy enough to see me when I brought you weapons to escape Huitzilopoctli," Senna said.

"I can be ruthless, too, sister. I needed you then."

"So. You guys all know each other, right?" I said, breaking the ensuing silence. "Senna, that's David, April, and Jalil. Everybody? I'd like you all to meet Senna. The witch. She brought cake! A very nice gesture, I'd say."

CHAPTER XXXII

We sat down. We ate corn cake.

Of all the many weird moments we'd encountered since we made the mistake of going down to Lake Michigan early one morning, this was one of the oddest.

Odd because it had such a superficial normalcy. Odd because we each had a million questions, so many questions no one seemed to know where to start.

Fortunately, that's why Jalil is good to have around. He knew where to start.

"You going to tell us what this is all about, Senna?"

"What all of it is about? Who can ever answer that?"

Jalil was unimpressed. "You can. And you know, I don't want to hear a bunch of metaphysical 'who can say?' b.s., so how about you start at the beginning and tell us what you're doing getting snatched off the pier by a mythical wolf and hauled into this alternate universe."

"You ask for simple answers to questions that even the wisest of the wise would —"

"Senna, cut the crap," Jalil snapped.

Senna's eyes went wide. David tensed involuntarily and shot Jalil a dangerous look.

Me? I could have kissed him. Exactly! Cut the crap. Answer the question. Final Jeopardy, Senna the Witch.

"I knew I would be taken," Senna said. "I had been resisting it for some time, but I knew eventually my resistance would fail. I knew it might endanger people near me when it happened. I found an isolated place and time, and allowed it to happen."

"Next question," I prompted Jalil.

"Fenrir was supposed to take you to Loki. What happened?"

Senna shrugged. "Loki is very clever. He is not all-powerful."

"Where did you go?" Jalil asked.

"Why bring us here with you?" David asked.

Senna chose David's question. "I didn't. That was an accident."

April snorted. "David told us how you asked

him to save you, protect you. You set this all up. We're not total idiots, Senna, although I know that's what you've always thought. Ever since we were kids and you . . ."

She stopped. Senna smirked. "Ever since what, April?"

Silence. They glared, eye to eye. Then April looked away. A red flush darkened her face.

Senna looked from one of us to the next, holding each of us in turn with her dark stare. "If you follow your fate, don't blame me because your path and mine run together."

"I'm still getting gibberish here," Jalil said. "I don't need this Tolkien-lite, pseudoprofound nonsense. I want more of that, I can go back and find what's his name. Merlin."

Senna jerked violently. I took a step back. It was like she'd been stabbed or something. Like she'd been bitten by a snake. I was looking for attackers, back up, head turning, adrenaline flooding into my muscles.

"Merlin," she whispered.

Suddenly I liked the old man a lot more. I liked the fact that the mention of his name could wipe the smug, know-it-all look off Senna's face.

She stood up, started left, stopped, started right. Stopped. She wrung her hands. Literally

"What did you tell him?" she demanded.

Jalil was liking this, too. "We told him we were looking for you, Senna."

Her face was pale in the golden firelight. "Do you think this is funny? Do you think Merlin is some feeble old man? I knew an attack was coming, I felt it, but from him? From Merlin?"

"An attack?" Suddenly David was alert and ready, grabbing the hilt of his sword.

Senna went to him and cradled his face with one hand. David blinked. "Save me, David," she said. "Save me, or he will kill us all."

She looked deep into David's glazed eyes. Nodded, like she was satisfied.

Then she came for me. I flinched. She smiled. A forced, hurried smile. She was trying to be unthreatening. Trying to look like the girl I'd thought I was falling for once. A shark with a big give-me-a-hug grin.

She put her hand on my face. I pulled away. No. No, I didn't pull away. Couldn't.

My mind flooded with images, memories. Senna, as I'd first seen her. Senna kissing me. Senna touching . . . Senna . . .

"Fight for me, Christopher. Be brave and defend me."

Her hand was gone. I was alone. But the enemy was coming! I had to save her. Had to try, had to try.

Swiftly she moved toward Jalil.

But then, above the soft wind-shushing of the trees, came a larger sound. Wind like a tornado. Louder and louder. Nearer.

Up. It was coming from above. Not from the jungle. Flying above the jungle just above the treetops.

It glowed against the night sky. It glowed like a coal when you blow on it. Like the red light that shines from within the flowing magma.

It was so big. A bird, but no, of course it wasn't a bird. No bird could ever be this big. No bird would fly with the sound of leather sliding over bone, no bird released the tornado with each downstroke.

A hundred feet from wingtip to wingtip. Longer still from its forked, whipping tail to its horned head. Teeth that were three feet long. Teeth clearly outlined, black against the liquid fire that ran like vomit from its mouth and left brushfires in its wake.

Senna quailed. Drew back from Jalil.

But even as she drew back I saw her face, just for a moment, a vision illuminated by the dragon's fire. A smile. A killer's smile, as though the lips might stretch still further and reveal vampire fangs.

She was afraid. But she was greedy, too. Hungry

for some chance that grew more possible with the approach of the beast.

I saw all this. And knew that this was not my fight. That Senna was not mine to protect. But my mind was no longer entirely mine to command. And my skepticism, my understanding evaporated, burned away by Senna's touch.

She turned and looked up at the monster. The dragon saw her. Its yellow cat's eyes glittered. Yellow wings beat the air, rustling the bushes, bowing the saplings. Talons spread wide, ready to grapple.

No need to fear, Senna, my mind said. *No need. I'll save you. I'll kill it, Merlin's monster.*

I'll kill the dragon.

EVER WORLD

#III

ENTER THE ENCHANTED

I was far from home.

As far from home as it is possible for a human being to get. Not a far place, a place apart, a place not touching reality, isolated.

Forget the normal. Normal was gone. Normal belonged to the real world.

There was magic here. Not magic like "ah, the moonlight was magic." Magic as in cause and effect didn't always cause or effect. The magic that negates all human knowledge, that invalidates ten thousand years of human learning.

Usually gravity worked, sometimes not. No way for that to be, of course, gravity isn't something you can turn on or off, if it was it wouldn't be gravity. If gravity could come and go, wax and wane, then things could fly when they could not possibly fly.

Like a dragon, maybe.

Can't possibly lift something as heavy and dense as a dragon, all that scaly skin, all that muscle, all that dense bone, not with wings, not with leathery wings like a pterodactyl. Wings that were not a tenth of what they had to be, not a hundredth of what was needed to raise this creature, this logic-killing monster into the air.

An elephant with wings! Dumbo, but not cute.

And fire. Could fire burn inside a living creature? Absurd. Ridiculous. Fire inside what, the belly? The intestines? The liver? Liquid flame spilling out of flesh, out of the monster's mouth, and that was supposed to be real? That was happening?

I stood, rooted, yes rooted, like my toes had grown down into the dirt looking for water and now I couldn't move them because my feet were attached to the earth itself, or whatever passed for Earth in this hideous, terrible place.

Run? How could I run from the dragon who pressed the tall trees down with the wind from his impossible wings and flamed the dry bushes in the night?

I could only stare. A miracle, that's what it was.

A dragon.

"Damn it, April, run!" Jalil yelled.

His face was wild, not like Jalil, eyes wide, mouth stretched into some indecipherable shape, half grin, half howl.

Only Jalil cared. About me. And that, not much. David and Christopher were mesmerized, bewitched. More magic. She had gone to them, touched them, spoken to them, and they had lost themselves.

They stood with pitiful swords drawn, defiant and foolish, waving their impotent weapons up at the killer from the sky.

Jalil grabbed me, pulled me, dragged me. My feet moved, missed a step, tripped, up again, and now I ran. But not far. I had to stop, to see.

"Go back to your master, Merlin! Tell him I am not his!" Senna screamed. Her voice was a tinny, faraway shout, a sound all but erased by the vastness of the noise, the howling wind, the bellows sigh of leather wings, the crackle of underbrush bursting into flame.

The dragon inscribed slow, tight circles above the clearing, a living tornado, flying like a bird of prey, an eagle with green and yellow skin, with talons that could carry away a child, a man, a horse, what couldn't it carry with gravity meaningless?

Jalil and I huddled in the woods, unprotected by bowed trees and whipped grass and dirt flying in little cyclones. But the dragon didn't care for us. It watched Senna.

Have her! Take her! I cried silently. This is her nightmare.